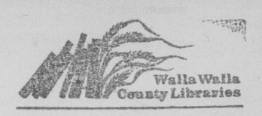

AND THE RIVER RAN RED....

The last *soldado* saw a huge, terrifying man charging him, a big pistol in his hand. The pistol barked. A puff of smoke and orange flame billowed from the barrel.

"El Gigante," the soldier said just as the ball struck him in the center of his chest, smashing through bone and gristle like a deadly seed, flattening as it coursed through his lungs and broke out through his back.

The big American mounted his horse, a fine black animal nearly seventeen hands high, and rode off toward the hut, an amulet bobbing against his massive bare chest.

A few seconds later, one of the Shoshones, riding a pinto, followed after him. He carried two fresh Spanish scalps, dripping blood and sweat, on his lance and carried a rifle made in Mexico.

It was late April of 1805 and the Rio Grande, like some amorphous lumbering beast, glistened in the sun, flowing quietly out of the mountains as it began its long and winding journey south, to the Texas border, to the sun-splashed Gulf of Mexico.

THE
RIO GRANDE

Jory Sherman

BANTAM BOOKS
New York • Toronto • London • Sydney • Auckland

THE RIO GRANDE

A Bantam Book / December 1994

ISBN 0-553-29925-5

Published simultaneously in the United States and Canada

Bantam Books are published by Bantam Books, a division of Bantam
Doubleday Dell Publishing Group, Inc. Its trademark, consisting of the
words "Bantam Books" and the portrayal of a rooster, is Registered in
U.S. Patent and Trademark Office and in other countries. Marca Reg-
istrada. Bantam Books, 1540 Broadway, New York, New York 10036.

PRINTED IN THE UNITED STATES OF AMERICA

RAD   0 9 8 7 6 5 4 3 2 1

For Jim and Wanda Fincher

Time is a sort of river of passing events,
and strong is its current;
no sooner is a thing brought to
sight than it is swept by and
another takes its place,
and this too will be swept away.

MARCUS AURELIUS ANTONINUS

Prologue

He crawled to the edge of the rimrock, peered down at the Ute camp. Dark people, no bigger than coneys, moved in slow motion across a wide, flat chunk of rock, unloading travois, clearing talus, gathering firewood. The hackles rose on the back of his neck, like tiny spiders crawling through the fine hairs. He had heard the Utes riding in the night before, in small bunches, moving slowly through the dark like phantom herdsmen, barely disturbing the rocks. They were like goats, he thought, climbing to high ground, well away from the bubbling roar of the big river. He had been following them for a month, ever since they left their winter camp on the Moonshell, what the French trappers called the Platte River.

They must have slept in the open the night before, because the women were just now setting up their lodges. Some of the men had crossed the river, what the Spanish, the New Mexicans, called El Rio Grande del Norte, the big river of the north. Here, the waters were shallow and the ford was easy. These were hunting parties, he knew. Ancient men at an ancient task, their bodies bronzed from the sun, rouged by ancestral pigments. He knew where they would hunt too.

1

Matthew Caine had been living near the headwaters of the Rio Grande for a year, avoiding the bands of Arapahoes and Utes who roamed the mountains. He had mapped the river, traced its course clear to the little pueblo of Taos, as far south as he dared go, as his orders would allow him. He had crossed and recrossed it, fished it, swam it, dreamed to the melody of its endless waters. He had named the creeks and mountains himself, recording these names in the journal he kept every night by the flickering light of a tallow candle. He had traversed the river from its source, plumbed its depths at every ford and in deep pools like a Sumerian measurer, undetected—until now. He'd made two fast trips to St. Louis, returning from the most recent only the week before. There, he sent his secret dispatches by way of special courier to an unknown destination, to a man he did not know but whose orders he followed.

Now, he wanted the Utes to know who he was. He wanted to make friends with them, if he could. He'd lived with Yellow Moon's Wind River Shoshones for most of a year and a half, had enlisted their help with his surveying tools, which they considered magical, and which were, by any man's account. He learned the lingua franca of the plains, sign language. Chief Yellow Moon knew what Matthew was going to do.

"You will not make friends with the Utes," Yellow Moon had said. "They do not like the white eyes."

Matt hadn't replied, for he didn't want an argument with his friend.

But he knew he must be very careful. During the winter, he left sign at their camp on the Moonshell—the Platte River—and knew that they wondered who he was. He left gifts of antelope and deer, a leg always tied with his personal totem: a lead .64 caliber ball, drilled through, centered on a thong, with three beads on either side—red, white, and blue. He wore such a totem around his neck, like an amulet. He hoped the Utes would remember, would think of him as a friend.

Now he followed three Ute hunters as they walked to a large meadow bordered by heavy timber. There, Matt knew, they would find elk, and that was where he would establish contact. Earlier he had put horses—good, strong mountain horses he'd broken to the rein and the bit himself—deep in the timber. They were hobbled there, waiting to fulfill their purpose.

Matthew Caine was a big man, standing six-foot-five in his bare feet. He was a great hunter, the Shoshones said, and he could build things with his hands. He left big tracks, and many who had only glimpsed him, like some giant ghost of the mountains and the plains, wondered about him, who he was. Before there were mountain men, he was a mountain man. The Indians of the Great Plains knew of him, and some called him friend, for he rode with the Wind River Shoshones and helped them catch wild horses or steal them from the Pawnee and the Apache. In truth, Matt had become half wild, his pulse pounding with the blood of forgotten ancestors who roamed the Anglo-Saxon lands and prowled the Scottish Highlands, drifted to the Irish glens and made poteen by firelight.

Long before he reached the settlements, he was a legend. The Spaniards in Santa Fe knew of him, and they worried that he was sent to Spanish territory by the United States government. In the spring of 1805 Governor Joaquín Reál Alencaster sent a small expedition to the Arkansas River and to the Rio Grande, to look for this man the sheepherders and hunters called "El Gigante," the Giant.

It was known that he had made friends of the Sho-

shone, but the rest was a mystery. And, from that little
piece of information, the Spanish governor of New Mexico wondered if El Gigante was trying to make allies of
the plains Indians before the United States invaded his territory and claimed the lands of New Mexico for themselves.

"If this man makes friends with the Utes and the
Arapaho," said Governor Alencaster, "then he could con-
trol the Arkansas and the upper reaches of the Rio
Grande." He ordered the *comandante* of the post at Santa
Fe to send soldiers to the north. "Find the Yanqui. Bring
him here."

The *comandante* sent out an expedition, a force of
thirty men, to find El Gigante and capture him.

Matthew Caine knew nothing of these plans, but he
knew that it was only a matter of time before he would
have to journey to the south himself, to enter Santa Fe and
try opening up trade with the New Mexicans.

For that he would need Yellow Moon and his Shoshones, and he would want to know that the Utes were
friends as well. He had already made friends of wandering
bands of Arapaho, traded with them, but he had met no
chiefs of that tribe.

Now, Matthew followed the Ute hunters. When they
had killed an elk with the bow and were gutting it out, he
strode out of the timber, his right hand raised in a sign of
peace, dangling the amulet. In the other hand, he held the
rifle, muzzle pointed toward the ground.

The Utes looked at him dumbly. They studied his
lake-blue eyes, the mass of dark hair on his head, the
bushy beard that hid a face tanned by the sun to a leathery
hue. They assessed the bulging muscles under his buckskins, the brace of pistols on his belt, the flintlock rifle he
carried in his hands, the Shoshone quillwork on his possibles pouch, the two powder horns dangling from his neck
on leather thongs.

He looked at the three Ute braves. They were short, round-faced, copper-skinned, with sunken dark eyes that peered at him owlishly. They could have been brothers, but he saw that there were differences. Their noses were shaped differently, one hawkish, another round and buttony as a mushroom, the other flat, Negroid.

Matt lay his rifle down in the grass. He put the amulet around his neck, made sign.

"I am the one who left food at your lodges on the Moonshell," his hands said. "I have horses for you. I would talk with your chief."

"You are the one of the lead ball and the beads," signed one of the Utes. "Do you know our tongue?"

Matt's hands, graceful and precise, told the Ute that he did not.

"What do you want?" signed another Ute.

"Come with me and take the horses. You can pack the elk and take the meat to your camp. I will come along as a friend."

"What are you called?"

Matt made the sign, and they knew who he was.

"Tu eres El Gigante," said one of the Utes, speaking in the Spanish tongue, while beginning to slice off the elk cow's hide with an obsidian blade, cutting downward on the neck and around the shoulder like a surgeon.

Matt nodded and grinned through his thick beard.

"I will go to the camp," signed a young Ute who had taken out the heart of the elk. "I will see if you can come back with us."

"Go," signed Matt.

By late afternoon Matthew Caine was sitting in the lodge of Bull Heart, the chief of the Muache Ute. The three hunters—Turtle, Black Beaver, and Deer Hoof— paraded the twenty horses around the camp, boasting of the giant who was their friend and even now sat in the lodge of Bear Heart, smoking the pipe, making good talk.

Before he left, Matt gave the chief an amulet like his own, and a little piece of colored cloth sewn with sinew around a smooth willow shaft.

"This will show that you are a friend to other men like me who will come from the place where the sun is born," Matt told Bear Heart in sign. "They will give you many gifts and will smoke with you in peace."

The cloth was like one that Matt had given to Yellow Moon of the Wind River Shoshones. He had hired a woman in St. Louis to sew him several just like this one.

It was a miniature flag of the United States of America.

Chapter
One

Rosa Seguìn felt the cords of her throat tighten. Her stomach knotted into a fist and her palms and forehead broke out in a Gethsemanic sweat. She uttered a small cry and turned from the window of the little *jacal* by the Rio Grande. She waded through the thin bar of afternoon sunlight that slanted through the window and headed for the shadowy doorway, her heart throbbing in her throat like a wounded quail.

"Pedro, *se vienen*," she called. *"Soldados. Ay de mì."*

Pedro Seguìn rose from the cot where he had been taking his siesta and rubbed sleepy eyes.

"Soldiers?" he said stupidly. "Coming here? *Porqué?"*

Rosa entered the room—there were but two—constructed of wood, grass, and mud, and he saw the anguish on her face—as if she had been stricken by a sudden blow.

"I do not know why," she said.

"Cuanto?"

"They are six," she said. "What could they want?"

"Do not be afraid," he said, rising from the mat that was nestled against the wall. He wore the summer clothes of the peon. Slipping bare feet into woven sandals, he reached for his straw sombrero on the barrel chair near the front door. Pedro was a shepherd. He summered his sheep above the big river, drove them back to Taos in the fall, there to market the fat ones. In the spring he harvested the wool, let the sheep lamb among the deep grasses of the mountain valleys, along the clear sweet streams of the Rocky Mountains.

"But why are they here?"

Pedro shrugged, but he knew. This morning up in the shepherd's camp they had found an elk hanging outside the *jacal* where the men slept. They all knew who had left it there. They had seen the man more than once, knew he was friendly. Sometimes he was with a lone Indian, sometimes by himself, but he lived up there, somewhere high up where the big river sprang from the giant thighs of the mountains, where El Rio Grande del Norte was but a trickle, where the Utes stayed and the Arapahoes roamed.

"I will talk to them," Pedro said. "Do not have fear."

"But I have fear. I do not like soldiers."

Rosa had Pueblo blood in her veins. Pedro was from the south, and his mother had been born a Yaqui. The soldiers did not like the Indians, even though some of them had the blood of Spaniards pumping through their black hearts.

Pedro went to the window, donning his sombrero.

"Do you see them?" asked Rosa.

He looked through the opening in the side of the *jacal*, cursed under his breath. "Spaniards," he said. He turned to Rosa. "Not just six. There are a dozen."

"Ai, Madre de Dios," she breathed. Flowers were arranged in little clay vases around the room. Now, they smelled like funeral bouquets, cloying and heavy in the lifeless, mud-floored room.

The soldiers were still some distance away, riding single file up the canyon. There were glints of light, silvery, as if one of the soldiers were holding a mirror to the sun, flashing signals to someone far away. There were no pack animals, so Pedro knew they were part of a larger force. They were cavalry, with lances, rifles, swords. One man carried a guidon, its pennant flapping in the light wind that blew down the canyon. Their brass buttons, the silver on their bridles and saddles, glistened in the sun. They rode with arrogance, bristling with a force that was like leashed lightning.

"*Hijos de mala leche,*" said Pedro. Bastards.

"What will you do, my cherished one?" asked Rosa.

"I do not know. We must see what it is that they want."

"They will have many questions."

"*Como siempre.*"

Pedro frowned. He looked at the machete that stood near the doorway. Its wooden handle was wrapped with string that had turned black with the grime of working hands, but its blade was still sharp enough to slice a hair in twain. It was a tool he used to chop wood, cut brush. It was a weapon too, but it would do him little good against soldiers. He stepped through the doorway, pushing his straw hat back on his head. He looked like a man swathed for burial, in his white peon shirt and trousers, his feet clad in woven sandals like a mendicant's, his toenails crammed with the dirt of mountains.

"Stay inside," he said to Rosa.

It would do no good. He knew the soldiers would search the *jacal* like ferrets, blood drops in their glittering eyes, teeth sharp as razors, the meanness in them boiling just below the surface, visible as cactus spines on their dark faces. He could feel their evil from far away, as if their breath had made a hot wind that blew against his face, shut off his own breathing.

"What will you do?" she asked.

"I will talk to the soldiers," said Pedro, his voice

steady despite the deep fear that was in him, that roiled his
senses like sour wine in the stomach.

"Ten cuidado," said Rosa. Be careful.

Pedro walked through the small doorway, stopped a
dozen paces from the *jacal* to wait for the soldiers. Rosa
stayed well back from the doorway, in shadow, watching
as the uniformed men made their way up the trail along
the river, like a snake crawling toward the hens, unhurried,
sure, deadly.

As they drew closer, Pedro saw the piping on their tu-
nics. They wore field sombreros and light summer trousers, but sweated dark like the horses they rode. The
leader held up his hand, shouted something to his troops.
The platoon flared out, drew rifles from stiff scabbards attached to their saddles.

Pedro felt a sinking sensation as the soldiers placed
their rifles across the pommels of their saddles. He wanted
to cross himself, to pray. He wanted also to curse so that
God would know his hatred, his fear.

He had seen soldiers in the territory before, of course,
but they were always riding on the plain, far off in the distance. He had seen them in Taos and Santa Fe, and sometimes along the trail to the mountains from Taos. He had
never encountered them like this, although he knew they
sometimes chased bandits or hunted Indians. Perhaps these
soldiers were looking for a bandit or an escaped prisoner.
But no, he knew who they were looking for. In Taos that
was all they talked about, and they disgusted him with
their lurid descriptions of what the soldiers would do to
the man when they found him.

"I am Captain Escobar," said the leader when he approached Pedro. "What are you called? Where do you
live?"

"I am called Pedro Seguín. I live in Taos."

"What are you doing here?"

"I have the sheep. I was taking the siesta."

The captain, a young man in his late twenties, was a Spaniard. Most of the other soldiers had the fair complexions of men born in the old country. The man carrying the guidon was a Mexican, like Pedro.

"Where are your sheep?"

Pedro cocked a thumb toward the mountains.

"In the high meadow, beyond that ridge," he said.

The captain frowned. "We will go there, but first I want you to tell me about the big gringo."

Pedro swallowed a hard lump in his throat.

"The big gringo?"

"The one they call 'El Gigante.' "

"I do not know of such a gringo," said Pedro, his mouth dry as a withered corn husk.

"You are a lying little worm," said the captain. He gestured to his men, and several dismounted and converged on Pedro.

Pedro started to back away. The captain pulled his pistol, aimed it at the shepherd's head. The pistol was large, with a big Spanish lock. Pedro could almost hear the powder sizzle in the pan. The captain had only to cock it and squeeze its trigger and he would be dead before he smelled the white smoke.

"Halt!" he ordered.

Pedro stopped in his tracks.

His hands trembled and he thought of Rosa inside the hut. The first soldier came up to him and raised his rifle. He struck Pedro in the chest with the brass-clad butt, knocking him to the ground. The sharp pain hammered Pedro's ribs and he felt the wind go out of him. He gasped as the second soldier swung his rifle, striking him in the jaw. He heard a crack and wondered if his jawbone was broken. He moved his jaw and the pain blinded him.

One of the soldiers kicked Pedro in the groin as the captain dismounted, pistol in hand.

Rosa screamed, startling the captain and his troops.

"Adentro," ordered the captain. "Bring whoever's in there outside."

Then Escobar turned to Pedro, put the pistol, a Spanish flintlock in .69 caliber, to the shepherd's temple.

"I want to know where El Gigante is," said the captain. "You talk or I will blow your brains to pulp."

Pedro tried to speak, but his mouth wouldn't work. The pain in his jaw made him wince, brought tears to his eyes.

One of the soldiers snatched Pedro's hat from his head, grabbed a clump of hair and pulled the shepherd's head back so that he stared into the gaping black eye of the flintlock pistol.

"I do not know this *gigante,*" said Pedro, his pulse pounding in his temple, the pain throbbing through his face with the drum of a thousand hammers, the searing hurt of a thousand knives. "Truly, I do not."

"But you have seen him?" asked Captain Escobar. "Do you know where he has built his fort?"

"I do not know of any fort, Capitán. I am a herder of sheep."

"Mentiroso," hissed Escobar.

Pedro heard Rosa scream. He heard the husky grunts of the soldiers inside the *jacal.* He winced again, but not from pain.

"They will violate your woman," said Escobar. "All of them. I want the truth."

"I—I have seen him. Once." Pedro's voice trembled. "I do not know him. He is very big. He lives with the Indians."

"The Indians?"

"Yes. Many Indians. Shoshones. I think he traps in the mountains."

"Shoshones? Or Comanches?"

"The ones who catch the wild horses," said Pedro. "I

think they trade with the Blackfoot and Crow. They hunt the buffalo."

"Shoshones," said Escobar. "This is very bad." He looked around him, nodded to one of the soldiers, held up his hand toward the sun and tilted it back and forth. The soldier took a polished metal mirror from his pocket. There was a cross cut in the center as a sight.

"I think this man, El Gigante," said Pedro, "is just a hunter. Maybe he is Indio."

"He is a spy," spat Escobar. "He is *americano*. He may be with the Shoshones, but he has been seen with the Comanches also."

"I do not know," said Pedro.

It was true. He had seen the huge man only a few times. He had the Spanish tongue. He spoke Shoshone and he made sign with his hands. He dressed in buckskins and beads and wore a bright red bandanna around his head in summer. He was a fearsome sight. Pedro did not know where the man came from, but one spring he saw him bringing packets of furs down from the mountains, and El Gigante waved to him as he rode wide of the sea of sheep moving up the slopes to the grassy meadows. One of the shepherds told him the Indians were Wind River Shoshones, that they lived on the Arkansas River and hunted buffalo, traded with the Indios of the northern plains. To Pedro, they seemed as fearsome as their cousins, the Comanche.

"What should we do with this *mentiroso*?" asked the captain of no one. "This motherless liar."

"Cut his tongue out," said the soldier, pulling on Pedro's hair. He gave his wrist a twist and Pedro cried out. Inside the *jacal* he heard the soldiers and Rosa's muffled sobs. He shut his eyes but could not shut out the obscene pictures.

"Slit his throat," said another soldier, grinning wide.

He looked at the *jacal* and rubbed his crotch. There was a hard knot bulging inside his pants.

"Beat him," said Escobar, turning away. He walked over to the soldier with the mirror. "Call in the scouts," he said.

The soldier, a young Spaniard, flashed the mirror in his hand. He flashed in all directions of the compass. The captain spoke to the other men on horseback. They dismounted. Two men held Pedro while two others took turns beating and kicking him. Pedro lost consciousness no more than two minutes after the beatings started.

The captain walked inside the *jacal*. He wrinkled his nose in disgust at the smells of sheep and cooked mutton, grease and smoke, the wildflowers reeking with the scent of graveyards.

The woman was spread-eagled on the floor, her private parts exposed. One soldier was squatting in the corner, watching as another took his turn with the woman, his trousers around his knees.

"Hurry up," said Escobar. "There are others waiting."

"Send them in, Capitán," said the man in the corner. "She will be very juicy for them."

The captain went back outside, gulped in fresh air. He nodded to the other soldiers. Pedro lay on his side, barely breathing, his face distorted from the beating, blood trickling from both nostrils, his lips crushed, bruised like trampled fruit.

"Where are those scouts?" asked Escobar.

"Already I see one," said a soldier, looking off to the north.

"And there is Chato," said another, looking to the southwest.

The two Indians converged on the patrol from different directions. Their bandannas, tied around their heads, were dull with dust; their features dark, leathery.

Chato arrived first. Then his *compañero*, Mosca, rode up, his face impassive, his dark eyes flashing with secrets.

"Where is Cholla?" asked Escobar.

"Muerto," said Chato.

"Dead? Where?"

Chato pointed back toward the mountains from whence he'd come.

"Who killed him?"

"No sabe," said Chato.

Mosca sat his horse, silent as stone. Cholla was his blood brother.

"How was he killed?" asked the captain, the anger in him burning his words like torches.

Chato held up a broken arrow. "Shoshone," he said.

"Did you see anything, Chato? Mosca?"

Chato looked at Mosca, his eyes expressionless, like buttons in a doll's face.

"Many pony tracks. There, there." Mosca made a sweep with his arm, covering a broad expanse to the north and west. Like Chato, he spoke simple Spanish.

"Many tracks also," said Chato.

"Indians?"

"Shoshone," Chato replied.

"Where are they now?" asked the captain.

"No sabe," Chato said again, but he looked to the mountains as if trying to see over the ridges and into the aspens, spruce, and pine.

"They watch us," said Mosca.

"Is this true, Chato?" asked Escobar.

"They are here," the Indian replied. "They know we are here."

"Hijo de puta," cursed the captain.

He gave rapid orders to his men. Three soldiers staggered from the *jacal,* and a fourth came out a moment later, tucking his shirt inside his trousers. Their rifles rattled as they mounted their horses. Leather creaked like greasy parchment.

Inside the *jacal* Rosa sobbed softly, holding her face in her hands, hiding her deep shame, hiding from the stern gaze of God.

The soldiers reined their horses into formation and retreated from the shadows of the mountains, following the sheep paths down to the plain. They crossed between two bluffs that bracketed the Rio Grande River.

The two Pueblo scouts rode on through, into the open, then clapped heels to their horses' flanks. The captain yelled at them: "Bring Garza, quick!" The scouts gave no sign that they had heard Escobar. In moments they'd disappeared.

Escobar cursed them in a liquid stream of Castilian Spanish.

"Corporal Espinoza," the captain called.

"Yes, my captain."

"Go and find Lieutenant Garza. Tell him to bring his men up. *Andale.*"

That was when the Shoshones struck. Arrows flew through the air from hidden positions, striking several soldiers. Men tumbled from their mounts. Corporal Francisco Espinoza took an arrow in the throat and slid like an oiled slicker from his saddle. Others began shooting at shadows. A big-bore rifle boomed, and Captain Enrico León de Escobar y Salazar grabbed his flaming chest as he fell backward over the high Spanish cantle. His horse kicked him as he fell over its backside, but he didn't feel the blow.

The Shoshones rose from their positions and screamed like devils from Hell as they charged the remaining soldiers in the column. The faces of the warriors were painted, and they appeared strangely demonic as the sun lit the hues, made the colors move like something hideous crawling on their flesh. The soldiers screamed too, in terror, and tried to reload rifles that had become useless. One swung his horse and pulled his lance free of its scabbard. A Shoshone arrow knifed into his belly and the skin parted easily, flowering crimson like some obscene red flower. He groaned in pain that was not human, but crude and animal, issuing from a torn mouth that already tasted hellfire. Another arrow sliced through the Spaniard's throat, cutting his vocal cords like twine under a butcher's knife.

It was over in seconds that seemed eternal in their agony. The last *soldado* saw a huge, terrifying man charging him, a big pistol in his hand. The pistol barked. A puff of smoke and orange flame billowed from the barrel.

"El Gigante," the soldier said just as the ball struck him in the center of his chest, smashing through bone and gristle like a deadly seed, flattening as it coursed through his lungs and broke out through his back, leaving a hole as big as a saucer.

The Shoshones took the scalps of the dead soldiers, snatching them from live heads and dead, then caught up the loose horses. The big American mounted his own horse, a fine black animal nearly seventeen hands high, and rode toward the *jacal,* an amulet bobbing against his massive bare chest.

A few seconds later one of the Shoshones, riding a pinto, followed him. He carried two fresh Spanish scalps on his lance, dripping blood and sweat, and carried a rifle made in Mexico.

It was late April of 1805, and the Rio Grande, like some amorphous lumbering beast, glistened in the sun, flowing quietly out of the mountains as it began its long winding journey to the south, to the Texas border and on to the sun-splashed Gulf of Mexico.

Chapter Two

The two Pueblo Indians rode a wide circle, keeping to the afternoon shadows, stopping to rest in places where they could not be ambushed by screaming demons painted for war. Their faces were grim, their skin stretched taut over fatless bones, and they did not converse, except, infrequently, in sign language. It took them a long time to reach the places where the soldiers lay dead and scalped, their bodies bloated by the sun, twisted in grotesque postures, like animals in the contorted shapes of colorless driftwood washed onto a last desolate shore beyond earthly comprehension.

Chato counted the dead, as did Mosca. They signed the counts to each other and nodded in agreement.

They recognized the scalping cuts. Shoshone. The soldiers' arms had been taken, and some of their clothing: shirts, boots, lances, knives, hats. Almost all of the men were stark naked, many with their groins mutilated, gaping bloody holes where their testicles and penises had once sprouted. Flies buzzed at open wounds caked with blood, and crawled across vacant glassy eyes. Ants trailed through nostrils, in and out of ears. That night, the coyotes would come and feed on the corpses. Tomorrow the buzzards and the crows would take out the succulent eyes and feast on what was left of the flesh.

"Should we go to the *jacal*?" asked Chato, speaking softly, almost in a whisper. "Maybe we should find Garza."

Mosca shook his head, signed the other man to silence. The two Pueblos looked all around, as if seeking apparitions, listening intently for any vagrant sound, for ghost whispers, death drums, ancient chants in an unknown language. A breeze riffled the gamma grass, shook the pods in the yucca, rattled the spines of the Spanish dagger plants. Each sound was magnified, ominous as distant thunder.

"This is a place of the dead," signed Chato. "Let us go and tell what has happened."

"Garza?"

"No. Not that *puerco*."

"Maybe the Spanish *locos* will kill us," said Mosca, speaking aloud.

"Ummm," murmured Chato. Even as Mosca voiced the words, they bloomed in Chato's mind, little cholla needles that pricked and nettled his thoughts. The *comandante* would be very angry. He would want to know about El Gigante. If they told him what the soldiers had done to that herder of sheep, that peon and his *mujer*, they would be called liars. They would be asked why they didn't report to Garza. Garza might kill them if they told what had happened. The Spanish pigs would blame him and Mosca for the deaths of the soldiers.

Neither man spoke for several moments, moments in which thoughts became tangled like nettles in a sheep's woolly hide. Chato felt uneasy, as if someone was watching him. His eyes scanned the plain, the nearby foothills, the dark mountains beyond. It was so quiet he could hear the breeze rustling in the smallest places, like women whispering in the winter lodges, like spirits in the wind that blows through the burial places. He could almost hear it moving grains of dirt under the *nopal*.

"We will go," said Chato finally.

"Good. I do not like this place."

The Pueblos followed the twisting waters of the Rio Grande, for they did not trust the trail. They had become like animals again, like hunted beasts imperiled in a hostile landscape far from their native haunts, and they became more furtive with each kilometer. They were suspicious of every shadow, every shape, and their eyes grew weary from searching the empty land under the big blue-clay bowl of sky fired by the sun's furnace into ceramic clarity.

After a time, Matt and the Shoshones allowed themselves to be seen. They appeared on the horizon just as the two Pueblos turned to look at the gathering shadows pooling up at every bush and clump of grass like the small warnings of night just before the sun went to sleep beyond the mountains.

Matt watched the scouts ride off, wondering again if he shouldn't have killed them too. Leave no trace. Maybe that's what he should have done, but if he had wiped out the scouts too, then no one would ever know what really happened to those soldiers. What the soldiers had done to a Shoshone woman and her child, to the sheep herder and his wife.

The sonsofbitches.

And what about what he had done? What he had become? He looked at the Shoshones, the pure warriors sitting their ponies in stolid silence. They were related to the Comanches, but unlike them, they had no treaties with the government at Santa Fe. Matt had made friends with both tribes, an alliance that he hoped would be valuable someday. The Shoshones thought nothing of the killing. It was almost fun for them. Almost a business. Certainly a way of life. As it should be for him, as well. One of his duties. Really? He needn't have killed them all. Just the captain, maybe. And his lieutenant. One or two of the noncommissioned officers. Or should he have let them all live?

Antelope looked at Matt, his glance so keen the giant felt pierced as if by a lance.

"What do you think, Big Man?" Antelope signed.

"My head is empty," said Matt in Shoshone. "Moss grows there. Wet green moss."

Antelope laughed. "You are crazy," the brave said.

Matt bulged his eyes out and rolled them, made his face into a demented visage.

Gray Deer heard them talking, rode over.

"We should have set the spirits of those two loose," he said. "We should have cut their hearts out."

Matt sighed. Gray Deer was right, of course. By his way of thinking. Once a Shoshone got the taste of blood, he wanted to stay at the trough.

"They will carry their fear with them," Matt said. "They will give it to the other soldiers."

"Maybe other soldiers will want to come back and get you," said Gray Deer.

"No. I am going to them," said Matt. "I am going to the big soldier fort in Santa Fe."

The two braves looked at him in puzzlement.

"When?" asked Antelope. "How many suns?"

"Now I go to the white man's town on the Father of Rivers. Then I will go to Santa Fe."

The two braves grunted.

"You have a woman there, in the Frenchman's town by the Father of Rivers?" Antelope was always the inquisitive one. And Matt had taught him so much, had learned so much from him.

"No more," said Matt, signing with the words, showing that his heart was on the ground. He knew that neither

man would pry into his locked life any further. They knew
he had many secrets and that he would tell them when he
wanted to. They knew that much about him.

Gray Deer had asked him once why he did not shave
off his beard and become a red man. The beard kept him
white, that's why. But he didn't tell them that. He had become a red man, gradually, unwillingly, over the
months—he almost said "moons" in his mind—more like
the Shoshone than he wanted to be. But he had hunted
with them, and eaten with them, and had taken one of their
women into his lodge, to replace the one he had lost.

He thought of Morning Lark then, but her image
blurred and he saw the face of the town woman, Emilie
Montaigne, with her coal-black hair, small, thin lips,
slightly aquiline nose, slender neck and waist. He could almost hear her voice, the rustle of her skirts. He could
sometimes feel the touch of her hand on his arm, taste the
flavor of her mouth when they kissed. Morning Lark
seemed like a dream person to him, someone he had come
to love but who was so enigmatic, so deep and silent, that
he might never know her. And worse, since he left the big
village in the mountains, he might never see her again. Yet
he felt a part of her too, as if she had given him a gift that
he could not see, could not feel. He felt the weight of it in
his heart, the tug of it at his senses. Her seldom smile was
part of it, so soft and hesitant, yet strangely warm and
wise. And he could smell the earthy fragrance of her body
nestled against his in the dark, the musk that scented the
night air from between her legs. Some of her gift was the
haunting look in her eyes, the light that was there whenever he looked at her, held her close. The look that he
could see now and feel pulling at him to go back, to throw
off the last vestiges of civilization and live like the red
man, live free and savagely, like the Shoshone and their
wild cousins, the Comanche.

Two women, so far apart in nature, in culture; and

both had made him happy. Emilie could not wait for him, that was what she had said, and he knew that she'd taken up with another man, a man who would never go anywhere, never do anything, but who was steady, hardworking, and wanted a family, like her.

"For one with an empty head, you think much," said Gray Deer finally.

Jolted from his reverie, Matt swore softly in English. "Hoopties," he said, knowing the word was incomprehensible to them. Almost to him. "Worldwide hoopties."

"Whoop-tees?" Gray Deer asked.

"Round, rolling things," said Matt, then made the sign. "Problems. Decisions. Hoopties. They roll all over the world, tangle things up."

Gray Deer spat as if he had tasted something sour. He signed that he did not understand.

"Big Man doesn't understand either," signed Matt.

"We can catch the Pueblos," said Antelope, not wanting to hear any more white man talk.

"Let them go," said Matt, peering after the two Indians. They were riding very slowly, as if reluctant to show fear.

When the two Pueblo Indians were far enough away and Matt was certain they were returning to Taos or Santa Fe, he called in his Shoshone friends and they returned to the *jacal*.

Pedro Seguìn emerged from the hut as Matt and the Shoshones rode up.

"What are you called?" Matt asked in Spanish.

Pedro told him.

"The soldiers will not be back."

"I know. We heard the guns and the screaming."

"Other soldiers might come."

"We know. They were looking for you."

"They found me."

"What they did to my woman," said Pedro, "that is not right."

"Nothing is right. There is no law here but the Mexican law."

"Why do the soldiers want you?" asked Pedro.

"They are afraid that I am only the first of many."

"Americanos?"

"Yes," said Matt.

"I have heard talk . . ."

"That is all that it is. Talk."

"They are afraid of you, I think."

"I am going away, Pedro. You take care."

"I will. It was good of you to avenge my wife."

"The soldiers killed a Shoshone woman and her daughter this morning. Because they did not answer the captain's questions."

"I thank you still."

"Go with God," Matt said, turning his horse.

"Vaya con Diós," said Pedro.

Matt heard the woman weeping inside the *jacal*. There was nothing more he could do for them. The Shoshones, as they rode by, held up the fresh scalps they had taken from the soldiers and grinned. Pedro shuddered, went inside the hut and closed the door.

When they were out of sight of the hut, Matt halted his horse. The animal whuffed and blew jets of steam from rubbery nostrils.

"I go now," he told the Shoshones.

"You go to the Frenchman's town on the Father of Rivers," said Gray Deer.

Matt nodded.

"You will return," said Antelope.

Matt nodded. He could not say the words. They might have known he was lying. The truth was, he didn't know if he would ever return. His orders could change. He wanted to map the river from Taos to Santa Fe, but those plans were contingent on what he was told in St. Louis. And despite what he'd become, he had an itch for civilization. Just to see if he could stand it, if he could shuck the savage skin he wore.

"We will wait for you where the tall grass grows in the mountains."

"Your eyes will see me," said Matt, his eyes steady on Antelope's.

The Shoshones grunted in approval.

There were no good-byes. Matt rode off to the east without looking back. The Shoshones did not leave right away. After a few moments Matt heard the pony hooves pounding on the earth as the warriors headed for the mountains. Then it was quiet.

Matt patted his bulging saddlebags. Inside there were documents, maps, notes, and survey charts that he had accumulated in a year's time on the upper Rio Grande. These he would deliver to a courier in St. Louis. After that he didn't know where he would go, what he would do.

He had hated to lie to his friends, the Shoshone. He thought again of Morning Lark. She would be in their lodge, waiting for him. He'd left all of his surveying instruments there. He could not be caught with them, should he encounter New Mexican soldiers again.

Matt did not know where his dispatches went after they left St. Louis, or the recipient. Neither did he know from whence his orders came. And no order given him had ever been committed to paper. The orders were always verbal, but they carried the weight of authority. He was given gold in payment and for his expenses, and had an open line of credit at several businesses in St. Louis, as well as money on deposit at a land office for special situations, should they arise. Letters of credit were also deposited in the same location, and he would need some of these for Santa Fe in case he ran into difficulties with the authorities there.

Matt was traveling light, plenty of powder and ball for his Mexican rifle and a .54 caliber Harper's Ferry rifle. He carried a brace of .64 caliber pistols with Spanish locks, made for him in St. Louis by a man named Eladio Gutierrez, rumored to have once been a pirate. His knife had been made in New Orleans, a single-bladed skinning knife with a buckhorn handle and brass fittings.

There was pemmican in a parfleche, water in his wooden canteen without markings. He had enough sun-dried venison and elk meat to last him a week. He was out of salt and sugar, and had not tasted coffee since his last trip to St. Louis. He had a bit of dried corn and some wild onions for flavoring. Having lived like a Shoshone and eaten as they ate, there was scarcely an ounce of fat on his giant frame.

Matthew Caine was, for all practical purposes, a wanderer without portfolio, a faceless man in a disputed country. He had lost most of his military bearing in the year he spent with the Wind River Shoshone. There was nothing on him to identify his country of origin or his allegiance. He spoke French, Spanish, German, Shoshone, and knew the sign language of the plains Indians. He could on occasion look like a dumb galoot. At such times he used his size as a handicap, appearing dull-witted and slow, as if his huge body contained a brain the size of a pea.

Once, when he first came into the country, he was stopped by a patrol of New Mexican soldiers scouting the upper Arkansas River. He spoke very bad Spanish then, and appeared to be lost. He played the fool. The Mexicans had laughed at him. They had also taken two bottles of very bad whiskey from him. One of the bottles was poisoned. The ones who had drunk from it were all dead, and the others knew they'd been tricked, but that was long after Matt made his escape. He'd gotten away with it then, but thereafter he avoided military patrols—until his encounter at the sheep herder's *jacal*.

One last trip, he thought. Then maybe he would know why he had been sent to the upper Rio Grande, and who had sent him. He knew that it had something to do with the Lewis and Clark expedition, that there was some kind of connection. At least, he had surmised as much. There had been talk that American traders had gone into Texas, while others had gone into northern New Mexico. Spanish frontier officials had orders to turn back all foreigners, but the country was big. Matt himself had entered Spanish territory, ostensibly as a trader, but knew now that he was a hunted man.

Now that Spain had given Louisiana back to France and France, in 1803, had sold the territory to the Americans, only the borders of the territory were in dispute. France claimed that the Rio Grande was part of its territory "from its mouth to about the thirtieth parallel." The big river was supposedly the western boundary of Louisiana. So far as Matt knew, the French had not pressed the matter with Spain. But Matt had a hunch that Thomas Jefferson would claim some or all of the Rio Grande inland from the Gulf. There were too many Americans going down there to believe that it was only coincidence.

Ever since Jefferson had paid Napoleon $15 million for Louisiana, the Spanish had been nervous, beefing up their defenses along the Rio Grande down in Texas, establishing garrisons and reinforcing their navy with Cuban and Mexican resources.

Matt knew that in some small way he was part of it. Else why all the secrecy? Why send him to the northern end of the disputed territory at the same time that Lewis and Clark set out from St. Louis? Surely, there was no coincidence here either. It was something to puzzle over, all right. Someday, maybe he'd find out the whole of it. For now, he was just following orders. Like a blind man. Like a blind man in harness, he thought.

*   *   *

Chato saw the patrol before Mosca. His heart seemed to fall inside his chest, like a pear from a tree.

"Look," he said in Spanish.

"I see them. They are all around us."

New Mexican soldiers had indeed encircled the two scouts, closing in on them with a pincer movement. Lancers rode ahead of the cavalrymen, who had their rifles aimed at the two Pueblos.

"Halt!" shouted a voice.

Chato saw the lieutenant, recognized him. The soldiers closed in with rifles at the ready, lances prepared to thrust.

Lieutenant Fidel Garza rode up, flanked by his sergeant and two corporals.

Garza had his saber drawn. He sat his horse stiffly, thoroughly military, irritatingly Spanish, his chest puffed out, his head held high in that Castilian arrogance that so many of his kind possessed.

"Where is your captain?" Garza demanded.

"Esta muerto," said Chato.

"Dead? And what of his troop?"

"Todos muertos," Chato said.

"How? Who?"

"Shoshones. El Gigante."

Garza's face purpled. "You deserted him," the lieutenant said.

"No."

"You are still alive and you say that Captain Jorge Escobar and all his men were killed? Just like that."

"We could not help them. The Shoshones let us go."

"Traitors!" Garza spat. "Kill them."

Mosca and Chato heard the ominous click of locks as a half-dozen rifles swung to bear on their chests. They stared at Garza in disbelief.

"Fuego," ordered Garza.

Six cocks snicked as six triggers were pulled. Tiny puffs of smoke rose from six pans as flints struck frizzen plates, shooting sparks into the main charge. Crimson flowers bloomed on the Pueblos' chests as the balls thudded into their hearts, pulping them before blowing large fist-sized holes in their backs. The two Indians twitched and spilled from their saddles, their eyes glazed over with the dull frost of death.

"Bastards," spat Garza. Then he began barking orders. His unit, a dozen cavalry, a sergeant in charge, filed in behind the lieutenant. He swore all the way to the killing place. When he saw the naked bodies, tears scoured his eyes.

"Let us now find this El Gigante," Garza said to his sergeant, Manolo Sanchez.

"Do we not bury these dead men?" asked Sanchez.

"Later. First they must be avenged."

"We have no trackers," said Manolo.

"There are tracks. Find the one that is heaviest. That will be El Gigante."

"You should not have killed the scouts," Sanchez muttered under his breath.

"What did you say?" Garza snapped.

"Nothing. I said nothing."

"Then find this man's tracks. I want to drag him back to Sante Fe like the dog he is."

"Yes, Lieutenant," said the sergeant. Sanchez barked orders to the men, who spread out and began examining tracks. There was much talk and pointing.

"They go this way," said one.

"And this way too," said another.

There were no iron shoes on any of the horses they were tracking. The sergeant finally figured out that the Shoshones and the heavy man had followed the Pueblos, then turned back. It took them over two hours to find the *jacal*. There was nobody there, but they saw the fresh tracks leading away.

"Well?" asked Garza after the men finished searching the hut.

Sergeant Sanchez had been studying the tracks.

"This is where Captain Escobar came. Then, when he rode away, he was attacked and killed."

"So, where are the savages now?" asked Lieutenant Garza.

"We will find them."

An hour later they saw the lone set of tracks leading away from the mountains.

"The Shoshones went into the mountains," said Sanchez. "The heavy man rode to the east."

Garza debated with himself only a few minutes. The Shoshones were many. The lone man would be easy to find in short-grass country.

"Sergeant," said Garza, "send a man to follow the tracks of the El Gigante. Another on point. Flankers out."

Sanchez relayed the orders. Corporal Eladio Fuentes rode ahead to follow the tracks. Private Porfirio Chamayo, a Mexican and the best shot, took the point. Two other privates rode out as flankers to protect the main body of the small patrol.

The soldiers rode until the sun set without encountering Matthew Caine.

By then, however, Matt knew that there were soldiers on his trail. He had seen the tracker and the point man, put his ear to the ground and detected the others following.

By the time the sun set, Matt was hiding his trail, dragging brush over his tracks, backtracking, circling. He knew of a drop-off where the tall grasses grew. Fed by a creek, it was a favorite feeding ground for buffalo and antelope. There wasn't much of it, he knew, but it was his only chance to lose his trackers. He had made note of such rare places when he had come into the country. The place was an anomaly. Protected from the heavy snows, the long-stemmed grasses had taken hold and grown as wild and high as any he had seen on the Kansas prairie.

He looked around, saw miles and miles of gamma grass. A man with a spyglass could be seen easily on the gently rolling ground. This would not do. He headed southeasterly, hoping he would find the brief stretch of tall-grass country that would make tracking him more difficult for his pursuers.

When he came to the stream he was seeking, he knew he did not have much time. It was already getting dark when he reached the tall grass, like an oasis in the middle of a vast, merciless desert. Before the moon was up, he had tied his horse in a stand of cottonwood by a stream that would lead him to the Arkansas River. He made a false camp there, laid out his bedroll, built a small fire. Then he walked away, found a shallow ditch and lay down to wait. He flattened the tall grass around the depression that hid him from view, laid his pistols beside him, then set his rifle on a line of sight with the campfire.

There, as the moon dusted the land with pewter, Matt waited, knowing that the soldiers were hunting him, that they would come like ghost shadows, like men riding to the tambours of war, hearing only the drumbeat of blood in their temples.

Chapter
Three

Lieutenant Garza watched the light fade away after a last holocaust of sun in the sky beyond the mountains. He saw the smear of golds and reds clinging to small clouds in the western sky, felt the first freshet of chill blow down off the mountains. The deerflies that had ragged them all day began to dissipate as the air cooled. Nighthawks sliced the sky as songbirds fled to dark thickets, trees already shrouded by shadows.

"Halt," he said. The tracks had led them in a bewildering maze through prairie grasses tall enough to hide antelope, deer, or even a man, but Garza had been through this country before. He knew where the streams and rivers were. He thought he knew where his quarry was headed, now that there was only a single track to follow through high grass. His quarry had left a maze of swales that looked like pathways leading nowhere. His men had learned to split up and follow each trail until they eliminated the false ones.

His men had done well. He'd deployed them well. El Gigante had tried his best to trick them, but by having the soldiers mark the giant's trail at the farthest points and track backward each time, they narrowed the course to a solitary path through the tall thatch of prairie grasses that rubbed against their horses' bellies, jerked loose and caught in their stirrups, stuck in their cinches. The big man had not tried any of his diversionary tactics for the past two hours of trailing him.

Sergeant Sanchez looked into the deepening twilight.

"We will lose him in the dark, Lieutenant. Unless he breaks out of this grass, we'll lose him."

"He is probably waiting for us to ride up on him," said Garza.

"The men are tired."

"We don't want him to get away," said the lieutenant, musing to himself. He was like a fox with the scent still strong in his nostrils; the rabbit, run to ground, twitching in a burrow. "*Maldita*, we are so close. And he can't stay in these thick grasses forever. He would suffocate, I think."

"He could pick us off, one by one," said the sergeant, who did not laugh. "We would never find him in the dark."

"Be quiet, Sergeant. Let me think." Garza dismounted. The soft leather of his Santa Fe saddle creaked in the crepuscular stillness. He looked down at the clear tracks, so fresh they seemed to have been made moments ago. The grass was sparser here and there were patches of open ground. The horse was carrying weight; the man who rode him was big. And dangerous.

Garza again thought of his orders. Escobar had made a mistake splitting up the patrol as he had. Perhaps he himself had made a mistake killing those two Pueblo scouts. But Escobar was dead, along with all of his men. Murdered savagely, scalped, robbed. He thought of their naked bodies lying there in the darkness. He shuddered when he thought of the coyotes that would come to sniff and perhaps tear the flesh. And tomorrow, the buzzards and the crows would come.

"We will spread out over a wide area," Garza said finally. "Two men to each post. One will sleep for four hours, then the other. No fires. No talking. One man will ride the perimeter, four-hour shifts. We will pick up the trail before dawn in the morning."

"Yes, Lieutenant," said Sanchez, knowing that it would be difficult to carry out the officer's orders. The men were tired, bone-tired and muscle-tired. But he knew that Garza was a man of experience. He had proved himself in battle with the Comanches, had fought Apaches, as well, and he was known as a relentless, persistent man who carried out orders from his superiors without question. Perhaps the lieutenant knew what he was doing.

"I will take the first perimeter watch," said Garza, as if reading his sergeant's thoughts. "Let the men rest and set up their camps. No more than one hundred meters apart. Rifles and pistols at the ready. Let them trample the grass down with their mounts, then lay out the camps."

"Yes, sir," said Sanchez.

He waited until all the men had reported in, then gave them their orders. Garza rode slowly in a great circle as the men split up and stripped their mounts, hobbled them, and set out their bedrolls. Those who whispered, he commanded to shut their mouths, those who clanked their tools or weapons, he reprimanded quietly.

"I will relieve you, Lieutenant," Sanchez told Garza when the men were settled and the darkness thick.

The long yodel of a coyote broke the stillness. Answering yodels spooled into the air from various directions. Insects yammered and sawed at Sanchez's ears as he lay down on his blankets, feeling his muscles give way to nagging aches close to the bone. The smell of crushed grass and horse droppings filled his nostrils. It was like sleeping in a hayfield, he mused, or in a roofless stock shed.

They should have gone to their field camp for the

spare horses, he thought. They should have sent a courier back to the garrison at Santa Fe ordering up reinforcements. They should have waited for help before pursuing a man who had killed a troop of trained soldiers as if they were so many flies to be swatted. This man they called El Gigante was a phantom. No—he was more than that. He was Death.

Sanchez closed his eyes and tried to picture the man they were hunting. Was he Indio? Was he an *americano,* as they said? He could not see a face in his mind. He could see only a shadow, a giant shadow with no face, and the vision was more terrifying than any he had ever seen in his life.

Caine waited in the dark, listening to the cries of the coyotes, strangely musical, oddly supernatural in the chill black air of night. He wondered if the men tracking him had given up and turned back, wondered if they had gotten lost in the high grass, amid the many trails he had tramped out to throw them off the track. He listened intently for the faintest footfall. He put his ear to the ground often and heard only the faint pounding of his heart, the pulse of blood drumming in his ears.

There was something about the soldiers who were tracking him, though. These were different. They undoubtedly knew that the captain and his men were dead. They had probably questioned the sheep herder and his wife. Perhaps tortured them for more information. These soldiers knew who he was, where he was going.

The moon's rise and its slow arc across the star-peppered sky marked the passing of time. And still no sound. Still no soldiers looming out of the darkness like nightmares of ancient wars. No creak of leather, no furtive footfall, no muffled hoofbeat, no scratch of grass against cloth or Chihuahua boot.

His eyelids grew heavy and he dozed off, only to jerk awake again, oddly disoriented, stars spinning in the skies, his quick breath of surprise and bewilderment loud in the prairie stillness. He felt around in the dark and found a chunk of rock. He pulled it toward him, placed it under his abdomen. He felt the pain of the rock when he lay on it. He stayed awake a while longer.

Matt's head bobbed downward as he drifted to sleep yet again. He rolled away from the rock, drugged by weariness, his senses shutting down, blotting out consciousness like a buffalo blanket thrown over a fire. He slept, dreaming he was awake and still waiting for the soldiers to come for him.

Garza slept for three hours, then awoke with a start, fully alert. One by one he roused the men, ordered them to saddle their horses.

"No talking," he said.

A private brought the lieutenant's horse to him a few moments later. The night was still black as pitch.

Sergeant Sanchez rode up. "It is still dark," he whispered.

"I want to move now," said Garza.

"I await your orders, Lieutenant."

"We'll go on foot. Follow the tracks. No doubling back. No column. Have the men walk fifty paces apart, following the tracker."

"We will not find El Gigante in the dark," Sanchez said. "Not in this high grass."

"Then we will drive him ahead of us until we wear him down," said Garza. "He'll have to break out soon to find a buffalo trail where he can ride without hindrance."

That made sense to the sergeant. He felt as if they had been riding through water, beating against waves of grass that clutched at them, beat at them like witches' brooms.

Sanchez spoke to the men. They led their horses, following the man he had assigned as tracker on this hopeless march, Corporal Lugar. He had the best eyes. He had been their best tracker so far. He was a Mexican anyway, part Indian. He was a good shot, adept at spotting game.

"I'll lead your horse, Lugar," said Sanchez. "You just follow those tracks."

"Yes, sir," said the young man.

Lugar moved slowly, the tracks so dim it made the corporal's eyes ache to look for them. At times he lost the trail where the grasses had risen back up almost straight, and his heart caught in his throat like clotted blood until he found it again.

And then the grasses thinned, and grew thinner, until he was tracking on hard ground. An old buffalo trail perhaps, wide and free of vegetation.

He was sweating, though it was still cool. And dark. Very dark. He could barely hear the men behind him, they were so quiet. Once or twice he looked back, feeling he was all alone, that he had gotten lost in the dark. Sanchez was leading his horse, so he didn't have that on his mind. Still, he felt somewhat helpless without his horse, even more alone.

Lugar almost tripped over the bedroll before he saw it. He had lost the track and was ranging at an angle trying to find it again when the lump rose up before him. He jumped back, flooded with fear. He swung his rifle up and grabbed the forestock, ready to shoot if anyone came out of the blankets. He smelled the lingering smoke from an earlier fire.

The blankets didn't move.

Lugar stood there, slowly bringing the barrel of his rifle downward until the muzzle pointed at the lump in the blankets.

"Levantase," he squeaked. Get up.

There was no answer. He turned, looking for Sanchez. That's when he heard a small sound, like someone blowing out a candle. Out of the corner of his eye he saw a flash. Thunder roared in his ears and he felt a sudden slap, as if someone had slammed him in the side with a twenty peso maul. The air rushed from his lungs and he smelled his own blood as it gushed up through his throat and spewed out his nostrils. He fell sideways, as if poleaxed, and hit the ground, gasping for air that couldn't get past the blood, couldn't get into his burning throat and down to his blasted lungs. He wheezed once, like a broken squeezebox, and breathed no more.

Matt Caine dropped his rifle, picked up his two pistols, and rolled out of the depression as soon as he had fired. Four rifles barked and he saw their flashes, felt the spray of sand as the balls kicked up dust all around him. He scooted backward, cocking the pistols.

He heard the liquid sound of Spanish voices as they came after him. He saw their dim shapes converging on him, men with loaded rifles, crouching. He cursed himself for falling asleep, for letting them get so close.

Horses whinnied in terror as rifles boomed. Matt found a target, squeezed off a shot. He started to run. A soldier blocked his way. He fired his other pistol at point-blank range and ran right over the man as he fell.

Men shouted at him in Spanish. He could almost feel their rifles swinging at him. He ran a zigzag pattern, still clutching the empty pistols, racing toward his horse.

"Kill him," shouted Garza.

Matt ran right through the ragged line of men, could hear some of them reloading their rifles. He heard a pistol fire, felt a rush of air past his ear. It sounded like a giant mosquito.

This wasn't going the way he had planned at all.

He heard a man's voice quietly giving orders to the soldiers. There was no panic in his tone.

Matt hunched over as he drew close to where he had left his horse. He threw himself down, went the rest of the way on his belly, then rose up, crabbing on all fours.

His horse was there, pulling hard on its tether. Matt shoved the empty pistols into his belt and drew his knife. He cut the horse loose and mounted him. He turned the animal, thinking he would ride across the creek, losing his pursuers in the brush and the darkness.

A shot rang out and Matt felt a tug at his hip, then the pain drove through him like a blade sunk to the bone.

He did not cry out, but his teeth slammed together like a vise. The pain wrenched at him. His mind begged him to scream. He fought down the hurting, drew a deep breath. Each jolt of the horse brought lancing spears of agony. The bone in his hip flamed like a blacksmith's forge; he felt the burning spread through his flesh as though he lay in hot coals.

Behind him, he heard fresh shouts, the thunder of horses as the soldiers took to their mounts and gave chase.

Matthew knew the Mexicans would finish him off if they caught him. He grimaced as he kicked his horse in the flanks. The horse picked up speed, and the pain in Matt's hip tortured his mind, flailed his senses.

The horse struck the creek, tried to gallop across it. Matt held him to the cobblestoned water, though the horse's uneven gait jolted the pain to an excruciating intensity. He felt dizzy, disoriented, but he knew he had to outwit his pursuers or go down with a ball in his back.

He slowed the horse to a walk and turned him out of the creek. He set the animal on a hard right angle away from the creek, away from his false camp. Each step was agony, but he heard the Mexicans floundering around in the creek, yelling to each other, asking questions.

He touched his side, felt the sticky clot of blood

around the wound. Fresh blood washed over it and he knew he was bleeding badly. His dizziness increased and he fought off the urge to stop and lie down. But he knew he had to tend to the wound or he would bleed to death before morning.

The horse made little sound as it increased the distance between him and the soldiers. Matt deliberately held him to a slow walk. Every so often he stopped and listened. Finally the sounds faded away and Matt turned the horse westerly. He was too badly hurt to ride to St. Louis. He had to find a place to hole up, tend his wound, stop the bleeding.

The sky started to lighten and a new fear arose in his mind. If he stayed in the open, the Mexicans could spot him. He started to look for cover, a place where he could hide his tracks and go to ground.

Garza called in his men when the sky began to lighten in the east. They searched Matt's camp thoroughly but found nothing useful. They confiscated Caine's rifle, packing it as evidence of the confrontation. By then there was sufficient light to see, although the sun had not yet cleared the edge of the world.

"Look for papers," Garza told Sanchez.

The sergeant barked orders. The men fanned out on foot, searching every square meter of ground.

"Nada," reported Sanchez.

"Nothing?"

"Just the bedroll. If El Gigante is carrying anything, it is on his horse."

"Then we must find him."

"Yes, Lieutenant."

The sun, a fiery gold disk in the morning haze, slowly slid up over the eastern horizon. Light sprayed the land, bringing shape to every living thing.

Sanchez ordered the troops to mount up and move out. They soon discovered that the man they hunted had ridden into the creek. This presented a dilemma for Garza.

"Does he go down the creek or up?" he asked his sergeant.

"We can split up and ride both ways," said Sanchez.

"I think this is what he would like us to do."

Sanchez shrugged.

"We will go up the stream," said Garza.

"That is in the opposite direction of Santa Fe," said the sergeant.

"Exactamente," said Garza.

The soldiers rode both sides of the stream, Corporal Montez leading one column, Sanchez the other. They rode slowly, examining the ground carefully for hoofprints, for any disturbance to the banks of the creek or the surrounding land.

Montez found the tracks where they emerged from the creek. He signaled to Sanchez, who passed the word along the column. Garza ordered the soldiers to cross over and join the others as they trailed El Gigante.

"There is blood," said Montez. "El Gigante is wounded."

"Spread out," Garza said. "Make no noise."

Matt sat his horse behind a sheltering copse of cottonwood trees. The light breeze blew the cottony blossoms from the tree limbs, streamers settling on the ground and on the horse's mane like vagrant flakes of snow. Carefully, quickly, Matt reloaded his pistols. Earlier he had cleansed his wound in the creek, packed soft mud around it, and wrapped it with a spare shirt. The bleeding had stopped.

He heard the Mexicans then. They were coming slowly, but there was the occasional ring of a horseshoe on stone, the snort of a horse. They had to be less than a mile away. His heart began to beat faster as adrenaline flooded his veins. He cursed softly under his breath. He looked at his saddlebags, knowing that their contents would incriminate him in the eyes of the Spanish. He looked around for a place to cache the documents.

He did not have time to dig a hole, and he was too far from the creek to submerge the papers, all packed in oilcloth, beneath the surface. A flurry of cottony tendrils floated toward him. One stuck to his nose. He snorted, blowing it away. There was his answer.

Matt rode around, looking for a suitable tree. He sought one with a hole in it, or a sizable fork high enough to reach from the saddle. He saw a pair of trees that had grown close together, their branches intertwined. He rode to it, stood up in the stirrups. There was room for concealment. He removed the packets of papers from his saddlebags and jammed them into the forks. They would hold for a while, but he wondered what a strong wind would do. He backed the horse away and looked. He could not see the packets at first glance. Anyone not knowing they were there would never see them.

He rode to four corners of an imaginary square. With his knife he notched each tree with a small X. These too were high and unobtrusive. Finished, he cut a leafy limb from a cottonwood and brushed away his tracks. Then he doubled back and took an angle toward the creek. The soldiers were getting closer. He winced from the pain of his wound as the sounds of horses became stronger, clearer. He stopped in an alder thicket and waited.

They jumped Matt a half hour later. His horse broke from cover two hundred yards ahead of the column. The Mexicans were ready for him. The soldiers fired a volley of shots. One of the balls struck his horse. The animal staggered and stumbled. Somehow, Matt managed to ride the horse a dozen yards more. But he began to lose ground. The Mexicans charged after him.

"I want him alive!" shouted Garza. "Shoot over his head."

Rifles popped like Chinese firecrackers. Orange blazes peppered the darkness. White smoke billowed from a half-dozen iron muzzles.

Then Matt's horse went down. His forelegs crumpled, his hind legs sliding sideways. The big man rode it clear to the ground, and Garza knew he had his man.

"After him, Montez," he yelled to the corporal.

The young trooper, his eyes ablaze with the youthfully certain glow of triumph, rode hard toward the downed man and his foundering horse, rode through the desolate *madrugada* of that place as the last close stars winked out.

Chapter Four

Matt clung to the saddle horn, felt the jolt jar through his wrists as the horse slammed into the ground. He lifted his legs to keep from being crushed. As soon as the horse was down, he slid from the saddle and took off at a dead run, heading back toward the last remaining acre of tall grass. His wound broke open again and he began to bleed.

Just inside the edge, Matt halted and spun around. A Mexican soldier rode ahead of the others. Matt raised one pistol, took careful aim and fired. He watched as the rider clutched his chest and toppled from his horse, his rifle clattering on stone.

Corporal Montez hit the ground head first. His neck snapped like an aspen in a blow, stubbing out the young man's life in a single, timeless instant. All impulses to the brain ceased, and when his heart stopped, all blood stopped flowing.

Matt scooted backward, holding his loaded pistol low, close to the thick, dry grasses. He did not look up, but listened to the steady, frantic drum of horses' hooves pounding toward him until they seemed inside him, more rapid than his racing pulse. In seconds the others would find the body of their companion and come after him with a bloodthirsty lust for vengeance, cursing him, calling down upon him all devils invented by man during a long history of savage blooding.

He hated to waste his last shot, but he knew that his only chance now was to elude the soldiers by using his wits. He was fresh out of horse, weapons, and good legs. He winced as his leg rubbed against a prickly pear cactus. Needles bristled from his torn trousers, burned at his capillaries like hot needles sterilized blue by fire.

"Now," he breathed, as he sighted a Mexican soldier coming on fast, a blur of horse and man, a lone fighting machine barreling down on him like the last shadow on earth.

Matt cocked the pistol, squeezed the trigger. Hot sparks flew from the pan into the dry brush. Flames from the muzzle shot into a clump of grass that had escaped the dew. Tiny coals winked orange. Matt blew on the grasses as a rifle boomed. He heard a ball whistle overhead, screaming his last name in a shrill monotone.

Other soldiers streamed through the brush, raced toward the sounds of the shots.

Matt tucked his pistols inside his sash and crawled on his belly, away from the crackling flames. Smoke billowed upward in pyrrhic plumes.

"*Fuego, fuego,*" yelled one of the Mexicans.

"*Buscanlo!*" shouted Garza. Find him!

Matt heard the confused Mexican voices, understood every word. He looked back and saw that the fire had spread rapidly and that the flames were high enough to hide him if he stood up. The thick smoke provided good cover. But how long would it last? He heard the Mexican commander shouting orders, telling his men to put out the fire.

Well, all that would take time, Matt knew. If the soldiers wanted to put out the fire with blankets, they'd have to strip their saddles from their horses' backs. Time. That was what he needed. The pain in his leg jolted him when he stood up. He took long strides until the stiffness diminished. Then he broke into a dash, running like a cripple with one leg shorter than the other.

Behind him the smoke billowed up. The light breeze spread the thick cloud spumes along a wide front. Matt heard loud hoofbeats, turned, saw two riders leap the flames like jumpers at a steeplechase and swing their mounts in tandem toward him. He ducked down, knowing the Mexicans would ride him down if he tried to outrun the powerful horses that galloped with the speed of Pegasus.

The pair of troopers brought their rifles to their shoulders when they saw Matt crouching behind the smoke. Matt swayed from side to side, dropping to a squatting position just as the two soldiers fired. The lead balls fried the air, sizzling past Matt's ears like maddened hornets, thunking into the ground a few yards behind him into ruderal near an old game trail. The soldiers charged toward him, sliding their rifles downward, to grip them by the muzzles.

Matt knew the riders meant to brain him. He sprang upward as the soldiers converged on him, rifles ready to swing. To the Mexicans' surprise, he charged straight toward the two horses. The soldiers tried to turn their horses, but it was too late. Matt grabbed the butt of one Mexican's rifle, jerked hard. The soldier, gripping his weapon, tilted to one side, lost his balance and tumbled to the ground. Matt wrenched the rifle from his hand as the other Mexican raced past.

Grasping the butt and forestock, Matt rammed the rifle butt into the downed Mexican's face. He heard the man's nose crunch. Blood spurted in a thick madrilene from the fractured nose. Matt drove the rifle butt into the man's throat, crushing his larynx as if it were pasteboard.

The man wheezed, trying to draw air in through the blood and mangled bones.

Matt jerked the man's ammunition pouch from the wounded soldier.

The other rider wheeled his horse, drew his saber. Matt dropped to one knee, dug through the dying soldier's pouch for a paper cartridge. He bit off one end of the paper, poured the powder down the barrel. He seated the ball over the muzzle, stood up and jerked the metal ramrod free. He rammed the ball down over the powder, brought the rifle up to his waist. He shook fine black powder into the pan, closed the frizzen and shouldered the rifle.

The charging soldier raised his saber for a killing swipe some ten yards from Matt's position. Matt calmly thumbed the cock back, taking deadly aim on the soldier's chest. He squeezed the trigger as the trooper bore down on him. The pan flashed, shooting sparks through the touch-hole of the rifle. The main charge ignited and propelled the soft lead ball from the muzzle in a blaze of orange flame, a cloud of white smoke. Then, blinded by the smoke, his face nettled with blowback, Matt dove to one side. He heard the saber's viperous hiss as it sliced the air.

Rising up, Matt watched as the horse sped by, its rider clutching his chest. The saber flashed silver in the sunlight and hit the ground with a metallic twang.

Matt sucked in air, feeling the pressure of time as soldiers fought to flank him, riding around the smoke, flashing through the blazing brush, scattering sparks as if they were riding over flint rock. He watched as the mortally wounded soldier eased over in the saddle and fell over the right side. His boot stuck in the stirrup as the horse galloped through flames. The Mexican's head bobbed up and down as it rumbled over the uneven ground. Matt turned away from the grisly sight, knowing that the man he had shot was dead as a stone.

The other horse, the one ridden in by the choking

Mexican, was pacing in circles, its eyes wide in panic, its nostrils flaring. Matt staggered toward it slowly, limping from his hip wound. He spoke to the horse in Spanish as he sidled up, one hand poised to grab a rein.

"Calmate, caballo, suave, suave."

The horse bunched its muscles as if to bolt from that burning place when Matt's hand lashed out. He grabbed the rein, pulled the horse's head down. The bit dug into the tender backside of the animal's mouth. Leaning over its neck, Matt grabbed the other rein, tightened both of them. Then he stuck his foot in the stirrup and swung painfully into the saddle, his hip hurting like a wooden stake through the ganglia of his brain.

He lay flat over the pommel and tapped the horse's flanks with the heels of his moccasin boots. The horse responded instantly, and Matt felt the ripple of the animal's muscles as the horse bounded away from the smoke and the flames that garnitured the rising sun with a bloodred intensity. Lead balls whistled like speed-maddened doves overhead, and Matt knew the soldiers were firing at sound, that they could not see him.

After getting his bearings, Matt rode southwest, knowing that he would eventually ride out of the deep swale. In doing so, he would rise up into the chaparral once again and make an easy target. He slowed the horse to a fast walk, which both muffled the animal's hoofbeats and conserved its flagging energy. Each minute that passed put distance between him and the Mexican horsemen. With luck, Matt figured he could get far enough ahead of them so they could not catch up without foundering their own mounts. It was a demanding hope, he knew, but it was backed by belief in his own ability and stamina. He gritted his teeth against the burning pain in his hip, and soon the acrid sting of smoke was no longer in his nostrils, no longer like cherry coals in his lungs.

He did not look back, but ahead, knowing that the

mountains would give him refuge, for he knew them well. And suddenly he realized that they had become his home, that they were in his heart, and that duty, obedience to authority, the ties to his country, were far less important.

Morning Lark heard the cries of the young boys who served as lookouts for the big Shoshone camp. Her heart beat faster and a familiar swirl in her stomach made her abdomen ripple in anticipation. She looked up, saw the small band of braves riding toward the circles of buffalo hide lodges, riding toward the center of the encampment. She strained her eyes to see if Big Man was with Antelope and Gray Deer.

The giant white man was not with the Shoshone braves. Big Man had told her that he must go to the white man's fort on the Father of Rivers, but Morning Lark had hoped that he might return—and stay for as long as he lived and breathed.

Morning Lark squatted in front of a tepee where her sister, Black Quill, lived with her husband, Red Elk. Black Quill, Two Lances's sister Basket Weaver, and an old woman named Broken String, were clucking over clay bowls of dye into which each woman was dipping porcupine quills.

Deer hides, staked taut a few inches above the ground, ringed the circle of women. A small fire smoked near the flensed and drying hides.

Her heart was on the ground that her husband-man was not returning. She fought back tears, compressing her lips into a thin, quivering, bloodless parchment. She stood up, turning away so that the others could not see her face, could not see the deep hurt in her now that she knew Big Man would not be lying next to her in the lodge that night.

"Where do you go, Morning Lark?" asked Basket

Weaver. "You are not finished staining the quills in your bowl."

"I am tired. I will go to my lodge and take some rest."

"Tired? Why, you have hardly moved a finger."

Lark felt her face turn warm with the rush of blood under her skin. She did not wish to fight with Weaver. She wanted only to gather her scattered thoughts and find that place inside her where it was calm, that center of herself where nothing could harm her, where the Great Spirit could speak to human beings and where human beings could hear the spirit voice.

"I will finish my work later," said Lark tightly.

"Her man has not come back and she wants to sulk," said Broken String. "Let her go."

"She is lazy," said Weaver.

"I am not," said Lark sharply.

"Lazy, lazy, lazy," prattled Weaver.

The other women grunted in assent, and Lark felt the anger scorch the tender flesh behind her ears like hot coals burning through a blanket. She was tempted to talk back, but these were her elders. And she did not know what to say, for she felt hollowed out inside, empty as a broken rattle that had lost its seeds.

Instead she turned from the women and walked disconsolately toward her lodge, clasping her hands together tightly, as if to hold herself together, to keep from shaking apart like a dry weed in the wind.

Antelope rode past, spoke to her. "Where do you go with that sad face?" he asked.

"To my lodge."

Antelope held up three Mexican scalps. He grinned.

"Do not tease me," she said.

"Your heart is on the ground for Big Man," he said.

Lark said nothing, just stared at the brave without blinking.

"He has gone to the white man's fort on the big river."

"He will not be back?"

Antelope shrugged.

"Go away," said Lark.

Antelope grunted and turned his horse to join the others.

Lark turned the buffalo head in front of her lodge the other way to tell everyone that she did not want visitors.

She hunched over, waddled into her lodge. Quickly she pulled the door flap closed, inserting the bones through the leather loops to latch it tight.

She sat in the darkness, the only light beaming down through the smoke hole. Motes of dust shimmered in the beam, like ghostly fireflies.

Lark scooted to her man's side of the lodge, knelt before a mound of deer hides she had tanned herself. Gently, caressingly, she lifted the hides and set them aside. She gazed down at the strange tools Big Man used, mystery tools that only he understood. Although they were wrapped in oilskin, she had seen them many times before. She dared not touch them, but she could picture them in her mind. They gleamed like the yellow metal when the sun struck them. One tool, like a hollowed branch, seemed to have water in it that would not run out even when tipped over, water that was frozen but not cold.

She knew that Big Man must be very powerful to carry such tools. With them he could measure the sky and the earth, and she had seen him make scratches on strange leaves that were square and even. He had taken these leaves with their mysterious markings with him, and this made her think that he might never return to her people.

She wanted to touch the tools, to take them out of their oilskin pouches one by one and lay them out so that the sun could strike them through the smoke hole, but she dared not tamper with Big Man's magic. Instead she carefully covered them again and patted the deerskins so that the lumps and wrinkles were gone.

She crawled to her blankets and uncovered a quilled pouch she had made from the skin of an elk. She opened it, pulled out the little beaded flag Big Man had given her and held it in her hand, as if to feel the presence of her man. She squeezed it gently in a tiny fist and began to weep.

"Come back, come back," she chanted, and the tears streamed down her face. She shut her eyes tightly and seemed to feel Big Man's arms around her, holding her close to him, smothering her with his bulk.

She looked upward through the smoke flap at the patch of blue sky above.

"Bring Big Man back to Morning Lark, Great Spirit," she prayed softly.

Chapter Five

Matt headed for a shallow, jagged arroyo, a place where over the centuries sudden floods had gouged a crooked furrow into the earth. There, he reasoned, he could rest and give his wound a better chance to heal. And anyone scanning the landscape for him would think he'd disappeared. Perhaps the Mexicans would give up on him, ride back to Santa Fe.

He had not seen the soldiers yet, but knew they were scouring the countryside, looking for him. He could almost see the Mexican lieutenant using his spyglass to search for him as if he were an ant under a burning glass.

For the past two hours, with the sun midway across the morning sky, crawling toward its zenith, Matt had played an elusive game of hide-and-seek, staying to the shallow draws, walking alongside the stolen horse to make his profile smaller. If he sensed that he might be spotted, he brought the horse to its knees, waited long enough to see if he had drawn any soldiers to his position, then continued on warily, his senses tuned to a hair-fine pitch.

He'd reloaded both pistols and the rifle he took from one of the soldiers he'd killed. When he searched through the dead Mexican's saddlebags, he found only a crumbling, dried-out tortilla, some rock-hard beans wrapped in dirty cloth, a small wooden canteen half full of some brandy, and two strips of dried beef that were gritty with sand, smelling faintly of saddle grease.

Water could become a problem, although he knew there were small watering holes scattered throughout that region. He knew how to dig below the surface in the arroyos, find the wet sand, the lingering pockets of moisture, but his strength was sapped from the wound in his hip. He had been bleeding off and on all morning. And there had not been time for the wound to scab over. As long as he was moving, he knew it would not; every time he mounted up, the wound would break open again and he would bleed.

Matt rode out of the arroyo into the blazing heat of the day. The sun was high in the sky, heading toward noon. He was hungry, tired, light-headed from the loss of blood. The horse kept snorting, sniffing the dry air for a whiff of water. There had been no grain in the Mexican saddlebags, so Matt let the horse snatch nourishment from the short grasses that grew on the plain. But each time he allowed the horse to feed, he knew, he was giving up a little more control should the animal decide to buck him off and run away on its own.

By late afternoon Matt thought he'd shaken off his pursuers. But he could not be sure. The Mexican patrol was out there somewhere, and he had long since been sapped of the energy to cover his tracks. He knew that if he did not find a place to hole up, with food and water, he'd leave his bones on the vast empty land that was dotted with the skulls and bones of other game.

The mountains seemed close, but he knew they were farther away than they looked. That night, when he found a place to bed down, in a shallow draw, he hobbled the horse, but was unable to strip it of its saddle, rifle scabbard, and bags. The Mexican rifle, with its large Spanish lock, was heavy. The brace of pistols dug into his flesh, and he was glad to lay them out and set the rifle down alongside. He slipped the straps of the two possibles bags from his shoulders, took off the powder horns. The thongs had dug into his shoulders too, but he was grateful to have the ammunition.

Too weary to face the prospect of eating the stale food in the soldier's saddlebags, he lay his head down on one of the possibles pouches and slept, his eyes burning in their sockets from an approaching fever.

Matt awoke before dawn, chilled, groggy from the dull pain in his hip. It took him a few moments to realize where he was, out in the open on hard, uneven ground. He listened to the soft sigh of the wind, looked up at the faint stars fading away from a glimmer of light in the eastern sky. He sat up, painfully, heard the Mexican horse whicker softly.

His hip was stiff and sore. Gingerly, he felt the wound. There was a hard knot where the scab had begun forming a crust, but it felt spongy to his touch. He knew it would break open again as soon as he stood up, unless he could brace himself and stand without jerking his bad leg. His stomach growled with emptiness and his mouth felt dry as a sun-baked stone. He touched his cheek, recoiling at the unexpected warmth. He was feverish and needed water to drench his parched flesh.

The horse whickered again, and Matt knew that it was hungry too.

He shivered from a sudden chill, then grew suddenly hot as the fever raced through his flesh. He touched a sore spot on his butt where he had lain on his knife during the night. Withdrawing the knife from its scabbard, he peered hard through the predawn darkness. He saw the shadows of prickly pear, hoped that they had not yet dried in the burning summer sun. He crawled toward one of the clumps, favoring his wounded hip.

It took him several moments to reach the cactus, but the light gradually intensified as the sun edged toward the eastern horizon. He was short of breath by the time he reached it, but inhaled deeply to smell its faded blossoms. Scooting in close, he steadied himself with one arm bracing his torso in a sitting position. He looked at the round, flat leaves of the cactus, barely saw their brown-gold spines bristling from the succulent plant. In its fibers was moisture, precious water that he and the horse might use to allay their thirst. Damned little of it, he knew, but it might mean the difference between life and death for both man and animal.

Matt began to saw at the base of one broad leaf. The work was more difficult than he had imagined. He felt his strength ebbing as he worked the blade of the knife back and forth. The blade was sharp, though, and he'd soon separated the leaf from its base. He set it aside, pricking his finger, then sucking at the tiny gout of blood that oozed from the skin. He grew more thirsty, but the salty taste revived his spirits.

He sawed through three more cacti before his energy waned. The sun cleared the distant horizon, drawing cold from the night-shrouded earth, and he shivered again before the fever took hold. He took one of the prickly pear cakes in his hand and began to shave the spines from its flat surface. When it was clean, he sliced it in half, then sliced the halves into strips. He put one of the strips in his mouth, chewing and sucking the moisture from its fibers.

He tried to swallow the chewed plant, but it was too tough, so he cut away the chewed part and continued to draw moisture into his parched mouth. He shaved away the spines from the other cakes. The sun rose higher, until it cleared the horizon, stood hovering in the haze of morning, ablaze with a golden-orange warmth that seeped slowly into him. He continued to chew until he felt he could stand on his feet.

Matt felt the scab tear loose from his wound as he stood up, holding the three remaining cakes. He sheathed his knife and walked stiff-legged toward the hobbled horse. The horse shied away from him at first. Matt held out one of the cakes. The horse's ears perked and its rubbery nostrils quivered. It extended its neck and nibbled at the cactus, then snatched the cake from Matt's hand and chewed it to shreds. Matt gave the animal another cake.

He managed to swallow some of the cactus he chewed, but it made him sick. He had to find water, he thought, and food, too, if he was to go on. He knew that once the sun was up high, he would lose the little moisture he had absorbed. Dizzy, weak, he staggered back toward the place where he'd slept. He knelt down, wincing at the pain in his hip, and slipped his possibles pouches over his shoulder, grabbed up his powder horns and put those around his neck. Using the rifle for a crutch, he walked back to the horse. He gave the animal the last of the despined cakes, removed the hobbles and placed them in one of the saddlebags. Painfully, he mounted the horse, which held fast for him. Sweating profusely, Matt steadied himself, waiting until a feverish convulsion had passed. The taste of the cactus was strong in his mouth. He chewed on the last of the strips and headed westward across the empty land, the sun at his back like a healing fire, burning into his flesh, warming the cold at his core.

His belly gnawed at him like a famished beast. He shook with chills, then sweated the poisonous fever through his pores. The land blurred as he tried to keep his bearings. He drifted in and out of consciousness like a sleepwalker. He heard the soft clop of the horse's hooves, and it sounded like a man's footsteps, like boots on hard sand. His leg throbbed with pain, and he wondered if he'd see the streaks that were the telltale signs of gangrene. Matt knew he had to treat the wound, had to clean it and dress it, or else it would fester and eat him alive.

The sun spun in the sky overhead, telling him it was afternoon. He jolted himself into a forced state of alertness, took his bearings. From the angle of the sun, he was heading south, too far south. He swung the horse to the northwest and saw the empty land all around him, deserted, desolate, without landmarks. The plain seemed to stretch forever, like a featureless sea. His heart sank with despair as the horse bleated pitifully, as thirsty as he under the scorching forge of the sun.

Matt took his mind away from his despair, took himself away as he rocked in the saddle, took himself back to the farm in Ohio, to green fields and the smell of newly mown hay, to the ponds and creeks of his family's homestead. He swam naked in the creek, diving off the grassy mud bank into cool waters, and he heard the laughter of his boyhood chums, the giggles of girls who had come to watch. And then he was marching to a vocal cadence and wearing a second lieutenant's uniform, riding a carriage to Washington to meet men with gold braid on their epaulets, men with blurred faces and deep voices.

He walked the streets of St. Louis in brume, heard the foghorns on the river, the chug of boats down on the levee, smelled the wet sandstone after a rain, heard the gulls cry forlornly in the nightmist that shrouded the waterfront, listened to the breathy voices speaking in French as he passed by, no longer in uniform, but wearing buckskins and carrying a Pennsylvania rifle, toting a backpack with all of his belongings so that his hands were free.

Matt heard his mother call out his name and he

opened his eyes. The horse had stopped, was standing hip-shot, his head drooping. Panic clutched at Matt's throat, seized his senses. Groggy from the short nap, he looked wildly around him, expecting at any moment to be charged by Mexican soldiers, shooting and shouting. But there was only a desolate silence, the soft brush of a dry wind against his cheek, so light and delicate it might have been his imagination.

His eyes strained to penetrate the distance as he gazed westward. Far-off clouds lay against the horizon. Were they masking the mountains? He did not know. He took his bearings, shook for a moment as he summoned his resolve, then tapped the Mexican horse in the flanks. The horse moved disconsolately across the plain, its head still drooping, its breath wheezing in dry lungs.

Matt felt swallowed up in the huge emptiness. A jackrabbit bolted from a clump of chaparral, and he did not feel so alone, but his mouth watered as he pictured the skinned carcass turning on a spit. He had been too slow to react, and the jackrabbit disappeared so quickly he wondered if he'd imagined it. But later he saw a small herd of pronghorns, standing like statues beyond a shimmering lake that danced and faded as he waded into it. A dust devil whirled across a wide expanse of land like some ghostly dervish until it blew itself out somewhere beyond range of his eyes.

The sun slid slowly down the escarpment of sky, blinding him in its glare the rest of the afternoon. Then, blessedly, it sank below the horizon, illuminating the far cloud banks, and hung there, a molten disk, lighting his way west as his and the horse's shadow stretched long behind him until it was as thin as a barrel stave. His mouth was dry as a corn husk and he couldn't swallow. His leg throbbed with every beat of his heart, but the wound had scabbed over again and he counted that as a small blessing.

The sun sank away beyond the distant horizon and its rays shot above the clouds, leaving a gold rim along their top edge. Matt watched the gold fade away to a purple, then blacken as night crept toward him, devouring all the shadows, turning daylight to dust.

He kept on going, because he didn't know if he would be able to get on the horse again if he ever got off. He had to keep kicking the horse in the flanks to keep it plodding ahead. Traveling blind until the moon rose, he felt as if he was riding through stars, the night was so black, the earth nearly invisible under the sliver of finger-nail that hung like a scimitar above the horizon. He tried to speak, just to break the silence, but his voice was a hoarse croak in his throat, would not pass his cracked and bleeding lips.

Sometime during the slow, dark night he smelled a change in the air. He had licked his lips dry, the salty blood only making him thirstier. There was a slight cool-ness to the air, and he thought he smelled water. But he could not see through the blackness, could not picture wa-ter in the pitch of his mind. There was a change in the air, though. He knew that.

Matt spoke to the horse, his voice a raspy whisper. "Water, boy, find the water. *Agua,*" he said in Span-ish. *"Buscalo."*

He clapped the horse's flanks with his boot heels. The horse whickered a throaty rumble and stumbled ahead. There was no gait to it, just an awkward plodding that was slightly faster than a walk. *"Andale,"* husked Matt.

The horse picked up speed, and Matt held on to the saddle horn, the high Mexican cantle pounding against his buttocks, sending shoots of pain through his wounded hip. He didn't care, though. The tang of water was definitely in the air. It seemed a long way off as he strained his ears to hear the sound of a creek or a river.

Where was he? Matt did not know.

Somewhere in the dark, lost. Somewhere in the middle of a vast desert, riding a dying horse. A dying man riding a dying horse. He started to laugh hysterically, but his throat cracked and he thought it might be bleeding like his lips had bled.

The stars streaked overhead as the horse broke into a gallop. The air was dank now with the tang of water. Big water, Matt thought. No creek, but a mighty river, perhaps the Big River of the North. Well, it was out there somewhere. He had mapped it, crossed and recrossed it, slept on its banks, dreamed its roaming waterpower as it rushed to the south, breathed its muscular depths under better skies than the one he rode under now. The horse slowed and Matt could hear it in the darkness, the gentle rush of waters, the slap of small waves against the banks.

The horse whinnied loudly, and under the moon's thin spray of light Matt caught the gleam of the river. Then the horse was at its banks, standing spraddle-legged, its neck bowed, slurping up water like a desert camel. Matt slid out of the saddle, touched the ground with his good leg. He let the reins trail as he hobbled to the bank, lay flat on his stomach upstream of the horse and found the water with his mouth. He sipped it, savoring the brackish taste, felt its coolness soothe his slashed lips and drench his parched throat.

His stomach contracted, rebelled, but Matt held the water down. He splashed his dry face, splashed water onto his shirt. He felt along the underside of the bank, felt the soft mud and knew that he could heal his wound, could rest there and regain his strength. He could wash the wound, pack it with mud and let nature take its blessed course. He wanted to shout with joy, but he had more thirst to slake and a mind to clear.

Matt cupped the water in his hands, brought it to his

lips. He sipped sparingly, feeling the water trickle down his throat. He didn't want to founder like a desiccated cow, but he knew he had to absorb enough water to clear his head, bring his body back to something resembling normalcy. He knew he was dry through and through, addle-brained, half crazy from the heat.

"Yes, yes," he breathed, and was delighted that his voice was back.

The horse stopped drinking, but it snorted into the water, blew air through its nostrils.

Matt laughed, and the horse jerked its head out of the water at the strange sound.

"We're goin' to make it, boy, you and me," said Matt. Then he ducked his head under the water, and when he emerged, blew his nostrils as the horse had done. He spoke to the animal in Spanish, said obscene things to it, discussed matters of life and death, talked about the stars overhead and the greatness of the river they had found together in the darkness. He knew it would sound crazy to anyone listening, but there was no one there but him, the horse, and God, and the great river rushing by, giving life to all creatures, bringing news of the mountains and the melting snows on the giant peaks, carrying messages of the high places in its powerful depths.

"I love this river," said Matt loudly, "love it as my brother, as my father. Horse, do you not love this grand river? It's God's own map put here to show lost travelers the way home. Horse, we are going to live, you and I. We will find grass and food to eat and we will live, by God."

Exhausted, Matt lay on his side, not minding the pain in his hip, and he heard the horse nibbling at the gamma grass. It would not go far, he knew. He listened to the river whispering by, heard it murmur at it sloshed against the banks. He smelled its musky tang and closed his eyes, feeling sleep tug at him like the current, like the deep currents in the river, pulling him down and under and along, along to wherever dreams could take him, up into the night and off to the high country, to the place where a woman waited for him in a rich grassy meadow under the stars.

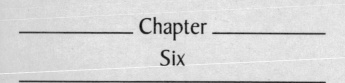

Chapter
Six

The man finished writing his report and put it in a large heavy envelope. He poured a small amount of wax where the edges joined, embedded his seal in the soft wax, then blew it cold. He turned the envelope over, addressed it to "General James Wilkinson via Courier," and wrote MOST SECRET in bold capital letters on the front of the envelope. He wiped the quill pen dry, put it back in its holder, stoppered the ink receptacle with a cork. The candle on his desk flickered.

Lieutenant Thomas Binder blew out the candle, strode from the room carrying the envelope. He wore civilian clothing, had grown a short beard. He locked the door to his room in the Alberge Reynard, walked down the stairs, emerged on a dark street in the Vide Poche, "Empty Pockets," section of St. Louis. He passed several women of the night who tried to entice him to their rooms, but he did not stop until he reached the open doors of the Rocky Mountain House. The windows were open, and Tom heard the saw of a violin, the jingle of a banjo from inside.

A man was singing off-key in French, trying to find the notes of the song as Binder stepped inside. Lamps burned brightly and the room was blue with pipe and cigar smoke. He scanned the room, saw his contact at a table near the front doors. He angled toward the courier, catching his eye.

"Sergeant," he said as he sat down.

"Lieutenant."

Binder handed the envelope to Sergeant Earl Fitzroy. "Leave as soon as you can."

"That's eight hunnert miles to Washington, sir."

"And General Wilkinson will have a fit when he reads my report."

"Caine didn't show?"

"No. I fear he's dead, or a prisoner. Proceed with all haste."

"There's a packet leaving at midnight. I got time to finish my beer."

"Suit yourself."

"Now what, Lieutenant?"

Fitzroy was a burly man, also wearing civilian clothes, who blended in with the rough crowd of mountaineers and pirates who filled the tables at Rocky Mountain House. His beard was longer and bushier than Binder's.

"I expect Wilkinson will send another man to take Caine's place."

"Who?"

"Zebulon Pike, likely."

Fitzroy drank from his glass, licked the foam off his lips and moustache. He let out a whistle. "Pike's out mappin' the Mississippi now. He won't like it much. The President's real serious, then."

"Well, the general is."

"Wilkinson don't have good sense."

Binder smiled, shook his head when a serving girl came up to the table. The girl went away.

"He's on a mission," said Binder. "He'll get us into war yet."

"I hate to go all the way to Washington." Fitzroy was looking at the serving girl when he said it.

Binder stood up. "I requested that you be allowed to return with the general's reply."

"Thanks, sir. I'd rather be here than there." The serving girl smiled at him.

"Don't spread the clap back home."

Fitzroy's face reddened and he laughed. He stuck the envelope under his shirt and stood up. "I'll pack my possibles and be on my way, sir."

"Give Wilkinson my regards, Sergeant."

"That I will, Lieutenant."

The two men left the tavern separately. The fog began to roll in. Binder felt the wetness on his face when he turned the corner. He wondered if Wilkinson would send Pike on an expedition. If so, there would be trouble with the Mexicans. Which was probably what Wilkinson wanted. The man was a mad dreamer who wanted to conquer the whole West for his government, but it was known that he was thick with Aaron Burr and had, at one time, been a paid agent for Spain while still wearing his general's uniform.

Binder wondered whose interests Wilkinson really had at heart. The government's or his own?

He strode the brumous streets, drawing his collar up around his throat as if to ward off the ghost of Matthew Caine, whose bones must now lie in a foreign land, with none to mourn his passing.

Governor Joaquín Reál Alencaster chewed the stub of a brandy-soaked cigar. The flame had gone out moments ago, but he savored the taste of tobacco and *aguardiente*

fino on his tongue. Indeed, he liked the taste of brandy itself and poured his crystal glass full once again.

"More brandy, Doctor?" he asked, holding the decanter in readiness.

"No more, thank you, Governor," said Surgeon
Larrañaga of the Santa Fe garrison. "I fear tomorrow, going among the river settlements."

"Ah, but you have not the fear of the soldier facing
smallpox, or the villager watching his child wither and
die."

"No, I have not that fear, Your Grace," said the surgeon. For years, since the coming of the Spaniards, epidemics of smallpox had broken out in all of the river
pueblos, decimating troops, people, especially children.
He had just returned from one sweep through the country, and tomorrow he was to travel farther south, taking
with him the smallpox vaccine that had recently been developed.

"Then it has been difficult? These vaccinations?"

They had avoided the subject all evening. Instead,
during the meal of roast lamb, potatoes, catfish, crayfish,
corn tortillas, and wine, they had spoken of politics.

"The people are ignorant of science," said Larrañaga.
"Both Indian and Spanish. They think I am being cruel
when I inject the 'poison' into their veins."

The governor laughed. He had been vaccinated himself, as had all others in the government seat at Santa Fe.

"They think it is dangerous to have me penetrate their
bodies," continued the surgeon, enjoying the governor's
glee. "They resist me and I have to use force."

"That is why I send the troops with you," said
Alencaster. "You are too small to use much force."

The doctor laughed. He was a small, officious man,
the only doctor for hundreds of miles. Some looked upon
him as a witch or a wizard. The Indians feared him. The

Mexicans, the mixed bloods, thought he was an evil man. Larrañaga ran a slender finger across his thin moustache.

"It is difficult to preserve the vaccine on these long journeys," said the surgeon. "I may indeed have killed a patient or two in my travels. When I return from the south, I will go to the pueblo at Taos. It will take more than a month to vaccinate all those to the north."

"Better than the epidemic," said the governor.

"True. There are other problems I have encountered, however."

"As if you did not have enough in your black bag," joked Alencaster.

"There are other epidemics besides the smallpox."

"To be sure," said the governor, not wishing the doctor to possess more knowledge than he.

"They have measles, the whooping cough, and there is always dysentery. The children, their little bodies burning up, their eyes too big for their heads, their lips parched, their flesh weak and ravaged. I dislike having to vaccinate small children who are already very ill."

"Still," said the governor, suddenly austere, sucking in his chest so that his large belly swelled against the table edge, his round face purpling slightly, "you have your orders. I wish to have a fair in El Paso this September. I want everyone under my jurisdiction to be healthy."

So, thought the surgeon, it was back to politics again. He sighed inwardly and reached for his brandy snifter.

"I believe I will have another taste of the fine *aguardiente,* after all, Your Grace."

The paunchy governor beamed, poured the snifter half full. He savored the fragrance before recapping the decanter.

"I have invited skilled weavers from New Biscay," said Alencaster. "That province needs some commercial organization. Their industry is pathetic."

"To be sure," said the surgeon, hoping the governor would not know he was being mimicked.

Alencaster frowned, however, and Larrañaga knew that he had probably gone too far. He downed the brandy without tasting it and rose from the table. But there was more, and he was bound to stay and hear what else was on the governor's mind.

"When you go to Taos, Doctor, keep your eyes and ears open."

"Eh?"

"There is talk of an American expedition to the north. I received a report of such from Chihuahua. And the Indios have spoken of a man they call 'El Gigante,' a Yanqui, I believe."

"I have heard the talk," said the surgeon.

"I have sent an expedition to the north to find this man and any others. I have heard of a fort on the Rio Grande del Norte."

"Am I to be a spy, then, Your Excellency?"

Alencaster laughed, but there was a sourness to it, like wine gone bad.

"Not at all. I would just like to know if you hear anything of this El Gigante or any American expedition to the north."

"If I hear anything, Your Grace, I will be glad to relay the gossip."

Alencaster frowned, then downed his wine as if to wash a bad taste out of his mouth.

"Thank you for a fine supper, Your Grace," Larrañaga said. "I must make preparations to depart on the morrow. I will vaccinate your people in El Paso, Cebolleta, Albuquerque, Laguna, and even Zuñi."

"To be sure," said Alencaster, dabbing at his cherubic lips with a napkin. Then he belched loudly, knowing he had made his point with the smug little surgeon with the bad manners to insult his host.

"Good night, Your Grace," said Larrañaga, with only the slightest bow before he pushed through the huge oaken doors of the dining salon.

Matt crawled to the riverbank, his hip so stiff he could not rise to his feet. The last pale stars shimmered in the murky waters of the Rio Grande del Norte, fragile mobiles in a wrinkled dance, caught in space and time as the river moved without taking them along in its current. He leaned over the bank and sucked water into his dry mouth, swallowed slowly. He seemed to draw strength from the waters, stiffened his arms and held his torso up as he gazed around, looking for signs of life, the Mexican horse. The pain in his hip was now a throbbing pulse that beat at his senses like some hideous form of torture.

The strength went out of his arms, and Matt crumpled to the ground, sweat beading up on his forehead like dew.

There was no sign of the horse. Or anything else alive. He felt like he'd been washed up on a desolate dream shore where no birds sang, no animals lived, no sun shone. But he was alive. He breathed. He drank. He hurt.

He lay there, eyes closed, listened to the sound of his breathing. He listened to the river, the chuff of its waters next to the bank, the soft lap downstream where it struck a root or a rock, the undertone of current that had its own strange hum, almost undetectable, yet audible beneath the other sounds. He felt the pull of the river, felt it beckoning to him, like a lover, to slide from the bank and let it carry him where it willed, to the southlands, to some warm littoral paradise where gulls flashed in the sun and shorebirds stalked the endless *arenosidad* of the Gulf, leaving their trident tracks in the sand until the gentle waves filled them, erasing the signatures of their passing.

Matt lapsed into a state of semisleeplessness, the water he had drunk seeping through his dessicated muscles, blending with his blood, assuaging the gnashing hunger in his empty belly. The river rush lulled him to sleep, soothed his fevers with a sonic balm until he floated on it, floated away on its surging tide, warm in its gentle embrace. The pain in his hip separated from his consciousness, became a separate part of him, something wooden, which could be taken away, could be left behind.

"Hoopties," he said softly. Everything round. Everything connected. A hoop for each man, a round life to be lived. The only way to get off the hoop was to die. For years now his hooptie had been duty, honor, country. He was on that part of the hoop, hanging on for dear life, although he felt a stronger pull in the opposite direction. Especially when he was with the Shoshones, living as the People lived. The People believed in the great circle, the absolute roundness of the universe and all the lives breathing in it. There was only one way out. Break away from the circle. Or break the circle. Grab another hoop, or die. Hoopties rolling everywhere in the world, sometimes touching, never connecting, except through magic, a ring trick that could not be explained.

Thinking of his imaginary hoopties calmed Matt, helped him collect his jumbled thoughts into a semblance of order. He could not stay in that place. He must heal his wound, clean it, pack it with river mud and . . .

He could not think beyond that for several moments. Just that much activity, just thinking about it, drained him of energy. Food. He must have sustenance as well. Fish? Could he find game in that empty place? Could he kill it and cook it? He could not set snares. It would be like tossing a knife into the air and hoping it would land on a rabbit and kill it. If he could even find a game trail, he would have to go another day without food, for the small furtive creatures came to drink only at night.

The morning light fanned out, spread like healing rays from some unknown source as Matt surveyed the stretch of river where he had found himself after a night of pain and darkness. He knew the stretch well, but it was far south of where he wanted to be. The cottonwoods, some still dark, lined part of the opposite bank and below the river took a meander, rolled over shallows filled with stones as smooth as darning eggs, and there was a shore where he could lie and bathe without fear of being swept away by the powerful current.

Matt listened, directing his thoughts upriver and down. Where was the horse? He pressed himself upward again on stiffened arms and gazed as far as his eyes could see, but he saw no sign of life, no dark shadow grazing along the river. It was quiet, the kind of quiet that makes a man apprehensive and fearful, for it was unnatural even in the midst of such emptiness of country. He gasped and fell flat once again, his energy sapped from just that small effort.

He lay there, breathing hard until his strength returned. Then he crawled backward, slithered toward the meander like a wounded lizard. He found a way to crawl and drag his afflicted leg so that he made better time. Still, it took him the better part of an hour to reach the slight bend in the river. He pulled himself down to the sandbar, stippled with stones, half-buried branches bleached gray as mortified skin, and managed to sit up. He shucked off his boots with great effort. He slipped his possibles pouch and powder horns from his shoulder, removed his shirt. He laid his pistols on dry sand, unbuckled his belt, with the knife in its scabbard attached, set it next to his pistols. He pulled his trousers off and sidled to the water. He eased himself in backward, a few inches at a time.

He felt the pull of the current on his legs, the chill of the morning water. He dug his fingers into the soft sand, gritted his teeth against the pain in his hip. The cold water numbed him after a few moments, and he eased himself out of the river. He looked at the wound for the first time. The ball had gone clean through, leaving an ugly hole. Skin hung like chewed meat from the exit wound, strangely paper-thin and translucent. He gingerly felt around both holes just below the hipbone, but could feel no bones broken.

He remembered shooting a young bull elk the previous fall. He had shot the animal in the neck and there was a lot of blood, but the elk did not go down. Matt had tracked the bull for hours. Finally it swam a stream, and when it emerged, there was no longer any blood. The stream waters were very cold, like ice, and when he picked up the tracks later, the bull had trotted off with a cow and calf, leaving no blood spoor. Matt realized that the cold waters of the stream had sealed the wound, stopped the blood flow. Now he saw that the same thing had happened with his own wound. It was clean and bloodless and he could feel the cold in his bones.

Matt stayed there at the meander all day, soaking his leg whenever the pain started in again. He drank to fill his empty belly, slept, and bathed until the sun disappeared beyond the mountains. That night, he dressed himself, crawled up to the top of the bank and made himself a sleeping wallow.

He gathered twigs and dry branches from along the shore, taking it slow, favoring the bad leg. When he had a large stack, he made a tepee from the smaller pieces. He sliced dry shavings from a small branch and placed these beneath the pyramid of salvaged wood. Before he started the fire, he took off his clothes again, sat Adam-naked, a man-frog flung back to the dawn of creation.

Matt hated to waste a ball, but he had no puller. He fired one of the pistols, reloaded it with a light charge, primed it. He shot orange sparks into the tinder. The shavings caught and he blew them into flame. The cone of wood blazed from the heat and fire of the shavings. When the fire was big enough and hot enough, Matt shoved the blade of his knife into the hottest part, turning it over and over until the edges turned blue-orange. He lay flat, took a sturdy, thin stick and placed it between his teeth. He poked the knife point inside the entrance wound, pressed it against the raw flesh. He bit the stick half in two. Tears streamed down his face through tightly shut eyelids. He reheated the knife again, barely able to stand the pain, then lay it flat against the entrance hole until he smelled the flesh burning. He passed out from the pain, awoke when sparks spattered on his bare chest.

He reheated the knife and put a fresh stick in his mouth. He seared the exit wound in the same way. This time he did not pass out, but his body was drenched with sweat and his mind exploded into a fireworks display with a pain he could no longer bear without screaming. His lost cry flared up and down the river and out over the plain like the anguished howl of a soul in torment.

He dressed in the dark, hungry once again, and thirsty beyond mortal belief. He drank at the river, able to limp down to the sandbar and kneel, scooping water up in his cupped hands. The pain was a different pain now, a pain he could bear, a self-inflicted healing pain.

He shivered all night long, but the wound did not break open, and it did not bleed. In the morning he lay in the sun until the wound scabbed over, then got to his feet. He stood there, not putting any pressure on his sore leg, waiting for the dizziness to pass.

He took his bearings by the sun, then headed upriver, knowing where he had to go. The Shoshone camp was far away, and if he made it, it would take him several days to hobble there. He had reloaded his other pistol, and now his uppermost thoughts were on food, any food, lizard or snake, rabbit or deer.

An hour later, his leg aching so badly he thought he could not walk another foot, he came across the tracks of the horse he'd taken from the Mexicans. The faint glyphs in the soil looked as ancient as fossil prints embedded in stone from another age.

Chapter Seven

Matt smelled the horse droppings in his hand. He cracked open the nugget and felt its insides as if it was a piece of fruit he had plucked from a tree in that desolate Eden.

Steam rose from the insides of the horse apple, morning fresh. But the horse was moving faster than before, not grazing, but roaming for better forage. Two hours later the tracks petered out, and Matt figured the horse had crossed the river, heading for the mountains. He began to look for a ford, hoping the tracks could be found on the other side. The morning wore on and the sun climbed high, beating at him, exacerbating his hunger. He had hoped to see game along the river, but he made so much noise, he knew that anything feeding upriver would have plenty of time to avoid him.

Matt had no idea how fast he was walking, but he figured less than two miles an hour with the stiff leg. It took him another hour to find a river crossing, and by then his hunger was a raging beast in his belly. The river was dissected by a large sandbar, but it was shallow where it widened. The water would come up a little past his knees in the deepest part. The danger was that the current would be so strong that, in his weakened condition, he would not be able to cross beyond the sandbar. Nevertheless, he had to try it. Without a horse, he was even more crippled, and he did not know if he could survive without something substantial in his stomach.

Still, he was walking better. He had learned how to step without putting strain on his hip, though the awkward saunter twisted his body so much that it wore him out. Each mile sapped his remaining strength and left him breathless, enervated. And there were tugs of pain in the hip that wasn't wounded, as the muscles there began to swell and flare with pain. That was a pain he understood, and he gladly suffered it, knowing that his ball-pierced hip had a chance to heal over and grow new flesh.

Matt waded into the river, felt its powerful tug when he was ankle-deep. He stepped carefully, knowing he could rely on only one leg to hold him up. It was treacherous going, until he got into deeper water and could bring more of his body to bear in holding him upright. He looked like a man walking a tightwire, his arms outflung like outriggers on a canoe, his wounded leg dangling uselessly in the current, almost pulling him down into the water with its deadweight. He rested on the sandbar, surveying the deeper water ahead.

He saw flashes of fish in the clear shallows, shadows that left impressions like afterimages in a dark room suddenly shed of light. When he had his breath and his strength, he stepped into the river again. This time his bad leg acted like a counterbalance in the swift current. He'd gotten the hang of it. He walked through, the water up to his pistol muzzles, but it was hard going. The weight of the river was such that he felt he would be lifted up at any moment and hurled like a rain-soaked log into the main current. It took him over an hour to cross a stretch no more than twenty feet wide, but he took steps that were so small it was almost like shuffling. He did not lift the foot on his good leg, but pushed it forward a scant inch at a time. Slowly, he made progress, and when he felt solid, swung his bad leg forward, knee bent, holding it there for balance. It was tricky going, and more than once his heart rose up in his throat and choked him for several seconds. When he reached the shallows, he had virtually no strength left. He collapsed on the shore like a man washed up from a shipwreck and lay there in the sun, deerflies tearing at his skin like small gray hornets, leaving streamers of blood on his sweat-soaked shirt.

Matt slept, and when he awoke his leg was stiff, the toes on both feet numb from the cold water.

"Should have taken off my boots," he said aloud, the sound of his voice strange to him.

When he walked, his moccasin boots squished, but his trousers were dry. He knew he must look a sight, shambling with a twisted gait like some wounded mendicant begging alms in a far, deserted country where even nomads seldom passed by. Downstream he found where the horse had emerged from the river. The animal angled off to the north and struck a stretch of woods. There, Matt saw signs where the horse had tried to rub off his saddle. Pieces of the leather rifle scabbard were embedded in the trunk of a pine, along with needles of horsehair, which looked like magnetized filings where the bark had been rubbed off clean.

The farther Matt got away from the Rio Grande, the more uneasy he became. The river was his map, his best source of food if he was unable to travel, and, in a pinch, transportation—to a village, where he could seek medical help. But he wanted the horse more than he wanted the security of the big river.

He found one of the scabbard straps several hundred yards away and knew it would not be long before the horse got free of that particular piece of impedimenta.

Two miles later he found his rifle, still in its scabbard,

none the worse for its mistreatment. One of the straps was still intact, but broken where it attached to the saddle. It would only be a matter of time, he knew, before the horse managed to rub the cinch strap loose and shuck the saddle.

The droppings were fresher than those he'd found that morning, and he came upon a place where the horse had grazed for at least an hour. Matt kept going, although he was ready to drop now that he was carrying the heavy rifle and its scabbard. But he felt that he had a better chance of surviving with the bigger weapon. Though he was a fair pistol shot, he knew he had little chance of dropping game at ranges more than fifty or sixty yards, and even at that distance he would be sore-pressed to hold a steady aim.

Over gently rolling land and into the foothills he followed the horse's tracks. He wasn't familiar with that section of country. When he stopped and looked back, he could no longer see the river. But he had an image of it in his mind, and he knew where it lay. To the north he saw the familiar mountain range and that was enough. But he was attached to the Rio Grande in some nameless, mysterious way. It was like an umbilical cord from his belly to the center of the earth, the center of the universe. A white man would not understand such a concept, but the Shoshones would, Matt knew. He had talked of this with Gray Deer more than once as he charted the Rio Grande.

"The river is good medicine," Gray Deer had told him. To the Shoshone, "medicine" meant mystery, magic, anything powerful that could not be fully understood. It was a grand concept, Matt thought. The Rio Grande had, over the past year, become a very complex river in Matt's mind. At first it was just the disputed boundary between two countries. Now he knew it was much more, that it was the very lifeblood of the country. It provided transport, served commerce, and provided sustenance for Indians and Mexicans alike.

The land became more rugged as Matt followed the track of the horse. The animal was headed south now, farther from the river, into thick timber beyond the foothills. Every time the horse found a tree big enough, he rubbed more leather away. Matt found shreds, bits and pieces, at each small stand of timber. The land here was vaguely familiar, and when he reached a high tor, he looked back and saw prairie, the thin ribbon of the river heading east before it made the bend and flowed southward. He crossed a stream that he knew fed into the Rio Grande, and the mountains got steeper as they rose to a peak that stood like a blue wall high above the surrounding crags and ridges.

An hour later he found the bridle, still clinging to the peg of a branch the horse had hooked it on. Late in the day, as the canyon he tracked through filled with shadows, Matt found the saddle, its cinch strap gnawed through. It was all scarred, the pommel wood cracked underneath the leather, the horn jutting cockeyed from its broken seat.

"Well, now you're free, you sonofabitch," Matt croaked, and realized he could go no farther. He was parched from lack of water, and the hunger had risen up in him again with its own sharp teeth, like some crazed ferret, razor-clawed and digging for the bone.

He reasoned that the saddlebags must have fallen off in the river and floated away, or sank. He could only think of the horse, or he knew the hunger he felt would hurl him into a despair so dark, like a deep night sea, that he might never swim out into the light. The horse, like man, never far from its savage origins, once back in the wilderness. It was ironic to Matt that he had been wrestling with just such an allure as the horse must now feel.

He tasted the air with his senses honed keen. He knew that he had descended, in a year's turning, to a more primitive version of the man who left eastern civilization: he had lived off the land; slept under stars that winked at him through the smokehole of a Shoshone lodge; eaten foods few white men had ever tasted, dog and buffalo, roots and berries without sugar or honey; he had shucked off the trappings of civilized society and become . . . what? He was still himself, but he saw the world differently. Could he go back? Could he don an officer's uniform again and stand obedient before his superiors?

Matt struggled with his thoughts as the canyon pooled with the velvet wash of night and closed him off in a blinding shroud. He could go no farther that day, could not see to hunt, was weakened by his wound and the strenuous climb into a wilderness that was harsh and merciless, uncaring as stone, bleak in those moments, like the shadowy thoughts of a man facing his own death.

Matt slept with his hunger and the pain in his hip, slept huddled up in a fetal position under an overhang to ward off the cold of the mountain night. He listened, for a long time, for a whicker or a whinny, but heard only the thin, fluting whistle of a young bull elk, and the howling of wolves who seemed to surround the canyon, intoning warnings into the chill wind that blew off the snowcapped peaks. The howls scattered like whispered laughter in an insane asylum, and it got so quiet he could hear his heart pound in his chest, and the sound basipetaled him in the ocean of sleep, carved the first strange shapes of his dreams.

Chapter

Eight

Before Matt went to sleep, the sky became a magician's cape, rent like a shotgunned drape, starsilver leaking through the eternal fabric in tiny pinpoints of light. As always, he was absorbed in the deep mystery of the sky, the smallness of the earth in that immensity, the smallness of himself so far from heaven, the place where the spirits of the dead journeyed along the path the white men called the Milky Way. He closed his eyes and for a long time could see the afterimages on his retina, dancing like silent fireworks, silvery fountains.

Matt dreamed of black horses like basilisks, and swarthy soldiers with death's head faces, all riding him down like Spanish conquistadors swarming over forgotten adobe villages, and he running through swamp muck so thick he could not get out of their way. He had two broken pistols in his hands and they would not spark or fire. And then he was wandering through huge empty rooms in a town like St. Louis, where the women called out to him and smiled, and some rubbed against him and filled him with hot-blooded desire, but the women all left under some vague pretense, and he followed after them to a great dining hall where people he had known in his waking life were eating daintily. He found a place at the long table, and all of the food disappeared as waiters came out of the walls and cleaned up everything in sight with magical precision.

And then he was in a grassy meadow, and there were Shoshone women there, their faces daubed with the colors of flowers, the blue of the sky. He asked about Morning Lark, and the women turned their faces away from him. He looked through empty lodges, and the men cursed him in sign language and showed him their genitals. He found another feast in one of the lodges and tried to get to the food, but women came up to him and he desired them, went away with one who reminded him of Morning Lark, and then she changed into the St. Louis woman and mocked him with her laughter, her teasing eyes.

In a crowded ballroom somewhere out of space and time, men and women, dressed in flowing robes, were jumping through large hoops, and then the hoops started rolling toward him, finally melding into a single hoop that made a sound like a roaring bull, and he ran away from it until all he heard was a rumbling, and so knew that the hoop was still following him through the tunnels of gigantic cities that seemed ancient and somber in their elaborate medieval structures.

Matt awoke several times, sweating and hurting, and when he fell asleep again he went back to the same dream: more rooms, more people, more food, and none of it obtainable, but snatched away before he could sup. And the women came after him, excited him and then left him before he could consummate his desire. And the real night became darker and colder, even unto morning when he awoke and was still in the dream and could not fathom his surroundings, but stared bewildered at the rock face of the overhang and thought he must be in his own sepulchre, buried alive in a stone tomb.

Drops of water fell on his face and the morning light

crept under the overhang, and Matt took his bearings like a man drugged with wine and crazy with not knowing where he had been, what violent worlds he had escaped by the skin of his teeth.

The eastern sky was a creamy gruel, daubed with faint clouds so thin they seemed translucent, and overhead a cloudless sky slowly turning a pale cyanic blue. The hunger now savage in his belly, his head still fuzzy with sleep and the shreds of nightmare dreams, Matt touched his hip and nearly fainted with the sudden pain. He smelled the air and caught traces of horse dung and wolf spoor faintly cloying inside the narrow canyon.

"Take it slow," he said aloud, both to convince himself that he still had life in him and to assert that he was still in command, though horseless, hungry, and wounded. He checked his weapons, knowing that he had to kill game that day or risk becoming too weak to hunt. He knew that he still had to track the horse, but it would now be a secondary mission. Food, water, then try to find the runaway gelding.

Matt listened, heard no sound but the persistent drip of water on stone. It was as if he had wandered into a corner of the universe that God had forgotten to invest with life.

"Goddamned hoopties," Matt said, and this time he felt foolish for talking to himself. The first sign of madness, he thought. But it was either look at his predicament as a joke or nurture a kernel of self-pity into a full-blown version of despair.

His head cleared with the gathering morning light. He checked his pistols, the rifle, reprimed the pans, tamped the lead balls to see that they were still snug in the barrels. He slung on his possibles pouch and powder horns and wrenched himself to his feet, using the rifle as a crutch. He knew that he had two priorities that summer morning: to find game and the Mexican horse. He would have to combine the two tasks if he was to survive. He looked up to the saddleback. It seemed a lot steeper than it had the day before. He could just make out the faint game trail that the horse had apparently followed.

The air smelled of spruce and pine, but the aromas only served to make Matt's stomach boil with hunger pangs. A savage desire to live beat in his chest like primordial tambors, and at that moment he knew he would do anything to survive, even if he had to crawl on all fours or climb trees.

Matt took a deep breath, steeled himself to the ordeal ahead. He glanced again at the saddleback, so near, yet so far he could feel its distance brooding over him like a barrier, like an unscalable mount.

His first step nearly drove him to his knees. A pain that was like being flooded with hot lava washed through him in a sudden comber. He broke out in a Gethsemanic sweat, feeling as if his very pores would gush forth blood. He almost gave up right there. He was tempted to throw down his rifle and take one of the pistols, put it to his temple and blow himself into eternity.

"This too shall pass," he breathed, his voice no more than a dying man's whisper.

He forced himself to take another step, but this time he eased into it. Like a man sidling past a scene of utter horror, Matt limped off the rock ledge and managed to hobble down the slope without breaking his neck. He struck the game trail and avoided looking up at the saddleback and finding further discouragement.

He walked, he crawled, dragging his rifle behind him like a crippled mendicant approaching a hilltop shrine. He rested often but dared not linger, lest he give up his quest altogether. Once, after more than an hour had passed, he did look up toward the saddleback again, to see how much farther he had to go.

He could no longer see the saddleback itself, but he

had made progress. Another five hundred yards, he figured, and over the steepest part of the trail. Finding the horse now seemed the most important task he must perform. Yet he knew he could not go far into the mountains. In his weakened condition, it would be an accomplishment just to reach the top of the trail. There, he could make another assessment, weigh his chances of finding game and catching up to the horse. It seemed imperative to him just then to complete his short journey, if for no other reason than to experience a sense of accomplishment.

It took Matt another two hours to reach the lip of the saddleback. Just before he reached the end of the trail, a lone Canadian jay, pale as a ghost, landed at his destination. The bird cocked its head and eyed him suspiciously. It pecked at the ground, strutted back and forth. Matt resented its arrogance, its wings, its freedom. He looked at the bird's spindly legs and wished his were as sound. With waning strength he grabbed a handful of dirt and threw it at the jay. The bird flapped off, the only sound a faint whap-whisper of wings.

Matt climbed the last few feet on all fours, like some ungainly scavenging beast, some outcast from the animal kingdom fit only to feed on carrion. At the pinnacle, he grabbed a craggy fulgurite and pulled himself the last few inches using the fused stone as a fulcrum.

Exhausted, he lay on his stomach and softly breathed the thin air of the mountains into his scorched lungs. He felt the cauterizing sun on his back, a radiant heat that suffused balm into his tortured musculature. His right foot felt numb, disconnected from the rest of his body but strangely present, like an amputated toe before a storm. He wriggled his toes and was rewarded with a steep current of pain in his hip. The feeling returned to his foot and his breathing returned to normal. He got to his knees and crawled over the rim of the saddleback, onto the narrow chine of bare rock that dissected its grassy bowl like the vertebrae of some ancient beast fossilized by scouring winds and raking rains since time began.

He stood up, surveyed his surroundings. The saddle-back was bordered by scraggy piñon and scrub pine, weather-blasted junipers twisted to skeletal stick men by the constant buffeting of prairie and high country winds. Matt felt the wind here, felt its pressure like a laying on of invisible hands against his back. He looked back down the way he had come, and the trail appeared less formidable, the slope not so sheer. It did not seem so far to the ledge where he had spent the night. Yet it had taken him almost three hours to climb what amounted to a pathetic few yards. Enervated, he swayed there in the wind, basking in the sun until his tendons forgot the agony and slowness of the climb.

He knew he would never find the horse until he could walk it down on two good legs. But he could not wait four, five, or six weeks to fully recover. He walked to the far edge of the saddleback, looked down the slope and scanned the opposite ridge. The little hills were bunched up there, and on the far hogback the first few spruce trees burned with a shadowy blue fire.

He knew what he was looking for, but doubted he would find it so easily. He scanned the far ridge, the small valley between. There was no sign of the Mexican horse, but Matt had no doubt that it had fed down there on the summer grasses. And unless it was doubling back for the Rio Grande, it would head for the nearest water.

The Rio Grande was fed by mountain streams, Matt knew. But this late in the summer, some would be dry, others underground. Where there was water, there was game, sooner or later. He stood there, leaning on the rifle, worrying the options in his mind like a man shuffling cards. He looked at the rumpled land between the saddleback and the far peaks, jagged, snowcapped, majestic against the blue sky. For now, the weather was clear, but he knew that sudden storms were birthed in these mountains and a sunny day could turn into a snarling, savage leviathan of the skies that would freeze a man to death in the middle of August.

The foothills seemed endless, and Matt knew he was seeing only a few of them, only a few of the many. If he followed after the feral horse, he would risk breaking his wound open, and even if that did not happen, he would have many hard miles to climb before he found a place where he might hunt and drink and set up a shelter.

Yet, Matt realized, that was what he must do—with or without the horse. And he must either stake out a homestead near where he stood, far from water, go back to the river, or go on, deep into the mountains.

He took his weight off the rifle, put it on his bad leg. The pain shot instant tears through his ducts and he quickly lifted his foot. No, he would never make it to the high country, not in time to save his life.

From where he stood he could see no spring, no telltale waterfall, no creek, no sign of a lake or a pond. Yet the horse was heading somewhere. Where? And why? Why not stay near the river and head south, back from whence he had been ridden?

Matt did not know the answers. He wiped the tears from his face and gritted his teeth. His hunger soared like something straining to be free to roam and kill. As the pain in his hip subsided, the gnawing ache in his belly deepened, chasmed like something terrible opening up deep in his bowels.

In his mind he could see the little creek near Ute Mountain; Lost Creek, he called it. Higher up he saw the beaver ponds in the alder thickets, water streaming everywhere, and meat in the ponds. There, he could find beaver and porcupine, mountain partridge he could kill with a stone. Here there was nothing, a no-man's-land between the Rio Grande and the plenty of the Rocky Mountains.

If he went back to the big river, he would be in danger of being discovered by a Mexican patrol, perhaps the same one that had chased him before.

Taking a deep breath and wanting to shout his defiance against the towering mountains in the distance, Matt stepped toward the edge of the saddleback, heading not back to the place where he had been, but forward, down the opposite slope and into a meadow that would swallow him up until he gained the next ridge. And after that there would be more ridges, and still more. But somewhere in those recesses, there was food and water and he could build a shelter and find game and heal.

It was time, Matt raged in his mind, to ignore the pain and just keep going until he found what he was looking for. And if the horse knew of such a place, perhaps he would ride to his final destination, that place where the Shoshone camped and summered the wild horses, where Morning Lark waited, where he could reconstruct his crude surveyor's notations and prepare, once again, the documents he had lost so long ago now, so far away.

Morning Lark hunkered barefoot in the slow, chill waters of Lost Creek, waiting until the parfleche was filled. She slung it over her shoulder and waded to shore. Black Quill, for she was married to Red Elk, carried two parfleches full of water.

"Do you still look for Big Man?" asked Quill.

"I do not look for him. Only a single moon has gone by."

"Almost two moons."

"It is a long journey to the fort on the big river," Lark retorted.

"Not long for a man who wants to get back."

"Why do you tease me, Black Quill?"

"Have you not heard Little Black Shoulder playing his flageolet outside your lodge?"

"I have heard dove flying and crow calling," said Lark.

"Ah, but Shoulder has many horses."

"I have a man."

"A man who is not here." The two women walked slowly back to their lodges. The chewed grasses were still damp, and the herdboys had driven the horses to another place where the grass was high. "A man who will never return."

"Big Man will return," said Lark stubbornly.

They both heard a thunder and looked toward the circles of tepees, then beyond to the trail that led to the plain. Riders galloped across the creek and over the greensward to the center of the big village. They were whooping and crying out.

"Who is that?" asked Lark.

"It looks like Blue Horse, Antelope, Gray Deer, and the other scouts who left here a moon ago."

Lark began running then, for she knew that the braves must have important words to say of their scouting on the plain. Behind her Black Quill, puffing, labored after her, the two parfleches swinging like pendulous breasts on the stick across her shoulders.

Lark reached the crowd milling around the scouts. She was not even winded, but her heart pounded like a stone pestle in her chest. She caught the eye of Antelope and he carved a path through the crowd. She saw the other braves holding up uniforms, Mexican rifles, a baldric, and a sword. Everyone seemed to be talking at once, and she could make no sense of what the scouts had found.

"Antelope," she said when the brave drew near. He was holding something in his hand that looked familiar. He put the bundle behind his back when he saw her looking at it. "Do you have news of Big Man?"

"We did not find him, but he had a fight with the Mexican pony soldiers."

"How do you know this?"

"We found his horse and the talking skins he took with him."

"Is that what you're hiding?"

Antelope handed her the bundle.

She snatched it from him and clutched it to her breast. "He is not dead."

"I do not know, Lark. There was dried blood, much sign. I think he may have captured a Mexican horse."

"Where did he go?"

"The trail was cold. But maybe he rode into the mountains."

"Then he is coming here. He would not leave his talking skins behind. He was taking them to the white man's fort on the big river."

"I did not see Big Man," he said softly. "His track has blown away in the wind. His trail is like smoke."

"I will keep the talking skins for him," she said.

"He killed many pony soldiers."

"He is very brave."

Antelope said nothing. Lark looked into his face, but it was a mask.

"You think he is dead," she said.

"The wounded bear goes to a secret place deep in the forest," said Antelope. "He sleeps until he is no longer sick or he lets his spirit fly away like a hawk to the stars. No man sees this thing. No man knows where the bear has gone."

"Big Man will not die," she said.

"Perhaps the bear will come back to where the berries grow and he will father many cubs before his spirit takes the starpath."

Antelope turned and walked away.

Morning Lark looked at the packet of talking skins.

She had watched Big Man make the marks on the thin bark, the signs that other white man could read and hear in their minds. She could feel Big Man's arms around her. She could smell his musk on the bundle.

She hurried to her lodge, the lodge she kept for her man, for she knew she was going to cry again.

But she would not tear out her hair or blacken her face.

Chapter

Nine

Matt stood there a long time, on a precipice of time and space, staring into his future. He might have been looking at a grave, his own grave, or an escape path, a trail to some promised land beyond his vision. At that moment he was not certain of anything. Except his own mortality. He laughed to himself at the seriousness of his thoughts. Antelope would have laughed too. As long as a man had his weapons, his knife, a good strong heart, he could not be defeated. He could find game; he could catch a horse. He could make everything he needed from all the things the Great Spirit had put on the earth for his children.

He was breathing; he was alive. Blood coursed through his veins. He felt pain, hunger. More than that, he felt hope. Mingled with doubt. Perhaps he should have doubled back, found his survey records, and just walked to St. Louis. Better late than never. But there was a greater risk down on the plain than in the mountains. Bandits, Indians, weather, floods, snakes. It might take him months to reach the Mississippi, and by then his contact in St. Louis would have given up on him, would have reported him missing or dead. No, he had a better chance in the mountains, he reasoned. Even if he never found the Mexican horse, he could find his friends, the Shoshone, and he would be mounted again.

A Gila woodpecker whipped past, attached itself to a pine and began a stuttering rhetoric as it hammered the bark with its beak. Yes, Matt thought, there was food everywhere if one knew where to look for it.

He had made his choice. Live or die, he was committed.

"Fool," said Matt, and the sound of the word made him grin.

Once a man started to feel sorry for himself, he was finished, Matt knew. The hills began to gentle as he wrestled with despair and self-pity, replacing those dark thoughts with the young green fiber of hope, the sunlight illuminating the hills until they seemed smaller than when he had first stood and looked at them like a cripple leaning on a crutch.

There was food out there, and water, the black Mexican horse if he wanted it, others if he lost the track of that one. In these mountains there was everything a man could need: food, shelter, clothing, safety. The leg would heal in time; he had fat aplenty on his bones. He would not starve if he kept his wits about him. It was all in the looking, all in the seeing.

Matt pulled himself up, squared his shoulders as if he was still wearing his soldier's uniform. A gray nutcracker swirled out of a nearby spruce and fluttered to a landing on a patch of bare ground. The bird strutted cockily back and forth, cocking its head toward him. The bird wanted food, Matt knew. The grin on his face faded to a smile and the smile curved deep into his heart, held there like a needle sewing him back together. He stared down at the thin line of the game trail and knew that if he stumbled, he could recover, if he fell, he would get back up. If he found no food this day, he would on the morrow. He squatted slowly, found a small round pebble that suited him, placed it in his mouth. It tasted of dirt and he swallowed the saliva, drew on the stone's nourishment, felt its magical powers assuage his thirst. He stood up, stronger than he'd been all morning. He started down the slope, sideways to it, his good leg higher than the weaker one.

There was not a hooptie in sight.

Matt did not eat that day. By the time the sun was setting, he figured he'd traveled no more than a mile or two, watched by a brace of mountain chickadees that fluttered from tree to tree a few yards ahead of him. He made a pine-bough shelter atop a ridge that jutted out over a meadow. While the light still lingered, he sat at its point, the rifle across his lap, watching for anything that moved. He hoped to see a mule deer or a coyote, perhaps a fox or lynx, rabbits. The way the wind worked, circling, flying at him from every quarter, he knew that his scent must be everywhere. But he sat there as the sky blazed like a blacksmith's forge beyond the snowcaps. He watched the colors fade and the sky go dark, bristle with pinholes of stars as the wind pillaged the trees like a pickpocket loose in a crowd of evening strollers. That night he lay beneath a spruce and chewed on a strip of pine he had cut from under the bark. The pine was moist and sticky with sap, and when he slept, he dreamed he was eating smoked pork.

The next day, Matt fought his hip and the land with equal ferocity. He began to follow the canyons northward and westward, conserving his strength, saving the steep climbs until the close of the day, when he took to the high ground for safety. He felt, at times, like the only man on earth, wandering through an untouched wilderness. He saw eagles and hawks, flying so high he envied them, and he found deer droppings and signs of sheep from other years.

He lost the Mexican horse's tracks, then found them again. The horse had kicked off one shoe from its left forefoot and was working on the right one. Matt found the tracks on ground softened by seeps from some stream farther up. In a wooded glen he found the tracks of other horses, and they were shod. So, the Mexican patrol had tracked the stolen horse, perhaps knew that he was trailing it as well. A chill riffled through the small hairs on the back of Matt's neck. He moved slowly, kept to cover during the day. He stopped often, listened.

One night he thought he saw the flame from a campfire, a pinhole in the fabric of night, and knew for sure that the soldiers were still looking for him. The next day he heard a rifle shot, and the hackles rose on his neck. He holed up for several hours and took to the high ground that night, but saw no campfire, smelled no smoke.

Matt cut notches on the stock of the rifle to mark the days. He began counting from the time he had left the security of the Rio Grande and chose the high country, not to mark his progress, but to remind him how long he'd been without food. He played games in his mind, keeping track of other signs of his progress. How many ridges had he climbed and crossed, landmarks, game had he seen, birds had he spotted flitting through the spruce and pine? He lost track from day to day, but each day, he counted his progress by the landmarks he gained on foot.

Two days after leaving the saddleback, he shot a rabbit early one morning. The hare had not seen him, but hopped past his bed beneath a blue spruce. Matt's hands shook so much, he almost didn't get off the shot when the animal froze. But he calmed himself, and the hare never moved when he cocked the hammer. He took careful aim, swallowed air, held it, and shot the rabbit's head off. Nervously, he made a fire, ate the rabbit slowly, knowing he could not afford to vomit his food.

When the rabbit was all gone—meat, bones, marrow—

Matt began to look more earnestly for small game. He hadn't seen a mule deer, and he finally lost the spoor of the horse when the animal coursed a stretch of rimrock. The agony of searching for hoofprints was too great, his stamina too sapped from the effort of climbing the hills, favoring his game leg.

He drank dew from the grasses in the morning, but his thirst continued to rage. He took his bearings each night from the stars and traveled by dead reckoning during the day, heading for the meadow where he knew the Shoshone were summering. On the fifth day, he found the carcass of a sheep that had been killed by wolves. There was little meat left, but he cut every scrap and cooked it over a fire he made that night, sheltered by spruce and pine boughs he cut and used to make a ringed wall.

He followed a small stream from which he filled his belly with precious water, taking two hours to drink enough to satisfy him, and followed it to the Rio Grande where it coursed through the mountains on its way to the plain. By then there were a dozen notches on his rifle stock.

The pain in his leg was no longer paramount in his mind. It had receded to some part of his flesh and brain where, like some subterranean worm, it gnawed him infrequently. He stayed away from the trails upriver, but kept the waters in sight, like a man hoarding food or gold coin.

Matt continued to camp on high ground at night. One morning, on his fourteenth day after leaving the plain, he saw the Mexican patrol. He did not know if this was the one that had ambushed him, but he counted seven mounted men. They rode single file along the river, then fanned out. One of the troopers pointed to something off the trail. Five men rode toward the pointer, and all six men disappeared. The lone man waited, watched. Matt held his breath as if he could be heard from such a distance. He hugged the ground, confident that he could not be seen if he did not move.

When the scouts had been absent for more than fifteen minutes, Matt wondered where they had gone. The one who was waiting seemed no more than a speck amid the profusion of yellow-eyed yarrow bordering the trail, and Matt judged him to be more than a thousand yards downstream, perhaps as far away as a quarter mile.

Two of the scouts returned. Matt watched them converse with the one who had stayed behind. One of the scouts pointed at the ground, then raised his arm, pointed his fingers directly at Matt's hiding place. Or so it seemed.

Spiders crawled on the back of Matt's neck.

The day before, Matt had stumbled on the Mexican horse's tracks again. The animal had thrown the other shoe. He found where the horse had bedded down, then lost the spoor again. He wondered if the patrol had found them. He knew, from watching the three soldiers, that they had come across his own tracks.

Matt waited, his finger caressing the trigger guard of his rifle, his thumb cocked to draw the hammer back.

The three Mexicans began to ride toward his position. They fanned out, scanning the ground as they rode. Matt had circled his present position before climbing to the ridge, and if the trackers were any good, they would find his trail. Sure enough, the three riders drifted off the trail, away from the river, and disappeared into the trees.

The birds went silent. Gone were the chickadees and jays. Time seemed to halt in its tracks as an eerie stillness settled around Matt. He scanned his surroundings for an escape route, knew that his chances were slim if the Mexican soldiers decided to storm his position. Yet, he stayed there, knowing he could not run away blind. He had to know what the patrol had found, why those he could see were moving toward him. The riders seemed sure of themselves, as if they had a destination in mind, or perhaps as if they knew where he was.

Matt blinked his eyes to relieve the strain of staring at the riders. When he opened them again, they were gone, melted into the trees and brush beyond the narrow game trail. As if he had imagined them, as if they had never been there at all.

He looked at the dazzling spangle of river that seemed to have swallowed the soldiers, as if he could penetrate its secrets and its silence and determine where the riders had gone. But the brightness blinded him, and Matt closed his eyes again to clear away the brilliance.

He strained to hear the soldiers, but heard nothing beyond the nattering saw of invisible insects, the soft rustle the breeze made as it flowed in a threnodic undertone through tree branches over the rocks and grasses. Sweat oozed from his pores, oiled his skin. His scalp began to prickle and itch, but he dared not move, even when the itch leaped to a corner of his nose. No amount of twitching could erase the irritation.

Matt concentrated on the possible movements of the soldiers, what they might know, what they might suspect. He had buried his offal, covered up his urine. He had left false trails, backtracked, circled. He could not hide everything, of course, but he had done his best to throw would-be trackers off his trail. Especially when he was forced to travel in the open, cross bare patches of earth where his moccasins left indelible images of his foot. With his limited ability to travel, he was not able to do much. But he hoped he had done enough so that the Mexicans did not know his present position.

Matt was surprised to see the Mexicans again. They emerged, in a body, from a shadowy grove of aspen and pine as if from a painting, as if they had been there, waiting, all along. The soldiers were no more than five hundred yards away. The last man in the bunch pulled something behind him, something large and dark. As the Mexicans rode into the sunlight, Matt saw that one man was leading a black horse, the horse he had stolen and lost. The gelding had a mouthful of harebells snatched from the soil between the trees. The men rode toward the river, the one in the lead staring intently at the ground.

"The sonsabitches," Matt mouthed silently.

The Mexicans had struck his trail. As he watched, they turned, rode toward him. The sleek hides of the horses shimmered with the dancing light reflected off the tumbling river as they rode close to its bank.

Then the troopers halted. Their leader spoke to the man in the rear who was leading the saddleless horse, who then rode up alongside.

"Oigame Gigante," yelled the leader. *"Aqui está su caballo."*

The leader pulled his pistol from its holster and shoved the barrel into the horse's neck, just behind its ear.

Matt's body jerked as the captain pulled the trigger. The explosion made his blood jump. A cloud of white smoke blew past the horse's head as it snapped with the impact of the lead ball. The animal staggered for a few feet, then its forelegs crumpled. The horse's hind end rolled and struck the ground, a half ton of deadweight. The Mexican horse quivered and twitched as the smoke broke up and wafted away like cobwebs blown by the wind. The Mexicans sat their horses like statues, their rifles at the ready. The sound of the shot echoed up the canyon, died as it was swallowed up in the trees.

Matt's throat went dry and his eyes narrowed to dark slashes as the anger rose up in him.

He put his rifle to his shoulder without thinking, lined up the sights on the Mexican leader who raised his pistol in triumph, a thin scrawl of smoke spiraling upward from its barrel.

He saw the Mexicans jerk in their saddles when Matt cocked the hammer of the rifle. The sound was metallic, soft, like a padlock opening to a key, but in the silence it boomed and crackled like brittle thunder.

Chapter Ten

Matt squeezed the trigger, heard the flint strike the frizzen. He felt the light sting of the powder in the pan as it threw off sparks, shot flame through the touchhole. The rifle bucked against his shoulder.

Garza took the ball in his neck. The lead pulped the carotid artery, flattened, tearing out veins, muscles, flesh, and bone. The spinal cord shattered like broken pottery, blotting out all pain, all sensation. The Mexican fell sideways off his saddle and struck the ground, blood spurting from his neck as his heart continued to pump.

The lieutenant's horse bolted and struck off through the trees, shearing yellow flowers like scythed wheat in its wake. The other Mexicans looked up toward Matt and brought their rifles to their shoulders. Their guns crackled like snapped twigs, and Matt heard the balls whistle over his head, speed past in deadly whispers like the whiffling ghosts of mourning doves. One ball thunked into a tree trunk, another splashed through spruce needles with the sound of a blade ripping a hole in bamboo curtains, a third ball lost itself in a tiny aperture of space.

Matt did not hear the other balls find resting places because he was sliding backward, slipping a precut patch into his mouth, digging a lead ball from his possibles pouch. He got to his knees, his heart pounding so loudly in his ears he was sure the soldiers could hear it. He poured powder around the ball in his palm, gripped it with fourth finger pressed to palm as he poured the rough equivalent of ninety grains of powder down the barrel. He spat the patch between his lips, mitted it around the ball. He set the patch on the bore opening, thumbed it down inside, his muscles bunched from the effort, sweat beading on his forehead, a string of minuscule beads transparent and golden as pine sap.

With his wiping stick, he seated the ball, rammed the rod back between its brass thimbles. He primed the pan with the small horn, blew away the excess powder. He heard, as he crawled back to the edge of the precipice, the rattle of ramrods and iron, the creak of leather from the river below. Two of the soldiers were already riding toward him in a pincer movement, trying to flank him. They were loading their rifles as they rode. Matt picked the nearer of the two, drew a bead on his chest. He slid the hammer back, holding the trigger in slightly so that the mechanism was muffled. He led the rider a fraction of an inch, prayed he'd read the windage right, and squeezed off the shot.

He did not feel the butt stock knock his shoulder almost out of its socket, but he saw, through the billowing smoke, the result of his aim. The soldier threw up both hands, tossing his rifle into the air as if it had suddenly turned hot in his hands. The rifle twisted awkwardly, fighting against gravity, as the soldier jerked backward in the saddle, then bent toward the saddle horn, a blaze of blood red as barn paint smearing his tunic. The horse stopped and turned toward its rider as the man fell in slow motion toward the ground, dying without a scream or a prayer.

The other flanker hesitated, then decided against further action. He pulled at his reins, turned his horse. Three shots exploded almost simultaneously, and Matt cursed as he realized he had not taken cover. Dirt and rock stung his face as two of the balls plowed the ground in front of him. The third shot struck his left arm, near the shoulder, tearing through his flesh. He relaxed for a second, realizing that the ball had not entered his body. He reached up as he felt the sting of the ball's passage, and his hand came away bloody as a woman's monthly rag.

He heard the liquid melding of Spanish voices as they cried out his position, cursed him and his gringo ancestors. Matt rolled out of sight of the troopers and winced at the piercing pain in his shoulder as it picked up grit and dirt. He backed off, more slowly this time, and reloaded his rifle. But he did not return to his former position. They would be after him now, and he had to outrun them, outcrawl them, outwit them, or they would shoot him to pieces.

Two minutes later he'd forgotten he had reloaded his rifle. His mind was a millrace of frantic thoughts. His legs were working, although blood dripped down his left arm and he felt giddy, as if he had taken too much wine on an empty belly. His leg was yet stiff, and if he used too much of it, there would be a slight tug, as if an unseen hand was trying to tear out his muscle. But he was fairly fit, if not as fleet as he once was.

He wondered what the soldiers were doing. They had lost their leader and one of their number. Would they tend to their dead first, or come riding, riding until their horses blew and foundered, their chests full of fire, their eyes rolling in their sockets like the eyes of horses mad on loco grass?

Matt was glad he had killed the leader. But there could be a heavy price to pay for that small satisfaction. He had paid some for it already, getting his arm ripped with a lead ball, leaking blood from dozens of tiny veins, shattered and smashed as if shot through with bird shot.

He would sure as hell leave some trail for the Mexican soldiers. He did not look back, but limped and staggered a zigzag course through the maze of spruce and pine, circling the deadfalls, holding his rifle with both hands, although he had little feeling in the left one, as if the blood, was taking too long to reach his fingers.

Well, he would take one or two Mexicans with him if they caught up to him. He might even wear out a horse or two, if his lungs and his legs held out. If he didn't bleed to death like a stuck shoat.

Matt stopped and listened for sounds of pursuit. There was a trembling in him brought on by the fear that he just might hear the pound of hoofbeats, the clatter of locks cocking like metal insects working diabolical mandibles. But he heard only the whiffle of wind in the trees, those maddening whispers that were wordless and all the more ominous for that, as if ghosts wandered the hills in warning for those who ventured there from the plain.

Light-headed, weakened by the loss of blood, Matt circled to his left, hoping to make a wide loop to the river, perhaps find the lieutenant's horse and catch it up. The animal should not have strayed far, and the soldiers might have forgotten it in their haste to find him and shoot him dead.

When he hit the slope, Matt started to trot, hoping to outrun the riders if they were close on his heels. He stumbled, almost fell, twisted his ankle in trying to recover and screamed silently at the sudden pain. He limped down the slope, favoring his right ankle, cursing the curse that he seemed to bear of late, wincing every time the ball of his foot touched the ground.

Matt ran out of the trees and into the raw sunlight that was so glaring it burned his eyes, and hobbled at a quickstep past the soldier he had shot. He smelled the stench of the man's death, the offal he had exuded when his sphincter muscle went slack, and he saw the lieutenant lying there all twisted up, his saber half out of its sheath, bent like a busted wagon spring.

The horse had left a swath through the flowers and grasses, and Matt followed the trail of the crushed fire wheels of the gaillardias, the heads of blue, leafy bract asters strewn among the trampled grasses, the shattered stems of shooting stars, the broken petals of spreading fleabane. The ground was moist and swampy from some hidden spring that seeped to the surface. The aspens stood stark and white amid the tall thin pines.

Matt saw that the horse had circled and was heading back to a point downstream. He cut a corner, hoping to head it off before it reached the open again. He crossed its track again, read that it had slowed and was picking its way through the trees, across a small open meadow bristling with wildflowers of red and blue and yellow, and was galloping on toward the river.

The horse stood there, streamside, its mouth dripping water, working the bit in its mouth. It bent its neck again to drink, and Matt slowed his pace, hoping the horse would not spook at the sight of him.

As he stepped from the trees, he heard the snap of a lock and ducked instinctively. He turned toward the sound, upstream, and saw the soldier standing there on foot, his rifle pointed toward him. So, at least one had stayed behind while the others chased him. He must have hidden in the trees and listened to him thrashing after the lieutenant's horse, making all that noise as if he hadn't a care in the world.

"*Alto,*" said the soldier.

"*Que vas a hacer?*" Matt asked.

"*Voy a tirarte.*"

Matt knew he had no chance. The rifle in his hands seemed big as a ceiling beam. If he went for a pistol, he would have to drop the rifle. Either way, the soldier had a bead on him, and his hammer was poised to strike like a scorpion's tail.

"Dejame," said Matt, and swung his rifle at the hip, cocking back the hammer. He stepped toward the soldier.

The soldier pulled the trigger. Matt saw smoke and flame belch from the rifle. He felt the hot wind of the explosion and the rifle was wrenched out of his hands as his right shoulder jerked from the impact of the ball.

Matt watched helplessly as the rifle struck the bank and cartwheeled into the river. He turned, saw the soldier still standing there, making no attempt to reload. Matt roared like a lion and charged the Mexican. The young trooper fumbled in his pouch for a paper cartridge.

Matt saw the man's face through the pain in his arm, just a boy in a Spanish uniform, a terror-stricken lad far from home, trying to chew off the end of a paper cartridge, pour powder and ball down the barrel of his rifle before Matt shot him dead.

The soldier rammed paper, powder, and ball down his rifle barrel as Matt closed the distance between them. He did not hobble or limp, but bounded in colossal strides toward the trooper. He roared again. The soldier looked straight at him—his eyes wide as silver pesos, white as goat's milk—and dropped his rifle just as shots cracked from the trees that flanked the two combatants.

Matt did not see the flame nor the smoke, but he could smell the burnt powder as it seared into his brain. He felt a ball burn across his rib cage, another slam into his left leg below the hip wound. In that split second of surprise, a drug of strength and magical powers flooded his bloodstream and he ignored the staggering blow to his leg. But he could still feel the ball flatten and gain weight, hammer through him like a sledge, mangling flesh and capillary, sinew and vein, and lodge somewhere in that trunk-thick leg like a poisonous capsule laden with death.

He swallowed up the soldier in his arms, and the

boy's scream mingled with Matt's roar as they grappled on the bank of the Rio Grande like ancient gladiators bereft of weapons except those that God had wrought: their arms, their hands, their teeth. Matt crushed the soldier, butted him with his head. The Mexican soldier twisted around and fell to the ground, robbing Matt of his prey. The momentum of Matt's charge carried him onward, past the fallen warrior. Blood streamed from his body in angry rivulets, tattered combat banners shredded by the wind of his charge, the terrible short flight through unconquered space. The prostrate boy cringed as the blood flecked his face and tunic, as the giant passed over him like a dark thundercloud, roaring still like a buffalo bull on a rampage across an ancient prairie.

Matt did not feel any pain as he lunged off the bank and fell into the river. The pain lanced into him as he struck the water, and then he held his breath as the water carried him away, floundering with one arm until he went under in a deep pool and was spewed out a few seconds later. The torrent swept him over the shallows, his butt bumping over smooth stones, and then he was in a millrace again and tumbling downstream, gasping for air, sucking in water until he choked and the sun turned dark in the pitch sky.

The river took a serpentine bend, then another, and Matt rolled like a sodden log as he tried to stroke for shore. The cold froze his wounds and chilled away the pain, but he knew the holes, the damaged flesh, the ball in his leg were all there, indelible as tattoos. His right arm was either shattered or numbed by the ball. He could not use it or feel it, and his left arm was weakened by its wound, weighted down with the weight of his drenched buckskin sleeve. His left leg had resumed its torment, and he wished he could summon the courage to draw his knife and slice it off, let it drop to the bottom like unwanted flotsam. He felt his pistols work loose and he tried to right himself, find the bottom with the slick wet soles of his moccasins.

The rush of water upended him, and Matt held his breath until he thought his lungs would burst into flame like paper thrown into a fire. Again the river spewed him out, and when he hit a rocky stretch, he flung himself toward the bank, grabbed a large rock and held on, his legs swinging downstream until they flapped in the current like the appendages of a dead frog. He grunted, pulled his legs up under him until he squatted in the river, felt its power surging against him, saw the water flowing around him in bubbled streamers as it did around the rock upon which he had purchase.

Steadying himself on the rock, using it as a center of gravity, Matt stood up. He shook from the cold and from trying to hold his feet to the bottom. The shore was only feet away, but the water was swift on either side of the boulder and he would have to wade through two feet of wild, deep water before he would be out of danger. He steeled himself to take the first step, leaving the security of the rock.

Stepping into the torrential tide was like stepping off the edge of the world. His right leg twisted away as his foot touched bottom, and he followed, hurled back into the stream like a scarecrow made of rags and straw, weightless when he struck the water. He had forgotten that his ankle was twisted, and the river twisted it again, left it swelling and useless.

But the water froze his wounds and stanched the blood flow better than any tourniquet, while the river battered him until his bones hurt in his teeth and in his mind like something eternal. His arms flapped like tattered ribbons, like spineless creatures, and he no longer tried to grab at the rocks or trees that jutted from the sandy bank and tore at his buckskin, ripping long slashes in his garments.

The river carried him down and down its twisting, breakneck course, whirling him around like a child on a berserk merry-go-round in dizzying whirlpools, making him into a water acrobat spinning off submerged rocks, shooting him through the shallows like a human cannonball and dashing him against rocks until he was half drowned and senseless. He no longer had the energy to fight against the river's powerful surge. His brain emptied of all desire to live, and there was just the scantest of sparks in the midst of its darkness, a tiny pinpoint of bleak silver flame that seemed connected to the tenuous thread of life to which all men are connected—until the filament breaks and releases their souls like cave bats blindly scuttling on ragged wings into the black maw of night.

Chapter
Eleven

Turtle, Black Beaver, and Deer Hoof watched from the trees across the river. They had heard the rifle shots, had skulked through the forest to watch as El Gigante charged the soldier, was shot, and fell into the river.

Now they watched as the soldiers buried the dead soldier.

"Should we kill them?" asked Deer Hoof.

"They have horses," said Turtle. "They are few."

"Let us follow them and kill them when they sleep," said Black Beaver. "Then we can take their horses."

"You two follow them," said Turtle. "I will return to camp and tell Bear Heart."

"No, let us not lessen our numbers," said Deer Hoof. "We will give a horse to Bear Heart."

The other two liked the idea. While Turtle caught up their horses, Deer Hoof and Black Beaver watched the soldiers mount up and ride downriver. The two Utes followed on foot until Turtle caught up with them.

The three braves tracked the soldiers for many days, waiting for just the right opportunity. The Mexicans posted a guard at night and were wary, like the fox. Finally the soldiers made a mistake. Before they reached the plain, the soldiers rode away from the big river. They became lost, and the Utes rode ahead of them to a narrow canyon where the soldiers would pass.

As the Mexicans rode single file through the narrow place, the Utes shot them with arrows. One tried to run away, but Deer Hoof rode him down and brained him with his war club. They stripped the horses and took the scalps of the dead men.

Then they rode to the Bull Heart's camp high on a barren plateau, a crag that jutted out from the mountain like the prow of a boat. They brought in four horses and showed the scalps they had taken. There was a big celebration in camp, for many had thought that the three braves had been rubbed out.

The heroes told their story to all who would listen.

"Did El Gigante give up his spirit?" asked Bull Heart.

"We do not know," said Black Beaver. "The river took him away. We did not see him and the soldiers did not hurry to go after him."

That night Bull Heart sent runners to the other camps, clear to the Moonshell, and he knew the news would spread to the Pawnee, the Arapaho, the Apache, the Comanche, and the Wind River Shoshone, to all tribes that crossed the plains or came to the mountains.

Pedro Seguín watched the sheep flow over the hillside like a woolly cloud, one animal composed of many. The herders walked along the flanks, dark apostrophes against the sea of white parchment. He watched the flock until it disappeared over the hill, then waved farewell to the last herder, who flapped his silhouetted sombrero against the agonizing blue of the sky.

Pedro did not look at his wife, who sat next to him on the wagon seat. He did not blame her for what had happened, but he could not get the images of the soldiers mounting her out of his mind. Had she enjoyed it? What was it like, with the first one? Did she enjoy the savagery of it and did she cry out in passion during the rape? These were questions he had not asked her, but they flowed like a litany through his mind and he could not shake them from his thoughts.

He would leave Rosa in Taos when he picked up a wagonload of supplies for his herders, the last he would bring to the mountains that summer. Life was not so dangerous there, and even so, he no longer had to worry about her virtue. In his mind the Spaniards had stripped his wife of all that was precious and sacred, had left her sullied and shamed.

The two-wheeled *carreta* creaked and rumbled over the stony path, its iron-clad wooden wheels jarring them in their seats. A single mule pulled the cart, its summer coat moth-eaten and shabby from neglect. The mule's ribs showed through its thin hide. Pedro rattled the reins on the mule's back, snapping them like suspenders. There was no reason to prod the animal, it was going as fast as it could down the slope. But Pedro felt like beating the mule to death.

"You take your anger out on the mule," said Rosa.

"I have no anger."

"Your words do not sound true, my husband."

"What do you know of truth?" The moment he said it, Pedro was sorry.

"Ah, it is me for whom you bear the anger."

"It was not your fault," he said, and the words were wrong again.

Rosa said nothing for several moments, but sat with her hands in her lap, folding and unfolding them like someone wrapping a gift, turning the object this way and that, endlessly and aimless.

"I am sorry it happened, *querido*."

"It happened."

"You must put it out of your mind, my husband."

"Jesus and Mary, I cannot."

"You did not see it. You did not feel it."

"I heard it. I knew what they were doing in there. Damn their black souls to Hell."

"You must not curse."

"I want to curse. Curse them all."

"They are dead."

"And I am alive and tortured."

"You are torturing yourself, *querido mio*."

"What did you do when they entered you, Rosa? What did you think? What did you say?" He could not stop the questions now. He had to know. His hands were fists holding the reins, and the mule was picking its way carefully down the crooked trail. Soon they would pass the *jacal,* and he would see it all again, hear his wife's screams and the grunts of the soldiers like pigs rooting in mud and dung.

"I prayed," she replied. "I did not think of what they were doing to me. I hated them and I prayed that they would not kill us."

"You should have prayed that they would die and go to Hell."

Rosa crossed herself. "I prayed for forgiveness," she said softly, and her words tore at Pedro like little daggers.

The *carreta* bounced over the rough trail and jarred them on the seat, sent shocks coursing through their bodies, rendering them speechless until the path smoothed out across a wide meadow that bordered the Rio Grande, forecast the prairie below and beyond.

The Rio Grande slid down through its water-carved bed with a lumbering force, a gray-green mass except when it frothed over shallows mined with stones, tossing suds into the sun, ejaculating creamy foam on sandy banks where they bubbled and seeped into the earth as if seeking seeds.

"And who will forgive you and why?" asked Pedro above the low rumbling thunder of the cart as they hit a stretch of smoother ground.

"God."

Pedro snorted. "And not I?"

"I did not betray you, Pedro."

"You gave yourself to them," he said cruelly. "You let them do it to you."

"I wanted to die," she whispered, her voice lost in her throat, struggling like a small bird tangled in a thicket. "I hoped they would kill me so that I would not have to live with my shame."

Pedro's silence filled up the mortal groan of the *carreta* straining over ground not meant to accommodate machines, things made by the hands of men.

"Maybe you should have died, then."

"Why? Can you not live with it? With me?"

"I don't know," he said, and there was the bitterness of sour brine in his voice.

Rosa began to weep then. She covered her face with her hands as if trying to hide her shame, to bury it in her own sullied flesh, to hide her face from God and the merciless light of the sun. The sobs shook her; tears poured from her eyes like the fragile warnings of the blood, portents of self-flagellation to come, leaving grief tracks on her face, temporary scarrings that would be wiped away only to leave indelible markings on the shadowy crust of her soul.

Pedro's mouth hardened and his eyes narrowed with a clenching hatred for an enemy he could not see, could not punish. The Spaniards, the filth. *Puercos. Perros. Sin verguenzas.*

And then Pedro's silence was filled with praying once

again as Rosa began to plead with her god and father, which were one and the same, and her voice carried the weight of her sorrow and shame and centuries of bondage and penitence, of acts of contrition and penances and corporal scourges with whips and thorns and nettles made to grow in the desolate landscape of the broken heart.

"Stop that," muttered Pedro.

But Rosa did not stop her praying. Pedro looked out upon the summer land that rose and fell and swelled like a sea captured and held motionless by unseen forces, and he sensed, with sudden illumination, the futility of man's life on such an earth that did not move or change despite the comings and goings of multitudes who left no tracks, their bones gone too, eaten by the wolves and worms of the earth. Gone, despite all the prayers and votive candles lit by shawled women with bony hands and drawn faces as death pulsed at the wattles of their necks and life dried them for the coffin, shriveled their flesh to remind them of the final skeletons they would become.

Rosa prayed to Jesus and to the immaculate and eternal virgin and crossed herself and touched the scapular medal enchained around her neck and kissed the image of the Virgin Mary cameoed in the pewter medallion blessed by the priest in Santa Fe as if all of it could protect her from evil and the lust of soldiers.

The cart rattled down the sloping road over its old tracks, through glades of aspen and pine, the solemn and graceful spruces, the scattered clumps of alder and gardens of wildflowers soaking green blood from the sun. Pedro tried to erase the images from his mind, the phantom shapes of priapic soldiers mounting his woman one by one and laughing as they spilled their seed in her womb.

They both smelled the carrion at the same time, but Rosa saw the buzzards before Pedro did, down the long narrow corridor of swollen hills. A pair of little jackal coyotes drifted from the carcass and disappeared into the timber. The buzzards flapped off, their pinions laboring, and drifted across the river, trailing their bent shadows through the water like shredded garments and finding roost in trees growing out of stone, bonsai jackpines shattered by wind, stunted by centuries of inclement weather.

"Look," cried Rosa. *"Ay de mi."* She pinched her nose between two fingers. *"Que peste."*

"Caballo," said Pedro as they rolled near the spoiling remains of the Mexican horse. The mule fought him, twisted in its traces like a trapped animal, struggling to turn back. Pedro took the small whip from its holder and cracked it across the mule's rump.

The stench of rotting flesh was overpowering, burnt the nostrils. Pedro rolled on past the carcass, downwind of the dead beast, stopped the cart and set the brake.

"Why are you stopping?"

"I want to look around. That is a soldier's horse, and I saw a fresh grave in the trees."

"I did not see it."

"Something happened here. I will be back."

Pedro climbed down from the cart, walked back to the dead horse. He knew the brand on its hip, like a Greek E. The horse was torn to pieces, but he could see the bullet hole in its hide. He walked to the mound of earth and stones that he had seen. Someone had made a crude cross of driftwood, two sticks tied together with a leather belt that had been cut in twain. The belt was like that worn by the Spaniards at the Santa Fe presidio. The coyotes had begun digging and pawing at the stones. In a day or two they would have the corpse. Pedro shuddered as he looked around. There were tracks everywhere, a day old, at least.

He crossed himself and walked back to the cart, the wind suddenly audible, like the keening zephyrs that coursed through graveyards, full of ghostly whispers and the secrets of metempsychosis. He shuddered again as he climbed into the cart.

"What happened?" asked Rosa.

"I do not know," he said, and looked at her. She seemed so frail and lost, frightened. He slid close to her and put his arm around her waist. "I am sorry, Rosa. I was cruel to you. I felt betrayed."

"I did not betray you."

"I know. It was the soldiers. There is one dead back there, buried."

He squeezed her waist with his hand, knowing they were alone in a wilderness and the smell of death was in the air. She trembled and he kissed her cheek.

"Cuanto lamento lo que ha pasado," he whispered.

"I know," she said.

"Let us go from this place."

"Pedro. I am afraid."

"Do not worry. They have gone."

But she looked around everywhere and into the inscrutable mountains that rose up around them like the walls of a great and mysterious city, and she gasped for air like a claustrophobe even though the wind was coming upcanyon and pressing against her face, fingering the shawl she pulled up over her head to block out the sun.

"I wish we were home in Taos," she said.

"Hush," he said, releasing the brake. He clucked to the mule, but the beast needed no urging and it stepped out briskly, following the track down to the plain, one eye looking ever backward over its shoulder as if pursued by demons, as if listening for the gallop of a dead and rotting horse hard on its heels.

They rode on into the afternoon and beyond, not speaking, but communicating through touches when the cart lurched and threw her up against her husband or when he patted her knee after traversing hard and dangerous stretches where the cart teetered and seemed sure to topple, and she put his coat about his shoulders as the chill deepened and the wind from the prairie met the wind from the high snowy places beyond their sight.

They reached the place where the Rio Grande took a wide bend before heading toward the plain as dusk was gathering in the secret hollows of the mountains, stretching long shadows from the trees until the earth was a jumble of stripes.

"Will we stay at the *jacal*?" she asked, a trembling in her voice.

"No," he said. "We will not go back there."

"Where, then? We must sleep. We must eat."

"A little ways. There is still light left." He looked back over his shoulder and saw the first dark clouds spilling over the mountains. "We will find a place," he said.

Rosa looked back to the mountains looming up behind them. "There is much wind," she said. "Many clouds."

"It will make a storm perhaps," said Pedro.

"Then we must hurry and find a place, make a shelter."

"Soon, soon," he said, wondering where the soldiers had gone, for the trail was laced with the tracks of shod horses, day-old spoor that brought him no comfort. The soldiers could be waiting, waiting for them just around the next bend.

The wind from the prairie died a little, and the one from the mountains freshened, bringing the chill of glacial moraines down on their backs until they drew their coats about them and huddled together on the sea like travelers who seek their bearings in a strange and hostile land.

But the dusk did not come quickly, and they drove on, past a placid stretch of river and down through steeper canyons that grew cold and darkened while the sun seemed to hang in the sky like some supernatural beacon

designed to light their way to safe harbor before the night
came down on them like some dark highwayman prowling
the lonesome stretches of an unmarked royal road, cloaked
and dangerous, his cape fanning out behind him like the
grim reaper's own flapping shroud.

Chapter Twelve

Matt felt the river pause as if taking a breath, and then it pulled at him, slow at first, then faster and faster until he hurtled onward, the sandstone bluffs blurring past him. He shot through a sepulchre of water, a flume that hurled him from one level to a lower one. He had the sensation of flying, of being propelled through a corridor of water yet somehow part of it and riding on it. The water was soft and swift until he struck the boiling froth at the bottom, where he tumbled over and over, out of control, inside a maelstrom that pulled at his clothes and blasted his face and tugged at his moccasins, a thousand clutching, tearing fingers that pulled him down and around until he was dizzy. His lungs were afire with the breath he was holding, until he turned black of face and could breathe only water and death.

The maelstrom ejected him and he popped up like a cork, then blasted into the shallows. His eyes burned from the battering water as he opened them. His butt bumped on the water-smoothed stones and his weight settled as his body stopped moving. He sat there, blinking like a sun-struck owl until his senses calmed and he could take his bearings.

At this place the river was broad and wide, taking a long bend before it gathered its strength again. Matt coughed and felt his lungs clear. He sucked in air, breathed heavily for several moments. Every bone in his body ached as if each one was gripped by a tightening thumbscrew. He looked up at the cyanic sky, the steep hills that rose all around him. He knew this place, had charted it, walked it, waded it. There was a lot more river beyond, before it reached the plain, but he had come a long way, even so.

He could not stay there. The soldiers would be riding this way, and they would make short work of him out in the open. He knew his wounds were bad, but the freezing water had stopped the bleeding, perhaps sealed some of the tissue for a time.

Matt tried to stand. The pain was enough to keep him down, but he realized that he was thoroughly exhausted. He could not walk, but he could crawl. He crabbed over the stones, soaking up water as he moved, looking like some mutant beast emerging from the slime of creation, slogging in his tattered buckskins through the shallow water until he reached land. He crawled toward a copse of trees, passed over a wagon-rutted trail, the tracks of sheep and horses. He felt like an animal on all fours. A wounded one at that, lumbering off somewhere to die.

He crawled into the shelter of the trees, found a sunny spot and lay down to dry and rest. He fell asleep. Later he heard the sound of hoofbeats, and when he looked up, saw the soldiers riding by, heading for the flat, silent and grim on their horses. They were not packing a dead body, so Matt figured they must have buried their leader where he fell. His heart pounded until they passed, and he thought his water trail must have dried in the wind and the sun.

He lay there a long time, listening, his mind raging with the pain in his body, and for hours he did not care if the soldiers came back and shot him dead. When they did not return, he began to think about survival, wondering how he could live in this wilderness without rifle, pistol, knife, or axe. His powder horns and possibles pouch had been ripped from his body by the river, and his buckskins hung on him in shreds. His moccasins had somehow clung to his feet.

For the moment, as the afternoon began its hushed deliberations in the trees, with the insects that burred and rasped in the grass and flowers, he was glad that he was alive. If he could survive his wounds, he would surely be able to find food, if that be only fish and lizards, bugs and snakes. If necessary he could return to a time when man emerged from the bog, naked and helpless, and began to fashion tools and weapons of flint and stone. He had advantages over that early pithecanthropus erectus, however. Matt knew things that progenitor never could have dreamed about.

Iron clouds armored the skies above the distant mountains, slowly rusted as the sun set, blackened in the coal char of the evening as the sun died in that day's turning, only to become reborn in another quadrant of the earth beyond these veridian foothills and dust-gray plains.

Matt listened in the soft, soft dusk and on into the no-man's-land of owl light, heard the coyotes crying like crazed jackals as they ran the canyons and ridges of the foothills like hunter robbers chasing after the shadows arranged by the funereal light, moved like prey under the fading afterglow.

And, upriver, he heard the solemn pronouncements of wolves arcing through the gathering dark like the ribbons of wind blown through the natural flutes of stone and walled canyons, hollowed-out deadfalls and certain formations of rock standing like the ruins of an immoral and plundered civilization that had died in one of the charted archeologies dimmed to shadows by time so vast it has no recorded history.

He lay in pain and cold, watching the distant lightning etching quicksilver hieroglyphics above the jagged peaks to the west, scrawling the names of gods over the Rocky Mountains in a crackling silvery shorthand no mortal could decipher.

Since he had crawled from the river to the copse of spruce and pine trees, he had been trying to make a shelter out of rotted bark, limbs torn from the bases of the trees, anything to keep out the prowling wind that had turned gelid with the falling dusk.

He heard the sound then, an alien thunder that was not issuing from the far-off storm descending toward the plain. He tried to sit up, but the pain in him kept him shriveled like a broken mendicant and he gasped at the sharpness of it, wondering if he would ever walk upright again.

He saw the mule first, then the dark figures on the seat, the *carreta* bobbing up and down on the trail he had crossed earlier in the day. They seemed to be headed straight for him, and for a long moment Matt's brain rang with the raucous off-key klaxons of warning. As they drew closer, he recognized the driver as the Mexican sheep herder he and the Shoshone had encountered being savaged by the soldiers from Santa Fe. The cart lumbered slowly off the trail, but it was heading for the very spot where Matt lay, still damp from the river, his wounds screaming in the peculiar yet articulate language of pain.

Did they know about his encounter with the troopers upstream? If so, how? What were they doing here? Why were they coming straight toward him? Matt saw that the clouds had skimmed over the high reaches of the mountains and were now invading the sky. Lightning flashed from the bowels of the black clouds like hurled thunderbolts from mythical gods. This time Matt heard the thunder follow the flashes, and knew that the storm would be on them in a scant few moments. It was then that he realized the two people on the cart were heading for shelter, without knowing that he was there.

The cart drew closer, until Matt could see the mule's eyes flaring as thunder rolled over the valley with the sound of empty cannons rolling on the wooden deck of a storm-tossed ship.

"Pare," yelled Pedro, and drew up on the reins. He set the brake and spoke to his wife. "Get down, Rosa. Find a place and I will try and bring the cart into the trees."

The woman descended from the cart and strode into the grove. She saw Matt and brought a hand to her mouth, but did not cry out. She stopped, stiffened. Pedro peered into the trees, trying to see what had startled his wife.

"What is it?" he said.

"No tenga miedo," Matt said in Spanish.

"It is El Gigante," Rosa said.

Pedro climbed down from the cart, ran into the grove. He stopped next to his wife.

"Que es?" he said again.

"He is hurt," said Rosa. She left the side of her husband, walked over to Matt, knelt down. *"Pobrecito,"* she said.

"Leave him there," said Pedro. "Let us go on."

Rosa saw the wounds through the tatters of Matt's buckskins, wondered how he could still be alive. She paid no attention to her husband, but looked into the eyes of the giant who lay under the boughs of the spruce. She saw that he had been building a shelter with his bare hands. She lifted one of them, saw that it was torn and bloody.

"Do you not feel pain?" she asked.

"A little," he admitted.

"Did they shoot you?"

Matt's eyes shadowed.

"I will take care of you. I have some medicines. Do you bleed much?"

"I don't know," said Matt. "The river brought me to this place."

"Come, Rosa," Pedro insisted.

"Bring me the medicines," she said. "Hurry."

"It is dangerous to stay here," said Pedro, hesitating.

"Go with your husband," said Matt, and he sank back to the earth, the pain flooding through him.

"No. You are hurt. I will be back."

Rosa rose and stalked back to the cart, passing her husband. Pedro grabbed her arm and she wrested it away with a defiance that surprised him.

"I am going to help the gringo," she said.

Pedro cursed under his breath, but his curiosity tugged him so that he moved closer to Matt. "Did the soldiers shoot you?" he asked.

"Yes."

"You killed one?"

"Yes. The others passed by a while ago."

"They have gone, then?"

"They have gone," Matt said.

Pedro looked at the pathetic figure on the ground. This was the same El Gigante who had befriended him, who had given him food, driven off the soldiers that raped Rosa. It would be an act of charity to help him, but it was also dangerous.

"There is a price on your head, Gigante."

"You might be able to collect it if you wait long enough."

"I would not do that."

"How much is it?"

"Many pesos. More than a thousand, I think."

Matt laughed until the pain doubled him up, shut off all thought, all reason.

Rosa returned with a small cloth satchel. She pushed Pedro aside, knelt once again by Matt's side.

"Help me take off his shirt," she said to her husband. "And we must remove his trousers."

Pedro was all thumbs, but he helped draw the buckskin shirt over Matt's head, and when he saw the wounds, he drew back as if blinded by them, as if scorched by the simple stark heat of them. Matt grunted and passed out before they got to his trousers. He heard their voices later, and the patter of rain, and then the wind came up like a hard shift of the earth on its axis and the dark swarmed in over them, but he saw the flickering light of a lantern and felt the woman's hands rubbing something into the open mouths of his wounds, and he heard the sound of cloth ripping and the cloth whisper as she wrapped him like a babe in swaddling clothes.

He smelled the ointments and the candlemusk, listened to the rain blast through the trees and tap against the cart like skeletal fingers on wooden shutters. The wind dwindled as it passed over them, until the rain fell straight down and soft, so that he could hear the river surge across the flat with a giant hiss as it swallowed stones and shore in its headlong dash from the confinement of the canyon.

Matt drifted in and out of consciousness. He could smell the woman next to him, a strange mixture of medicants and flowers, of female musk and wet earth, and the man too, smeared with the oil of sheep and the sweat of fear, and once he heard them whispering and he thought they might be making love, but the delirium took over his dreams and he no longer knew what was real or imagined, what was dreamed of quivering shapes that drifted past on unseen missions or had become oddly concrete in the void of the night.

Later the fever burned at him and he broke out in a clammy sweat. The woman opened his mouth and put something into it, forcing him to chew by working his jaws with her hand. She gave him water to drink, to wash down the tasteless mold she had crammed between his teeth, and when his stomach had settled he drifted away into that netherworld between sleep and waking and heard horses in the distance, thundering over a high plain, and heard Shoshone voices flagging them on, driving them over airy distances like graceful shadows borne on the wind, their manes streaming behind them like pennants scissored from hammered gold until they shone in the sun that lay beyond the dark plain.

Rosa gave Matt water throughout the night, put wet cloths on his chest and stomach, and he basked in the sweet smell of spruce and pine, lolled in the music of the rain dripping from the branches, wandered in and out of places he had known, others he had never seen. He wafted through dark corridors after wavering lights that disappeared in brumous alleyways, in some where souls sobbed and reached out for him, their faces shrouded in dark cowls, their voices like the hooty cries of owls.

The morning broke over them and cracked open Matt's eyes. He expected the Mexican couple to be gone, thought that he might have dreamed them, but they were still there, Pedro tending to his mule, feeding it grain and rubbing it down, Rosa at the river filling parfleches with water and lugging them to the grove on a stick braced across her back.

"How does it pass this morning?" asked Pedro in Spanish.

"It passes well," Matt replied. He still had the fever and his body felt like one huge boil that needed lancing. He could feel the poison inside him.

"We are going to leave soon," said Pedro. "I will take you to Taos."

"Why?"

"Maybe if you go there, you will live."

"Is there a doctor?"

"No."

Matt said nothing. He closed his eyes and drifted off again. He was awakened by Rosa putting something into his mouth. She made him chew again and then she poured water down his throat. He choked, but did not throw it all back up. The medicine this time tasted foul, like something green and moldy. He felt himself being lifted, and then he was floating somewhere, and finally he lay on something soft, but he could feel wood underneath and then the cart was moving and he dreamed that soldiers were tearing off his flesh in huge crimson strips and he was trying to scream, but they had filled his mouth with mud and moss and he could make no sound and the pain was so loud it would have drowned out his voice anyway.

Something inside Matt made him cling to life that first day in the *carreta,* and took him into that night where the dreams were more horrible than any he had ever encountered, and he thought Rosa was tending to him but he could not be sure. The pain rode beside him, slept with him, and finally entered him like a shadow twin of himself, and after that only the pain could think, only the pain could scream, and Matt tried to slide away from the shadow and find death, for he knew it was waiting for him somewhere in that madhouse of the mind where there was no sound except the silent howl of that interminable pain that was no longer his shadow, but himself, limbless and mute on a journey through a limbo catholic and eternal.

Chapter Thirteen

D ays of pain and delirium, dreams of being flayed alive with sharp lashes, strapped to the rack with the drum turning, the rope tightening, hung on a gibbet. Matt Caine wondered if he was in Hell or suspended somewhere in between earth and Hades. He was certain the Mexican couple were torturing him deliberately, and he cursed them in three languages, uttered vile epithets and blasphemies at every jounce of the *carreta*. He raved, awake or asleep, his skull full of horrible images, his body gorged with an ungodly venom from some vile serpent that threaded through his dreams. At times he felt himself skewered on a spit above a roaring fire, turning, turning at every roll of the cart with no respite, no respite, no place where his skin did not feel as if it had been boiled in hot oil and slowly pulled from his body in fine strips until he was a single raw wound screaming and screaming somewhere in the dark reaches of his mind.

Sometimes he heard the voices of his captors, and they made no sense to him, as if he were a disembodied wraith forced to listen while his agony raged on.

"His fever does not break," said Pedro.

"A little," replied Rosa. "He has a lead ball in him that must come out."

"Take it out."

"I have the fear of doing that," she said.

They followed the Rio Grande down its twisting course through the mountains, afraid to strike for the plain where the soldiers might be. Each night, they stopped and made camp and Rosa cooked. She fed the delirious Gigante soups made of leeks and onions and mutton, forcing little morsels of meat into his mouth which she had already chewed.

"I miss our little Domingo," said Rosa while feeding Gigante.

"Your mother takes care of him."

"I miss her too."

"I do not," said Pedro.

Rosa swatted him with a wooden spoon.

"Well, only a little," he said.

Through the pain, there was the heady scent of balsam, the aromatic fragrance of sage that Rosa sprinkled on the cookfire in some ritual known only to her. Matt waited for those moments when the cart was not bouncing, took some comfort in knowing that the pain would not move over his body like a blacksmith's maul, but linger in isolated compartments where each could throb separately and without competition. Sometimes he opened his eyes and saw the stars so close he thought he was floating among them, riding on the pain itself through the diamond dust of the Milky Way, but gritting it back down when he closed his eyes, clenched his teeth.

Rosa changed Matt's dressings every evening, continued to give him boiled herbs and treat his wounds with a special salve made by a bruja in Taos. She tried to make him comfortable in the cart, but knew that his suffering was great. She wished for a stack of buffalo robes to ease his ride, but there were none. In camp she made a bed of pine boughs, and after a week of travel, El Gigante seemed to be sleeping better during the night.

"He did not awaken last night," Rosa said one morning.

"He was awake," said Pedro.

"He made no sound."

"He was weeping."

"Ai, que pobrecito."

After three weeks of travel, they drove down onto the plain late in the afternoon under a cloudless, lazulite sky. It was like coming into another world, a landscape of sand and sage and smoketrees, clumps of wild zinnia, patches of nopal and cholla, their heads haloed and spun with the mist of their delicate spines, an illusion created by the slanting beams of the sun. The plain stretched out under the falling sun, shimmering in a lilac haze, full of muted shadows and a desolate silence that made them feel small and insignificant.

"In two days we will be at the home of your mother," said Pedro.

"Thanks to God."

"What will you do with El Gigante? It will be dangerous to be with him."

"I will see if the *bruja* can take out the lead ball."

"That old woman will kill him."

"We owe El Gigante a chance to live."

"If the soldiers know we have him, they will hang us all."

"Then we must hide El Gigante from them until he is well."

Pedro said no more. They left the road that morning and struck out across the high plain, avoiding any contact with soldiers who might be patrolling the road. The wagon lurched and rolled like a foundering ship on a restless sea, and they had to clear brush from the wheels and push the cart over sandy swales. Long after dark, three days later, they drove into Taos, a city of mud and sand risen from the big river, where Pueblo Indians yet plotted the overthrow of their Spanish captors. They kept to the shadowed *calles,* little more than cart trails, away from the plaza where the soldiers would be. The night air smelled of tobacco and woodsmoke, of burnt corn and candlewax. Bullbats knifed the darkness on silent wings, their wakes when they passed like whispered vespers in a midnight graveyard. Somewhere in the adobe maze of the village a goat bleated, followed by the yips and yammerings of two or three dogs. The Seguíns came in behind the adobe house of the widowed Carmen Velazquez, down a narrow alleyway. They carried El Gigante inside, huffing and puffing from the weight of him, and awakened Rosa's mother, Carmen, and their son Domingo, who was seven years old, eyes black as agates, unshorn hair sprouting tufts in all directions like the wire whiskers of a cat. He was small-boned, resembling his mother slightly, with his open flat face and high cheekbones.

"Eh, what is it you have there?" asked Carmen. Once beautiful, she looked like a figurine made of parchment retrieved from some Babylonian cavern. She was a Pueblo Indian who had married a Mexican, so that the bloodlines were confused, scrawled from tribes lost to the earth, murdered and scalped in arid lands to the south.

"Ssssss. *Callate, Mamá,*" said Rosa.

Domingo hugged his mother, circled the giant gringo on the floor warily. Pedro patted his son's head, made sure the windows were curtained before he lit the candle set in a brass lantern case. The house reeked of incienso, the dried sap of the brittlebush collected in vessels set in every room. There were wildflowers in clay vases everywhere, some alive, some dead and dried. If not for the florals, the place would have looked like an adobe vault.

"Bless the Christ. Holy Mother of God. It is El Gigante," said Carmen. "Is he a Yanqui? The soldiers are looking for him. You will gain much money from bringing him to them."

"He saved our lives," said Rosa. "We did not bring him here for the reward."

Pedro carried the lantern over to where Matt lay, held it high so that his mother-in-law and son could see the man they had carried down through the mountains.

"He is a very big man," said Carmen, her speech thick from drinking the cheap *tepache* all day. "What is the matter with him? He is a Yanqui, no?"

"The soldiers shot him," said Pedro, shooting a warning glance toward his wife. "Yes, he is an *americano*."

"Why did you not leave him to die?"

"Because God would not want us to," said Rosa quickly. Her mother, she knew, would pry and pry and build up suspicions in her mind until she and her husband would be forced to tell her the whole story of El Gigante and the soldiers. She did not want her shame to spread any further than it had.

"Domingo," said Rosa, "bring me a mat and help me fix a bed for El Gigante."

"There are many soldiers in the pueblo," said Domingo. "There is a doctor and he gave us the vaccinations."

"A doctor? Here in Taos?"

"Yes," said Carmen. "You and Pedro must see him tomorrow. He says everyone must feel the sting of his needle. His name is Larrañaga. He is a surgeon."

"A surgeon?" Rosa looked at her husband with pleading eyes. Pedro shook his head.

"It is too dangerous," he said.

"But he can save El Gigante," said Rosa.

"For the hangman, perhaps. And the Spaniards would stretch our necks at the same time."

"Please, Pedro."

"I must think," he said. "Domingo, do as your mother

has asked you. Prepare a bed for the gringo. In the morning I will decide what we will do with him."

Matt heard them talking, but he could make no sense of their words. They spoke very fast, and the pain twisted everything they said. He floated somewhere deep in the pain, too far down to come up. He did not want to come up, because awake, the pain separated from the dream and could not be handled. In those waking moments he was insane and suicidal, a wretch begging for death, a hopeless cripple with no desire to live. He felt sorry for the woman who believed that a witch-woman could heal him. The man knew he was going to die. He had said as much, unless Matt had imagined that too.

Carmen filled the air with a flutter of questions, but Rosa refused to answer her. She said that they were tired. Pedro and Domingo put the mule in the little corral with the adobe stables and set the cart under a lean-to, unloading the few things Pedro and Rosa had brought with them from the mountains.

Rosa, Domingo, and Carmen made a pallet for Matt. Pedro sent Domingo to bed, then retired himself. Rosa changed Matt's dressings with her mother looking on.

"Ah," said Carmen when Rosa took the pus-caked bandage from around his arm. "You draw out the poison."

"A little. There is a ball in his leg. I can feel it."

"I will make some hot water. We should wash these wounds."

"He will scream," said Rosa.

Carmen looked at Matt's face. "He is screaming now," she said, then glided from the room toward the rear of the dwelling. Rosa heard the slap and clack of kindling wood as her mother threw it into the mouth of the *horno*.

The two women stripped off the clothing and bathed the wounded man, their faces lit by the lamp glow. In the dark cavern of the room, they resembled women tending to the crucified body of the Christ, smearing him with oils and unguents, wrapping him in white linen in a long-ago cave.

"Where is the ball?" asked Carmen.

"Here," said Rosa, pointing to Matt's leg. They could see its dark shape through the almost translucent skin.

"It is not very deep."

"From the other side," said Rosa, "it is deep."

"But a small cut."

"There is a big vein there, an artery."

"Yes, that is so."

Carmen handled Matt's manhood. "He is very big, no?"

"Mother, stop that."

"I was just looking," said Carmen.

"What if he wakes up?"

"What could he do? What could I do?"

Rosa blushed with shame. She covered Matt's loins with a cloth. "Help me dress him," she said.

"No. I will clean his clothes and mend them. Put a blanket over him."

Rosa nodded at her mother's wisdom.

"Who will watch Gigante?" asked Carmen later, when they were going to bed.

"There is no need to watch him," said Rosa.

"What a pity," said Carmen, and shuffled off to her room, wide-awake now and humming to herself.

Surgeon Larrañaga dabbed the sweat from his forehead with a white linen handkerchief, stuffed it back in his waistband. The sun slanted through the windows of the adobe building, warming the room, which had been cool that morning. The walls were affixed with official posters, government warnings, instructions that few of the townfolk could read. His satchel, the boxes of serum, bowls of raw alcohol, an array of syringes on a folded cloth, all lay on a rustic table as the villagers passed by him for their vaccinations. His nurse, Elena Cuevas, and his aide, Federico Morales, stood in the doorway. The room smelled of disinfectant, alcohol, vaccines.

"Is that the last for the day?" the surgeon asked as an old woman hobbled away from him toward the door.

Esmeralda stepped outside. Federico leaned out as the old woman passed through and peered up and down the plaza.

"Two more," said Federico.

Elena escorted Pedro and Rosa through the door. Larrañaga looked at them. They appeared nervous, but were clean, their faces washed. The woman pushed the man ahead of her.

"Have you had the vaccinations before?" asked the surgeon.

Pedro shook his head. He wore the white cotton garment of the peon. Rosa wore a cotton skirt, the lavender faded to a dusky violet, and a simple peasant's blouse of pale yellow with short sleeves, no frills or ribbons.

"Are you man and wife?"

"Yes."

"Any children?"

"No," Pedro lied.

"Roll up your sleeve."

Pedro pulled his sleeve up. The doctor washed a spot on his arm with the alcohol.

"Don't move or touch this spot."

Pedro stood there while the surgeon opened a vial and filled one of the syringes with the dark fluid. He injected the serum subcutaneously, then scratched another place on Pedro's arm and Pedro felt a stinging, a burning. The surgeon wiped the blood away.

"Don't wash the arm for a day."

"Yes, Doctor."

"Next."

Rosa stepped up to the doctor. She looked pleadingly into his eyes.

Pedro stepped between Rosa and the two people in the doorway, blocking their view.

"Roll up your sleeve."

"Doctor," Rosa whispered, "I must tell you something."

"What is it?" Larrañaga asked loudly.

"Please, I am afraid."

"What are you afraid of?" The surgeon lowered his voice.

"There is a man. He is hurt very bad I think."

"Who is this man?"

"Have you heard of El Gigante?"

Larrañaga's eyes narrowed. He did not speak for several seconds. Of course he had heard of the gringo. That was all the soldiers who were with him talked about. He had not paid much attention to them, for they spoke of El Gigante as if he was some mythical creature, a giant rumored to be either Indian or Yanqui or both, living in the mountains, a wild, uncivilized beast.

"What about El Gigante?" the surgeon asked very quietly as he swabbed Rosa's arm with alcohol.

"He is here. In Taos. He has been shot. There is a lead ball still in his leg."

"What do you want me to do about it?"

"Can you cut out the ball?"

"Why should I? The man is a criminal, is he not?"

"I do not know. He was shot by soldiers from Santa Fe."

"I see. That is very serious. Why did you come to me?"

"This man helped us."

Larrañaga saw the fear in the woman's eyes. He saw it on her face. He gave her the injections and told her not to cleanse her arm for a day.

"Stay," he told Rosa and Pedro. "I will send those two away."

The doctor rose from his chair and walked to the door. He spoke softly to Elena and Federico. As they left, he closed the door.

"Well, now, where did you find this El Gigante?"

"In the mountains," said Pedro. "We are afraid. If the soldiers find out we brought him here, they will kill us."

"I truly believe they will. There is talk that this man you speak of killed several soldiers sent to kill him."

"We do not know if this is true," said Pedro.

"I believe it is true. The governor would very much like to talk to this man, to question him, perhaps bring charges against him."

"We do not care what happens to him after he becomes well," said Pedro.

"Then why save him?"

"It is a thing we must do," said Pedro. He looked at his wife. She lowered her head, and Larrañaga sensed that there was more to this story of El Gigante than he would ever learn.

"Can the man walk? Can you move him?"

"He is very sick. He is dying, I think," Pedro replied.

"I will look at him. I will have to bring the soldiers with me."

"We do not want them to know that we brought him here. We have a son and we are at the home of my mother-in-law."

"Then you will have to take him to a place where I might examine him and treat him."

"Where?" asked Pedro.

The surgeon sighed, rubbed delicate fingers over the ridges of his forehead and down into his brows. "I will send my man Federico home with you. He will bring a handcart. You can trust him. You help put the wounded man in the cart, and he will push him back here."

"But—"

"That is the best I can offer. I am sticking my neck out to do this much."

"Yes," said Rosa, relieved. "Let this man come with us, Pedro. I am so nervous I could die."

"That's fine, then," said Pedro. "I trust you, Doctor."

Larrañaga opened the door, gestured to someone outside. Federico Morales came inside. The surgeon spoke to him so that he could not be overheard.

Federico left and the doctor turned to them.

"He will be back with the handcart very soon. Take him to El Gigante. If any soldiers ask you where you are going, tell them that I, Larrañaga, have ordered you to bring me a sick person who cannot walk. Federico will tell them the same. Now go."

Rosa and Pedro went outside like two bewildered children, and stood in the gathering shadows of the plaza, lost and afraid, until they saw the surgeon's man pushing the cart across the cobbled plaza. Everywhere they looked they saw soldiers, standing, smoking, sitting in chairs outside the cantinas, and all staring at Federico Morales and the noisy chart, with its iron-clad wheels, rattling across the plaza. The cart, long-bedded and empty, seemed to shriek the secret of its destination for all to hear.

_____ Chapter _____
Fourteen
_____

E lena Cuevas breathed through the gauze cloth masking her mouth. The room, a small one in the apartment where the doctor resided while in Taos, reeked
of chloroform and disinfectant. A streak of rust stained
one corner of a gypsum wall, stretching from ceiling to
floor. A hospital cot, made up especially for the giant, took
up an entire wall. The palette that served for a bed stood
on sturdy crates and was soft and big enough for Caine,
with clean sheets and blankets. Federico Morales stood
aside, also masked, holding a small bowl containing a
cloth soaking in chloroform. A half-dozen lanterns, two
hanging from wooden tripods above the patient, threw saffron light on the operating table as Larrañaga made the in-
cision in Matt Caine's leg. Elena sopped up the blood with
a towel. She threw it onto the floor, grabbed another one.

"Probe," said the surgeon. Guitar music floated
through the windows, plaintive, muffled. Down the street
a woman laughed, and children called to one another
across streets and alleys blackened by night.

Elena slapped a metal probe, curved like a brain
spoon, in the surgeon's hand. Moths swirled around the
lanterns, fluttered at the light, some perishing in the

141

flames, hissing as the fire consumed their fluids. Others fell to the floor, where they were crushed underfoot, or flapped broken-winged and singed across the room.

"Ah," the surgeon said.

Matt stirred. His bad leg jerked slightly. The surgeon pressed down on it with all his weight while he dug the lead ball out of the leg. He did this with delicacy, moving it through the flesh, careful not to rupture the nearby artery. The ball popped out and fell onto the bloody towel. Larrañaga picked it up, held it between two bloody fingers.

"Round as a berry," he said. "This man has the luck."

"It did not flatten," said Federico.

"Not one bone broken." The surgeon spread the wound, looked through it to see the extent of the damage. He stuck a finger inside, felt for lead fragments as a man would seek a pearl inside an oyster's gelatinous mass.

The surgeon laved the wound with alcohol.

"There. Clean as can be."

Larrañaga finished quickly, sewing the wound closed with thin black thread. He had examined the giant thoroughly, cleaning up his other wounds. The woman had tended him well. The man was healing. Had the ball been removed sooner, he would be in much better shape. As it was, El Gigante was a magnificent physical specimen.

"Not a word of this just yet," the surgeon said.

Federico and Elena both nodded. She began picking up the bloody towels while Federico put away the chloroform, going outside to wring out the anesthetic-soaked cloth. When he returned, the surgeon was slipping out of his operating garb, washing his hands in a bowl of warm soapy water.

"After a few minutes, we'll move him to his bed. One of us will have to watch him around the clock. I'll take the first shift, say three hours. Federico, you and Elena get some sleep. You'll take the next shift, Federico.

I want him watched carefully. If his wound breaks open, it will be very bad for him. If he awakens, tell him to lie still. Come and get me immediately."

"Does he speak Spanish?" asked Federico.

"I don't know."

"What are you going to do with him, Doctor?" asked Elena.

"We'll see," he said. "First I must make him well. Then he and I will converse, if we are able to find a common tongue."

Elena smiled. The surgeon was an educated man. He spoke, besides Spanish, French, English, and German. She knew that he had even picked up a few words of the native Pueblo dialect. It was difficult for her to conceal her admiration for Dr. Larrañaga. At eighteen, and unmarried, she hoped that someday she would find a man as courteous, accomplished, and intelligent. So far, in Santa Fe, she had met only arrogant soldiers and lazy Mexicans. She had been promised to a man in Guadalajara, where her parents lived, but he had been killed by Apaches, and her family had made no other arrangements. At times she felt like an outcast, for she was of marrying age and, because of working long, hard hours for the surgeon, in danger of becoming a spinster. She pulled a light coverlet over the unconscious giant on the operating table, resisting a sudden impulse to touch his face, stroke his thick beard.

Matt awoke in darkness, his head full of cotton and cobwebs, swirling with dense fog.

"Hoopties," he said.

Federico, a young, lean man from Chihuahua who was studying to be a doctor, walked over to the recovering patient.

"*Que dices?*"

"Hoopties," Caine muttered.

"Que es juptis?"

Caine's eyelids fluttered but he could not open them. He lay there, floating just below wakefulness, trying to isolate the pains. He felt a burning in various parts of his body, a deep throbbing pain in his leg.

Federico stood there, watching the man to see if he would awaken. After a time he walked back to the bench and sat down. He heard a stirring in the room above him. Footsteps. After a while the door opened and a sleepy-eyed Elena entered the room.

Federico rubbed his eyes, yawned.

"How is he?" she asked.

"He started to wake up, but did not."

"Better get some sleep," she whispered. She checked the bandages after Federico left, felt the patient's forehead. He was feverish, but that was to be expected. His face was pale. The candle fluttered and she looked at it. The flame was guttering. She replaced it with a fresh candle, then sat in shadow watching the sleeping giant in rapt fascination.

He might have been lying in state, but his massive chest moved up and down with the slow, steady beat of his breathing. Once in a while his face would contort, his lips move, but he made no sound.

Federico had swept the room of dead moths. Elena was impressed with his conscientiousness. There was fresh water should the patient awaken, and some medicine for the pain, powders that the surgeon had brought from Santa Fe.

She listened to the sound of Matt's breathing. Strong and steady.

Matt knew there was someone in the room with him. He imagined that it was the woman who had carried him in the cart. But he was sleeping on something soft and there was no movement, no hard boards battering his back. He thought he might be lying in a room where someone was waiting for him to die.

The dreams confused him. He wandered through deserted barracks, picked up a rifle that was broken. The stock was scored with deep gashes and the barrel was bent. He tried to find ammunition for it, but instead of powder, his pouch was filled with milled white flour. He tried to straighten the barrel, but the rifle fell apart in his hands.

Mexican soldiers came into the barracks, hunting him. Matt hid behind a wooden footlocker and found a pistol. The lock was loose and he tried to screw it down tight as the soldiers prowled the barracks, calling his name. Several soldiers rolled large metal hoops in marching formation. The soldiers wore hideously frozen grins on their faces. The hoops made a sound like breathing, and when they started wobbling on invisible axes, he crawled away from them still carrying the broken pistol.

Through mazes of barracks he ran, seeking a way out, and then he was chasing a broken two-wheeled cart across a landscape of ruin, shell holes smoking like tiny volcanoes, the rubble of war strewn everywhere, cannons and surgeons' wagons, broken swords and tattered uniforms, stumps of arms and legs riddled with bullet holes, and the sky aflame, pulsing with cherry-red coals, black horses gutted and maimed, their eyes bulged and glistening like polished agate, muskets and rifles all a-tangle, and the wagon rumbling over the dead, drawn by a man and woman in torn leather harness, their feet cloven like the devil's own hooves.

He dreamed variations of the same dream over and over, and it felt so real he knew he must have drifted from the real world and into some nightmare dimension from which he could not escape until, in the last frightening segment, he lay chained on an iron cot in a dungeon crawling with rats, red eyes winking out of the darkness, snakes slithering over human skulls that were still alive and screaming, and people stood around him and sunk knives into his flesh until a troop of skeletal soldiers appeared in their place and fired volleys of bullets into his arms and legs.

Then there was a great roar and the dungeon walls burst and he was borne by a flood that carried him through the walls and out onto a barren cliff where men in black cloaks stood waiting and hurled him over the precipice, and he struck a river raging at floodtide and sank like an iron anvil deep into the murky waters, where he strangled, straining at his bonds, and could not breathe, could not free himself from the river's grip, and tumbled over and over on an iron slab that pounded him until he screamed in agony and broke free of the river and the dream in one explosive instant—

Matt's scream startled Elena, jolted her so, she jerked in her chair as if electrified. His was a scream of someone in mortal agony, of a man tortured beyond comprehension. She gathered her scattered wits and ran to Matt's bedside, her features stricken with the furrows of worry, distorted in abject confusion.

"Que pasó?" she asked as she stared into Matt's wide eyes.

He saw the woman and closed his eyes, opened them again.

"Un sueño," he said.

"Do you have pain?" she asked in Spanish.

"Much pain," he replied in her own tongue.

"Where does it hurt?"

"All over. My legs, my arms, my head."

"I will give you some powder for the pain."

"No," he said, gritting his teeth. "Where am I?"

"In Taos. It is like a hospital."

He breathed slowly and let the pain course through him as he stared at the adobe ceiling. He looked at the woman's face very carefully, as if memorizing it, watching the way the candlelight played with shadows over her features. She seemed young, was pretty, with her hair tightly bound and braided, no makeup, even white teeth, high cheekbones, fair complexion, blue eyes. Not a Mexican. Her speech had the softness of the Castilian Spanish, was very correct and crisply pronounced.

"Who are you?"

"I am called Elena."

"You are not Mexican."

"Yes, I am Mexican. New Mexican."

"Did the man and woman bring me here?"

"I do not know. The surgeon removed a ball from your leg, tended all your wounds."

"I am grateful to him."

Matt moved his arms. He was not bound or shackled. He wiggled his toes, tried to move his legs. The pain stopped him in his tracks as if all his muscles were ligatured, connected to a central source from which all torment emanated on invisible wires.

"He will be here soon." She looked up toward the window as if seeking a sign in the night, as if looking for dawn's gray face.

"I would like to talk to him," Matt said slowly, hoping that the pain would subside, glad that he could feel, that he was alive.

"He will want to talk to you."

"There is no doctor in Taos."

"No. We have come from Santa Fe with the vaccines. We will return when our duties are completed."

"Are you a nurse?"

"Yes."

"I would like a drink of water."

"It might make you sick."

"My mouth is very dry. My tongue feels thick."

"It is the chloroform. The surgeon did not want you to feel the pain."

"He is a good surgeon. I did not feel much pain."

"You are weak. You have lost much blood."

Matt looked at her closely. She seemed without guile, but he dared not ask her any more questions. Perhaps the surgeon did not know he was a wanted man. Perhaps news of him had not reached Taos yet.

"I feel weak," he said in English.

"What?"

"*Nada.*"

He closed his eyes. He felt her hand brush across his forehead, then she was taking his pulse. A door opened, but he could not open his eyes. The girl walked away, leaving him alone with the pain. The pain held him down, held him down tight, and he had to squeeze himself through it, concentrate on riding over it or he would surely scream again.

Voices. Conversing softly in Spanish. One a man's, the other belonging to the nurse. Matt stayed down there, with the pain, trying to decipher what they were saying, but the whispers sounded like leaves rustling in the wind, like the far-off songs of birds flying over white-crested ocean waves on a somber winter's day.

The door closed again. Footsteps across the dirt floor. Different this time. Matt clamped his lips together tightly, as if to keep the pain from roaring out of his mouth like flame from a foundry furnace.

"There is much pain," said the surgeon in Spanish. Matt felt the man's hand on his, gentle, soft, comforting. "I am sorry that you suffer."

Matt opened his eyes. Standing there was a small, wiry man dressed in a suit. His eyes crackled as he drew a slow smile across his mouth.

"I am Surgeon Larrañaga."

"Matthew Caine."

"You are an American?" he asked in English.

"Yes," Matt replied in his own tongue.

"Are you a soldier?"

Matt's eyes flickered. The surgeon's bored into his like a pair of gun barrels. But his look was not unkind.

"No. Trapper," Matt lied.

"A good one?"

"Not very good."

"Ah, a pity. And do you have permission of the Mexican government to trap in this territory?"

"I didn't know I needed permission."

"Tell me. What are these *juptis* you talk about in your sleep."

"Hoopties?"

"Ah, an English word. I am not familiar with it. Elena thought it was important, so she told me."

"Hoopties ain't important, 'cept to me."

"Who shot you?"

"Injuns, I reckon."

"Well, that is a good story."

"It'll have to do."

"Today I must speak to the lieutenant who is my escort. I will tell him that you were lost and shot at by wild Indians, say Comanches or Apaches, and that you are my personal responsibility. When you are well enough to travel, I will take you with me back to Santa Fe, introduce you to the governor and beseech him to grant you papers so that you can return to your own country."

"Why would you do that, Doctor?"

"Otherwise, I'm afraid, all my good work on you would be wasted."

"How's that?"

"Oh, I'm quite sure that the governor would hang you, sir."

"Hang me?"

"Yes. He's had soldiers hunting El Gigante for nearly a year."

"But—"

The surgeon put a finger to his lips. "There's no need

to explain, Mr. Caine. I will give you something for your pain. Rest is the best medicine. You'll want to be at your best when you meet Governor Alencaster."

"Maybe the governor will hang me anyway," said Matt.

"Perhaps he will," said the surgeon.

Chapter

Fifteen

A week after Caine's deliverance into the hands of the surgeon, the patrol rode into Taos; the adobe dwellings rising above the sunstruck plain like stacks of white cartons. They sat their dark horses like broken men, their faces drawn to an unflinching grimness, daubed with dirt and sweat as if touched by the mortician's brush, their uniforms dirty and wrinkled, their boots sun-cracked and coated with a thin patina of dust.

Their horses stumbled through the coarse and tangled ruderal at the edge of town as if they no longer could find the road, or perhaps they avoided the cart ruts on sore hooves that had ground the iron shoes down to lean crescents that granted them no protection.

Peons in the fields looked at the sad procession that had ridden in from the north and then bent to their hoes and rakes like large white birds pecking for gravel and seed. Goats wandered in their path like mythical creatures with cloven hooves, bearded like senators, horned like demons exiled to some wasteland. Chickens scattered like feathered balls ahead of the bedraggled horses.

The troopers rode to the center of the village, halted in front of the adobe where flew the company banner, where stood two guards with rifles who presented arms and stood rigidly at attention. The troopers dismounted and staggered to shade, except for three men who entered the headquarters building, none bothering to tamp the scurf of dust from their uniforms. The lieutenant in the fore tossed off a salute, and the guards ordered arms as they passed like prisoners going to the dock.

Lieutenant Don Facundo Melgares sat at the table in the makeshift headquarters in Taos and listened in silence as Lieutenant Felix Candelaria gave his verbal report. With him were his sergeant, Nestor Camacho, and corporal, León Ferros. They had led the scouting expedition out of Santa Fe to find out what had happened to Escobar's expedition.

"We found one man alive, who was badly wounded," said Candelaria. "Private Porfirio Chamayo. Before he died, he told us of the tragedy of Captain Escobar and a dozen men—the death of several other soldiers and Lieutenant Garza. They did encounter El Gigante, sir."

Melgares could not mask his fury, the pain he felt inside. "All dead?"

"Yes, sir," said Candelaria. "We believe so. Chamayo said that El Gigante killed Captain Escobar and Lieutenant Garza. Chamayo was shot and scalped by three Utes, who left him for dead. We found him and the other two men. Their horses were gone. We found the grave of Lieutenant Garza."

"There were thirty men on that expedition."

"Yes, sir. I know, sir. According to Private Chamayo, El Gigante was responsible for all their deaths."

"And El Gigante?"

"Dead, sir."

"Where is his body?"

"He fell into the river, Lieutenant, according to Private Porfirio Chamayo. His body was washed away."

"We never found it," said Camacho.

"One man killed thirty," muttered Melgares. "I cannot believe El Gigante could do such a thing all by himself. He must have an army."

"We found no sign of an army. No fort." Candelaria looked uneasy. "But no one man could kill thirty seasoned men unless he had help."

"Exactly," said the lieutenant. He turned to his sergeant-at-arms. "Confine these men to separate quarters. Under guard. Give them paper and pen. I want full and separate written reports from each of them."

"Sir," said Candelaria, "do you not believe my report?"

"Don't be insubordinate, Lieutenant. I want specific details of where you went, what you did each day, where you found evidence of our dead. And I want a verbatim account from each of you concerning Private Chamayo's story about the death of El Gigante and Lieutenant Garza."

"Yes, sir. With your permission."

"Well, what more, then?"

"I am under direct orders from the *comandante* of the presidio of Santa Fe. I only stopped at your headquarters to give you my report out of courtesy. My men are tired. We wish to rest up and return to Santa Fe early in the morning."

"You wish to get drunk?"

"That too. It must have been a horror for those men."

"Dismissed. You will carry out my orders, Lieutenant."

"With your permission, sir."

Melgares waved the troopers away, rubbed his forehead until his fingers came to the bridge of his nose in a strong pinch as he closed his eyes.

Captain Escobar and Lieutenant Garza were friends of his, hand-picked for the expedition to find the Yanqui they called El Gigante. He dreaded relaying this failure to Governor Alencaster. But he had been assigned to escort the surgeon to all the pueblos in the river kingdom, and it was not his fault that they had not returned with their quarry.

The door slammed and it was quiet in the room for a few moments. When the knock came, Melgares was already into the brandy.

"Who knocks?" he asked.

"Corporal Santos, sir. Surgeon Larrañaga wishes to see you."

"Send him in." Melgares retrieved another glass from the tray on the table.

"Will you have some *aguardiente*?" the lieutenant asked as the surgeon entered the room.

"Not this early, thank you."

"Seat yourself, Doctor."

"Very well, then." The surgeon sat in the rustic wicker chair some soldier had appropriated from the village. The room was as spartan as any he'd seen since coming to Taos over a week ago. They had been in the village only a day when Matthew Caine was smuggled into his quarters. This had been done at night, and word of the surgeon's patient had not gotten out. At least the news had not reached Melgares's ears.

"You are ready to return to Santa Fe?" Melgares asked.

"No, the vaccinations go slow. The villagers are afraid of me."

Melgares laughed harshly. "That is nothing new. My troops stand ready to herd them to your hospital like cattle."

"There are farms and ranchos flung from Taos to the Rio Grande and to the east."

"I will send my soldiers to bring them in."

"That would be most beneficial."

"How much longer, then? I wish to return to Santa Fe as soon as possible. Orders may be awaiting me."

"Orders?"

"It is military business, begging your pardon."

"We will be another three weeks, I estimate."

"Three weeks?" Melgares poured himself another brandy. The man hated idleness, the surgeon knew. Taos was a village full of somnambulists. There were no clocks and there was not much to do. There were no parades, no formations, no balls where the soldiers could preen themselves in front of the ladies.

"At least."

"I must leave here within a week," said Melgares. "You do not have enough vaccine for three more weeks of injections."

"That is why I came here. I need more vaccine. Would you send some troopers to Santa Fe, order more medical supplies? I have a list here."

The surgeon slid a piece of paper from inside his coat, laid it on the table.

Melgares picked it up, looked at it suspiciously.

"What are these other things? They are not vaccines."

"Supplies I need. Some of the people have become my patients. They are very ill."

"Let them die," said Melgares. "Let them beseech their own witch doctors."

"They will die if I don't treat them. I am a physician, Lieutenant. I am bound by my oath as a surgeon to treat the sick."

"And I am bound by my military obligations. I will not send for these things. That will take weeks."

"Very well, then. I had hoped you would cooperate. I will find men to go for me."

"Dr. Larrañaga, I am under orders to escort you, not to provide a supply train. If you do not have enough vaccine or medicines to treat these filthy Indians, these *poblanos,* then that is their ill luck. We must return within the week."

The surgeon rose from his chair, seemingly unruffled. He had found out what he needed to know. Now he would know how to proceed. He had lost this battle, as he had surmised he would, but the final one was yet to come. Melgares would throw a purple fit when he had to escort the Yanqui back to Santa Fe. But Caine would not be able to travel such a distance in a week, even two. Larrañaga needed time, time for his patient to heal. In the meantime, he'd have to stall Melgares and prevent the lieutenant from killing the American on sight.

"Go with God," said the surgeon, heading for the door.

"One week, Doctor."

"We'll see," said Larrañaga, the trace of a smile flickering on his lips.

The door closed behind the surgeon.

"Damn that son of bad milk," cursed Melgares, finishing off the brandy as though it were water. "He's up to something, that bastard. Three weeks my royal ass."

Matt Caine gradually became aware of his surroundings as he experienced more and more lucid intervals between drugged bouts of amnesia and thought-shattering pain.

The woman, Elena, was there with him like a ministering angel, and she became part of his dreams during the long, suffering nights when his body was somehow an alien creature, a huge boulder he pushed up a mountain like Sisyphus, only to have it roll down again, thundering with a hundred violent torments when he reached the top.

She bathed him with soft cloth and warm water, gave him powders for the pain, held his hand when he sweated through his own Gethsemanic garden, touched him when the pain broke beyond his lips into a savage scream of agony, and sometimes both she and Federico had to hold him down on his bed lest he break his wounds open and bleed to death.

Matt knew too that the surgeon came to see him often, and they would talk, in Spanish and in English, but he never retained any memory of the conversations. He knew that he was guarded in his answers because he did not trust the surgeon or his staff of two. He smelled of raw alcohol and liniment, and he dreaded those times when Federico and Elena turned him over in his bed and rubbed his flesh with unguents so that sores did not form. The worst times were when they changed his bedding and had to lift him from his pallet and place him on blankets set directly on the floor.

The surgeon was seldom there during the day, but tending to the endless vaccinations in another quarter. Sometimes, however, he stopped by on his way to the *clinica* and saw that Matt was clean and not reeking of infection.

Elena fed him broth, and at times there were bits of tender meat, chicken, fish, beef, and pork in the stew, and potatoes, leeks, and some kind of grain that he couldn't identify but might have been barley or bleached corn. Elena gave him cool water to drink and talked to him of pleasant things, the *bailes* in Santa Fe, the feast days of saints, the celebration of Christmas, the fair in Chihuahua each September. She told him what the days were like in Taos, and when it grew hot in the afternoon she fanned his face and helped him drink tea made cool in the *olla*, tasting faintly of lime.

Matt grew dependent on Elena, missed her when she was not there, grew angry when she was late in relieving the taciturn and officious Federico. In his sickness, he became like a baby, petulant and demanding, moody and withdrawn. His hunger increased as his body healed, and Elena gradually added more red meat to his diet even though she continued feeding him a thick broth that filled his belly while leaving him hungry for more substantial fare.

After a week Matt awoke to find Elena sitting next to his cot, holding a cup of hot tea.

"Buenos dias," she said.

"Buenos dias, Elena."

"Will you take some tea?"

"I want to get up. I want to see if I can walk."

"No, you must not."

"I have the bad itch," he said. "All over. If I don't get up and walk, I will turn to stone."

She laughed, forcing the cup of tea into his hands. "The surgeon will tell you when you can get up."

"I want to rise now, like Lazarus."

"If you do not calm yourself, Mateo, I will summon the surgeon and Federico. They will strap you down."

"Damn them."

"Ay, such curses so early in the morning."

"They'll get worse if you don't bring me my clothes."

"I will not bring you your clothes."

"Then I'll walk naked upon the land and frighten all the little old ladies and the small children."

Elena laughed again, pushed gently at the cup so that he would drink and forget about his ambulatory desire.

"Drink the tea, Mateo."

She held his head up so that he would not choke.

"You make me feel like a big baby," he said. The tea was just warm enough to swallow. It was sugary and roiled his appetite.

"I want you to feel like a baby. A spoiled child. I am here to spoil you until you get well."

"I feel fit."

"Those are only feelings. They are of the mind, not of the body."

"So, you are a philosopher, are you?"

"I am a nurse."

"And the nurse knows best. *Claro?*"

"Claro que sí."

He liked her laugh. He finished the tea, drinking even the brackish dregs. They too were sweet.

"I'm hungry."

"What would you like to break your fast?"

"Eggs, beefsteak, green chilis, tortillas."

Elena laughed. "Would you also like some tequila to drink with your breakfast?"

"With nails in it."

She made a chiding sound and tapped his lips with a finger, took his cup from him. "Someone will bring your broth, soon."

"Broth again?"

"You are getting better, Mateo."

"I would like to sit in the sun, feel the fresh air on my face."

"Soon, soon," she said.

After he had eaten, he was exhausted and he knew that Elena was right. He wanted to be a man again, but his body was corrupted by lead and damaged further by the surgeon's knife, and the pain was so immense he closed his eyes and spoke no more that day. He wallowed in the pain like some chained beast rolling in a sea of fire, and each wave was more agonizing than the one before, and he was glad when night came and Elena gave him the powders and he could sleep in a place where the pain was far away.

The door closed behind the last patient of the day. Federico was with Caine at the surgeon's quarters that day, since Matt had been restless the night before and Larrañaga thought he might need to be restrained.

Elena was cleaning up the syringes, picking up the soiled *toallas,* straightening up the clinic for the next day's endless stream of the lame and halt.

"Let's talk a little," said the surgeon.

"Why, of course," she said.

"Here's what I would like you to do. I am going to send two men back to Santa Fe for some medicaments and supplies I will need to treat our incognito patient."

"I am at your service, Doctor," said Elena.

Elena listened to the surgeon's instructions. He had told her not to take notes.

"I wish you to cut the patient's hair, shave off his beard."

"How shall I cut his hair?"

"Cut it short, but not in military style. A gentleman's haircut. Shave his face until it is soft and smooth as a newborn's butt."

Elena laughed nervously. "What if he does not wish me to do this?"

"I will talk to him first. It must be done right away. I do not trust Lieutenant Melgares. He will come sniffing around here before long."

"Is Mateo Caine the one they call El Gigante?" she asked.

"Probably. Can you keep this a secret? All of it? How he got here, who he is?"

"For certain," she said politely.

"I am sending Federico to fetch a tailor. I want Senor Caine to be measured for a couple of suits, so that he does not look like a derelict. I want you to throw away those filthy buckskins he had on him. And see if you can find a cobbler to make boots large enough to fit him."

"Ay de mi," she said. "Who is to pay for all this?"

"I will pay," said Larrañaga.

"You are a generous man."

"There is something about Caine that fascinates me. He is not what he seems, not what he pretends to be. He speaks excellent Spanish, yet he affects an English that is lowborn. I feel that there is a gentleman under those filthy buckskins, behind that beard."

"He is probably a spy," she said, so quickly it startled her.

Larrañaga laughed softly. "I have no doubt he is. But that is why we must protect him."

"I don't understand, Doctor."

"The Americans are a land-hungry people. Since secretly buying the Louisiana territories from that scoundrel Napoleon, they realize that the boundaries are in dispute. Mexico is very nervous about this brash young nation. Caine may be the first of many to cross our borders with the intent to lay claim to New Mexico. Then they will pounce on Texas and all the lands between."

"It is treasonous to talk so," she said, "begging the surgeon's pardon."

"Yes, perhaps. But there is a change in the air. If the Americans do cross our borders and Chihuahua loses its hold on New Mexico, it might be good to have a friend in court."

"Why are you telling me this? We could both be killed for harboring a spy."

"We are but small people, Elena. We do not know who this man is. He is just a patient who sought our aid and comfort." He patted her hand.

"I'm afraid," she said.

"Do not have fear, Elena. I have a feeling that Governor Alencaster will be just as fascinated by this strange man as we are. You are fascinated by him, are you not?"

Elena looked sharply at the surgeon. Her heart seemed to skip a beat. "He is somewhat interesting," she said lightly, but could not control the slight quaver in her voice.

"Take good care of him," said the surgeon, closing his satchel.

Before she could say another word, Larrañaga was gone and she was alone in the empty room, a bar of sunlight slanting through the window, motes of dust dancing in its hollow and diaphanous chamber.

Chapter

Sixteen

Elena did not come to Matt's rooms for three days. A Mexican woman gave him water and food during the day, and emptied his slops. A different one stayed with him each night. Each woman was more ugly than the one before. Matt did not talk to them, nor did they pay him much attention. They sat in the chair and sewed or dozed, chewed on tobacco or strange misshapen comestibles that were either dried fruit or piñon nuts. Federico stopped in once to see how he was faring, he said, and to take his measurements. He brought with him a small, humpbacked man with a cloth tape and paper on which to write.

"What is he doing?" Matt asked Federico when the little man laid a tape across his chest.

"He is measuring you for some clothes."

"What happened to my buckskins?"

"They have been taken away. Burned, I think. Or buried."

"Why are you giving me new clothes?"

"The surgeon wants you to look presentable."

"Why?"

"For when you go to Santa Fe and go before the governor."

"Am I prisoner, then?"

Federico shrugged. The little tailor measured Matt's waist, the length of his legs, the girth of his torso. When he wanted Federico to do something, he made small twirls in the air with one hand. Federico turned Matt over, careful not to touch any of the wounds. Matt's dressings had not been changed in two days, but he was used to the smell by then. Everything in the room smelled bad, and even the air that came in from outside smelled of urine, feces, goat and dog, and great unwashed hordes of people who made sandal noises as they passed by.

"Elena will shave you when she returns," said Federico. He seemed very nervous, anxious to leave. "The surgeon says you must remove your beard and have your hair cut. I would change your dressings, but I have to help the surgeon. We are very busy."

"What happened to Elena?"

"Nothing. The soldiers brought in many people from beyond the pueblo. We must get them all vaccinated within the week."

"Why?"

"The soldiers want to return to Santa Fe."

"And take me with them?"

"We will all go under their escort," said Federico. His eyes were furtive, could not settle in their sockets, nor focus on Matt for more than a split second. He kept looking toward the door like a fugitive at the scene of his crime.

"Shit," said Matt.

"*Como?*"

"*Nada.*"

"Are you feeling better, Senor Caine?"

"Well enough."

"Have the patience."

"You mean lie here like a stone and listen to these old women snore and fart at night."

Federico did not laugh. He told the humpback to hurry, hurry. The tailor wrote down his figures and stepped away from Matt's bed without speaking.

"Are you finished?" asked Federico.

The tailor, who seemed to be mute, nodded. His hands made motions in the air, but these were not like Indian sign-talk. They made no sense to Caine.

"He doesn't say much, does he?" asked Matt.

"He has no tongue."

"What happened to him?"

"He is probably not a very good tailor. The Spaniards, I think. He was exiled here from Santa Fe."

"Ah," said Matt.

Federico and the humpbacked tailor left, and Matt lay listening to the sounds of the world outside, the crow of a rooster, the bleating of goats, the tramp of feet, the cries of children and the yells of their mothers. The church bells tolling the masses and benedictions at all hours, the distant bugles at dawn and sunset, the braying of burros and the sad lowing of skeletal longhorn cattle ever on the forage. An old woman came and brought him tortillas and beefsteak, but she picked through the meat and ate most of it herself before she gave him the basket.

"You eat," she said, thrusting the basket at him as if he was a dog.

"Are you sure you do not want all of my food?"

"I have enough."

Matt ate and then the woman took the basket and left him alone.

She sat in her chair like some shadowed creature, her mandibles working as she chewed tobacco, her teeth clicking like darning needles. After a time, she brought out a rosary from the deep folds of her skirt, and these rattled in maddening counterpoint to her murmured sotto voce prayers.

Matt turned away from her and folded an arm across his eyes to shut out the wavering, flickering, erratic, feeble, and equally maddening light from the wall sconce. He tried to shut out the sounds coming from the woman, or assign them to different sources. He imagined only that a large hoop was rolling endlessly around the room, clicking on objects it encountered: small stones, rosary beads, chicken claws, eating utensils.

He longed for Elena, for someone to talk to, and he wondered why he did not think of Morning Lark anymore until just that moment, but it was too late, for sleep crept up on him unawares and he drifted away from the room, with the sounds becoming other noises in nature and of no consequence to his rapture at having escaped from that desolate prison at last.

Matt ate and slept off and on all the next day, when he was visited by still another woman, uglier than any who had come before, and more sullen, if that were possible. He was beginning to think that none wanted to be with him two days or nights in a row. A small boy and a girl brought him supper that night, a small boiled chicken, tortillas, beans, and chili peppers so hot they burned his eyes, his tongue, his throat, his stomach. But he felt some need for them, as if for penance.

He heard the rumble of a water cart as it passed by his window, heard the sloshing in the *ollas,* the clank of the jugs against the wood and against each other. The boy and girl fidgeted and watched him choke on the chilis, and they scratched themselves, cracked moving lice on their heads, crunching them under dirty fingernails and tasting their acids on their tongues.

When Matt was finished eating, the children took the bones and broke them open with their teeth and sucked

them until they whistled like flutes; they chewed the skin
and pieces of meat and tortilla he had left on his plate,
their cheeks bulging like the fat faces of feeding squirrels,
and Matt wished they would go away so he could mourn
for Elena or just be alone with his desolate thoughts. He
was at that stage in his healing when he could not find a
comfortable spot on the bed. Even though it was soft, it
felt hard, from coverlet to underbedding, as if the cloth
had been sewn over thin sheets of hammered iron.

Elena came and sent the children away with a few
whispered words and coins pressed into their hands. She
carried a bowl with her and scissors, a straight razor, a
large comb wrought from a tortoiseshell, towels and soap
and other things that she laid out on a table. Matt watched
her in silence, admiring her tawny skin under the light, the
bones of her face under her translucent skin, and he
thought she must pulse with the blood of Andalusia, and
he could hear the distant wind moaning among the sad ol-
ive trees of Iberia.

The young woman barred the door tightly, stood there
for a long time, listening.

"What passes?" asked Matt in Spanish.

"I have taken care that the soldiers did not follow
me," she said.

"Why would they follow you?"

"The surgeon says they are suspicious." She let out a
long breath and walked toward him. "All week they have
sent out patrols, bringing in people without vaccination
marks, and watching us. That is why we would not come
to see you."

"Is the surgeon hiding me out?" Matt struggled for
the proper words. "Keeping me out of their sight?"

"Yes. But did you not see him?"

"No."

"I think he came down from his bedroom to check on
you each night, but you were asleep."

"He was very quiet," said Matt.

"I am going to take off your bandages and bathe you. Then I am going to shave your face, cut your hair."

"I like my face and hair the way they are."

"It is a thing that must be done." She was whispering, and her words were like the shadows in the room, soft and vagrant. Pale saffron light flickered on the white mud walls. The oily cloy of candlewax mingled with the scents of sickness and the spangled bonds of medicines, thick smelly pastes and thin strands of alcohol all straining for recognition in a room that had gone sour and dank from lack of air and sunlight.

She pulled his covers back, took off the smock they had made for him from a sheet. Her hair was braided and made her look very young, emphasized her high cheekbones. She smelled of fresh flowers, and he knew that she had bathed herself before coming over. He imagined her naked and wet, her body sleek with scented soap and the thicket between her legs dripping water when she stepped from her tub. She leaned over him to remove the musty, blood-threaded bandages, and her breasts came very close to his face.

Matt's arousal was visible, and Elena clucked to herself as she carefully and tenderly pulled the bandage from his hip, untying the cloth and laying each flap aside.

"Ay, you are getting better," she said.

"I am sorry about that."

"Why? You are a man. We are alone. Perhaps you have thoughts that are manly." *Pensamientos machismos.*

"I have missed you."

"And I have missed you."

"Did you pick out the women who came here?"

She laughed softly. "Why do you ask?"

"They were ugly. Crones, every one. *Brujas.*"

"Were not the children a welcome change?"

"Not much."

She laughed again. She soaked the bandage to separate the dried blood from the scab, then worked it back and forth so that there was little pain when she separated it from his body. She examined each wound carefully, and he could not make his penis unswollen. Each time she touched him, it engorged itself with blood like some night-feeding animal.

"I will cleanse and leave these little wounds unwrapped," she said. "They are healing nicely."

"What about the big wound?"

"It is still seeping, but not so much. Be still now. I will bathe you with cold water and alcohol. You will shiver."

"A cold shower, huh?" he asked in English.

"Como?"

"Una broma."

She was merciless with the water and alcohol, and doused his passion. She rubbed dirt from his pores and sopped away the dried blood and made him turn himself. His leg was stiff but full of feeling. The pain made him wince, but he did not show her how bad it was.

"I do not mean to hurt you," she said.

"You clean very well, Elena."

Her name was like a song, a lyrical trill issued from the throat of some magical bird in a green garden. Like the woman of Troy who launched a thousand corsairs across the wine-dark sea in ancient times.

She washed his hair and cut it, and her caresses made him sleepy. His locks fell to the floor like small dark birds' wings, and the snip-snip of the scissors lulled him into a languorous state where he floated just below the surface of night. She soaped his face until it was snowy with lather and began shaving his beard with a surgeon's deftness. The razor made a sound as it scraped across his skin,

hacked away the hairs from the temples to his chin. She
sloshed the razor in the water to clean it, and stropped it
on a leather strap like a barber.

"Samson," she said, her voice a whisper in the quiet
of the room.

"What?"

"Samson and Delilah. I am shearing you of your
power."

"Do not make any dear wagers on that, Elena."

She laughed again and finished the shaving, laved his
face with a wet towel, then dried it with a fresh one. He
reached up, felt his jaw. It was very smooth. He felt even
more naked than he had when she bathed him.

"You look beautiful," she said, stepping away from
him.

"You mean handsome."

"It is the same thing. But you look very handsome,
Mateo. I wish I had brought a mirror."

"I do not want to look at me." His eyes bored into
hers.

"Even your blue eyes look more beautiful now that
the black beard is gone." She combed his wet hair, and
that too felt good, felt soothing and relaxing. He felt pam-
pered as he lay there, naked and once more aroused.

"You have not been with a woman in a long time,"
she said, and there was a dry husk to her voice that made
him want her.

"That is so."

"Perhaps I should go and get one of the hags to stay
with you tonight."

"That would be cruel."

"For both of us, Mateo."

"I want you, Elena."

She leaned over, touched his lips with her index finger. Her touch was soft. "Shhhh," she said. "You must not
talk this way."

"It is the truth. You know it."

"I know," she whispered, taking her finger away from his mouth. "You are not well enough yet."

"We could go slow."

She laughed, a quavering, nervous laugh. "Could we?"

"Don't tease me, Elena."

"No," she said. "That would not be nice."

"*Te quiero,*" he said again.

"*Momento,*" she replied, and in the soft whisper of her voice he heard a promise and a longing, the sensual tone of a young woman in season, and so a conspiracy was born, a pact sealed. She crossed the room to the sconce and snuffed the candles, and he could smell the fumes, see the images of the flames for several seconds, indelible in the sudden darkness.

Then a whisper of cloth, and her form vaguely illumined by the soft pewter light of the moon washing through the windows, bathing her in smoky veils of gauze.

She came to him in the darkness and climbed atop him, so light and feathery he was afraid she would float away before he could embrace her. Yet she was warm and her breath on his face was hot with desire.

"Do not move," she whispered, and then kissed him, and fire flooded his body like a surging lava stream, a bright liquid orange sea that engulfed him, transported him on a slow steaming river through its bubbling depths.

They held each other like desperadoes clutching to life's last moment, like drowners, and she took him inside her so gently and delicately that the blood drained from his skull and left him light-headed and woozy, like a man plunging from a great height, like a soaring Icarus falling wingless and lost to the sea.

Yet in those moments, Elena returned him to health and vigor and reason, taking him into her depths slow and gentle, until they soared together far beyond the reach of the world, deep into a universe brimming and pulsating with stars, into a benighted ether hallowed with their presence, where they became one soul, one radiance, immortal for one single moment in a blinding detonation of flaming and ancient suns.

Chapter
Seventeen

The surgeon set the pricking needle in the tray, heaved a weary sigh that was like the last wheeze of a sailor's squeezebox, and waved the patient toward the door. The peon, in dirty shabby shirt and baggy trousers, shuffled off on worn sandals, holding his tattered straw hat in his hands, just as bewildered and concerned as all the others who had been brought to the *clinica,* forced to undergo the witchery of vaccination.

"Is that the last?" Larrañaga asked Elena.

"Yes, Doctor."

Larrañaga poured water from a porcelain pitcher into a wooden bowl and began to wash his hands, slowly, carefully.

Federico took the tray away, with its bloody cotton wads, scratchers and needles, and began to clean up the soiled detritus of the clinic. Elena started to join him, but Larrañaga stayed her after drying his hands, grasping her arm just above the wrist.

"Then that is the last one we vaccinate. We must leave Taos tomorrow," he said.

"So soon?"

"I wish we had another week here. You know what that means."

"Yes. How will you explain Mateo to Lieutenant Melgares?"

"Did the suits arrive?"

Elena nodded toward a table near the front of the room. There was a large bundle atop it, a much-washed flour sack wrapped in crude brown twine.

"The tailor brought it while you were taking your siesta," she said.

"Good. Take them to my quarters, see that Senor Caine is dressed and groomed. Can he walk?" The surgeon had been coming to his quarters late each night, leaving early each morning.

"He has been pacing a circle in the room for the past two days. Like a caged puma."

"Good, good. Has he got his story straight?"

"He will say that he was ambushed by bandits, robbed and left for dead. Some Indios found him and brought him to Taos. He is a businessman who was on his way to Santa Fe to collect a debt."

"That is the only way that he, or any American, could come to Santa Fe. Otherwise he would be arrested."

"He understands that, Doctor."

"Then he must convince Melgares, and when we get to Santa Fe, he must also convince Governor Alencaster."

"But he has no papers."

"He was robbed. You told him that, did you not? Bandits along the trail."

Elena smiled. So did the surgeon.

"Do not bother to clean up. I will help Federico. Take the suits to Mateo. You barbered him well. He does not look so . . . so formidable anymore."

Elena said nothing, but her face flushed slightly.

"Have you lost your heart to this Yanqui?" asked the surgeon.

"What do you mean?"

"It is of no import. Just take care, eh?"

"I know what I'm doing," she said, but did not meet the surgeon's searching gaze.

"The heart knows," said Larrañaga, "but does the head?"

For that, Elena had no answer. "It seems sad to leave Taos," she said. "Life has been . . . less complicated these past couple of weeks."

"You have cared for our wounded trapper well," he said. "There is no higher calling."

"But now his fate is in the hands of the military, it seems."

"Elena, do not be sad. Life is full of twists and turns. There are changes in the wind. Mexico lost its territory here once before, when its colonists were abandoned and there was trouble between soldiers and civilians."

"I did not know that," she said.

"They did not know whether to treat the Indians as Christians or as conquered peoples. The Indians took matters into their own hands, under a leader named Po-pe, and revolted. They killed everyone except those in the Piro villages and at Isleta, south of Albuquerque, besieged the survivors in Santa Fe. The land ran with Spanish blood. That was in the year of our Lord, 1680, and they held dominion for a dozen years."

"There is much unrest here in Taos," she said.

"And so it is," said the surgeon. "The Indians have long memories, and so does our esteemed governor. I am quite sure that our Senor Caine will make Governor Alencaster quite nervous."

Elena shuddered.

"You'd best go now while there is much of the afternoon left, so that you can dress your patient and perhaps take him for a walk."

"I was hoping I could do that," she said.

"Go," said the surgeon with a benevolent smile.

She picked up the bundle with the new suits inside and left the clinic, strolling through the bowered alameda, across the adobe-bricked plaza, while bronze-faced men— Indians, Mexicans, soldiers—all watched her pass and made crude remarks, leered at her. She walked proudly, her head held high, her chin outthrust. She was a striking sight in a light cotton dress, pale white with evenly spaced blue flowers sewn to the hem and waist, which fitted her gracefully curvaceous form, flared with her movement so that the onlookers caught splendid glimpses of her slender legs, her trim ankles.

She walked through the mud-daubed warren of adobe buildings, her heart half full of feathers, half full of lead. She wanted to see Mateo in his new suit, but she dreaded his meeting with that martinet of a lieutenant, Melgares. The soldier might clap the *americano* in irons just to exert his authority. There was no telling what Alencaster would do when Caine was presented to him.

There was a small *tienda* with no name on one of the back streets. It bore a sign that read: ABARROTES, CARNES, DULCES. The sign leaned against the adobe wall, was taken in each night. Elena entered the dim interior of the store, with its secret scents, walked to a counter made from a wooden door sawed in half, set on crossed logs that had been peeled of bark and tied together with rope and raw-hide.

Streamers of dried chilis hung from the beams in the ceiling, chunks of salted rabbit, antelope, goat, and pig lay in boxes swarming with flies. On shelves there were arrays of beads, spools of thread, and tin mirrors; combs of bone and turtle shell; hand-ground knives, clay and wooden bowls, woolen blankets, buttons of antler and hide, hundreds of what-nots and pretties. Sacks of flour and sugar stood against a wall. The smells were impossible to decipher. Masa flour, corn tortillas steaming on *hornos,* tequila and *aguardiente,* mashed fruit and sour wine, fresh sausage and sage, fowl boiling in a pot, bubbling *adobo* sauces and pickled eggs floating in vinegar-filled jars, apples and figs, onions and cilantro, a million aromas all blended and summoned from kitchens near and far, vagrant in the trapped air of the room, a conspiracy of scents and substances roiling at the nostrils, triggering hunger and desire and memory.

"Buenas, senorita," said the owner, a small-bellied man of mixed blood.

"Have you the pipe?" she asked.

He nodded, turned and stooped to retrieve it from a wooden box.

"A very fine pipe," he said, "made of pipestone from the north, hard and sweet." The pipe was carved out of pink pipestone, threaded with white veins, deftly notched at the square bowl, light in the hand for all its bulk, the stem gracefully curved, all of a piece, like something a sculptor would fashion to stay his hands from idleness between more ambitious creations.

"And the tobacco?"

"Two kilos," said the merchant. "Very dear, very dear, the tobacco."

"We aren't finished yet," she said.

"Ah, yes." The man walked down the counter, rummaged among some cartons and returned with several items.

"This is the serape you ordered. Very, very large. A pair of well-made sandals, very fine leather. Very, very large, also. Two shirts, both for a huge man. And a pair of shoes. Very dear. And very, very large."

"How much for everything?"

The bargaining began. Elena set the bundle of new suits on the counter and engaged in a monetary discussion until she was satisfied she wasn't being cheated and that the store owner was making a fair profit. She counted out the pesos and centavos, spread them on the counter like inlays for a belt.

A small woman entered through the doorway leading to another room, carrying a basket. With her floated smells from her kitchen, piñon smoke, the fine sharp aromas of sugar and baked flour.

"Ah," said Elena. "You have my basket, senora."

The old woman handed Elena the basket, its contents covered with a clean cloth. It was heavy.

"The squabs, the *pan dulce,* and the *papas fritas* are still warm. There is a fine bottle of wine, another of *aguardiente,* and some sweets, as you wished."

"I thank you," said Elena, setting the basket on the counter.

"Dos pesos," said the woman.

Elena gladly paid her. The woman pocketed the coins and left the room.

The store owner dropped her merchandise into a large sack that once had harbored frijoles, and wrapped it tightly.

"You must not tell anyone where you bought the tobacco," he said.

"Por seguro." Elena walked back outside, carrying her two bundles, a jaunty lilt to her step.

As she approached the surgeon's house her heart beat faster, drumming an apprehensive tattoo against her temples, plucking a tendon in her neck so that it throbbed in rapid time like a metronome.

Three boys raced in front of her, rolling willow hoops, propelling them with sticks. They threaded back and forth, one darting in front of another, as if they were braiding invisible rope.

One more corner and she would be on the street where Mateo was staying.

*   *   *

Matt, garbed in a sheet from his bed, the cloth wrapped around his naked body like a Roman toga, one shoulder bare, hair tousled, leaned against the outside adobe wall of the house, his face turned toward the sun. He was barefoot. His chest was a great swelling bellows as he breathed the sweet air of health and freedom. He sucked deeply on the cigarillo, blew a fragile plume of blue smoke into the air. From inside, from the room where he had lain so long, the old woman muttered toneless maledictions as if she was chanting her matins. Matt smiled. The sun felt good on his face. He had paced his room long enough. Yet he dared not venture far from his hospital prison. He knew he faced other travails, and he owed the surgeon some cooperation. Besides, he had no money, no papers, no proof of his identity. Not that this would have done him any good. If his true identity were known, he would be put to the wall or hanged, most likely. Elena had been most insistent that he follow the surgeon's plan and lie through his teeth. After he faced up to Lieutenant Melgares, he would still have to stand before Governor Alencaster and lay the lies on him with a trowel.

The street where the doctor had taken quarters was quiet, nearly vacant at that late hour of the afternoon. Gaunt, mangy-hided dogs lazed in the shade, out of the heat. Matt wondered what month it was. July? August? He did not know. The past weeks were a blur in his mind; time a warped and meaningless fraction in some mathematical Pascalian puzzle.

"That cigarillo is contraband," said the old woman, poking her face outside the door. "You will be arrested by the soldiers if they see you smoking. Besides, you stole it from me. I will be arrested too."

"You will be paid, senora," he said. "Do not worry."

"*Ladrón,*" she spat, her face a wrinkled and toothless mask, then disappeared back into the room.

She had told him that tobacco was illegal to possess

in New Mexico. Except for the *ricos*. But she had given
him the cigarillo on his promise to pay a dear price for it.
She had objected only because he chose to smoke it outside, and was fearful that she might be arrested for selling
him the unlawful tobacco.

Elena had said she would return early that day. Matt
missed her. He had missed her all morning and could not
even sleep after eating his noon meal. The old woman
slept, though, taking her siesta in the chair next to the table by the wall. Her snoring had driven him mad. When
she awoke and lit a cigarillo, he had a sudden craving to
draw smoke into his lungs. He missed his pipe too.

He savored the cigarette, smoked it down to a stub.
When it burnt his fingers, he threw it down and watched
it burn itself out.

Movement caught his eye. He looked up, saw three
boys with hoops racing toward him. He watched in fascination as they flashed by, dashing erratically back and
forth, brown skins sleek with summer sweat, grins white
as starch.

"Hoopties," Matt declared as they whizzed by him.
Then Elena turned the same corner from whence the hoop
racers had come, weighted down like a pack mule with
packages. He grinned and loped toward her, dragging his
sheet in the dirt, holding it tight to keep it from falling
away.

At the sight of him, Elena started to laugh. She
dropped two of the bundles, but held on to the picnic basket.

"Mateo," she shrieked as he, like some Roman sena-
tor, unkempt and barefoot, lumbered toward her, huge
hairy legs appearing from under the sheet, grinning like
some half-mad Cicero.

Matt took Elena in his arms, cocooned her in his
sheet like some huge winged creature swarming at her, and
she let the basket drop to the ground, lest she be smoth-

ered and kept prisoner right out there on the open street in front of God and everyone who lived there.

"Elena, Elena," he breathed in her ear, "you have come to rescue me from the witches of Taos, deliver me from the evil clutches of the meanest woman in New Mexico."

She pushed him away, laughing. "I have come," she said, "to dress you decently, and to take you to the river for a very private meal before anyone takes you off to the insane asylum."

"I thought this was the asylum," he said.

"Help me carry these packages," she said, "and try to behave with some dignity until we get inside your room."

"I want you," he said softly. "Right here. Right now."

"Oh, you savage," she said, picking up the basket.

Matt grabbed up the bundles, hardly stooping to retrieve them, and he followed after her like a worshiping anchorite, his sheet slipping from his one shoulder until it hung only at his waist, held there by the bundles he clutched to him, and trailing like an obscene and meretricious bridal gown in his ungainly wake.

Chapter Eighteen

Elena paid the old woman for the cigarillo she had given Matt and shooed her away. The crone grumbled and cackled like a disturbed nesting hen with the croup as she scurried through the door, sewing basket clinging to her arm like some grotesque appendage.

"Nice lady," said Matt.

"With a mouth like a freight hauler," said Elena.

"She was very eloquent."

"Be quiet. We have many things to do, Mateo."

Elena made Matt try on all the clothing, first the suits the surgeon had instructed the tailor to make for him. They were the suits of a gentleman, one made from coarse heavy linen dyed black, the other from a finer material, a royal blue. She dressed him as if he was some huge doll. To her surprise, there were shirts from the tailor, too, that fit him perfectly, of fine white linen, blue and red and green, four of them, all delicately embroidered, with flaring cuffs of different design.

"You look like a caballero," she said.

"I've never worn anything so fine," he told her.

"The surgeon has good taste," she said.

"I feel like a dandy."

"What is this dandy?"

"A kind of gentleman coward," he said, not knowing a word in Spanish for "sissy."

"When we get to Santa Fe, I will take you to a boot-maker."

"How will I pay for boots? I have no money."

"Do you have a trade?"

Matt considered how much he dared reveal about himself to this woman. "I am a carpenter," he said finally.

"Good. There is plenty of such work. Do you make cabinets?"

"Yes." He had learned the skills from his father, but it had been a long time since he had used chisel and plane, worked with wood. But he loved the trade, and had he not gone into the army, he surely would have pursued that profession, as his father had before him.

"Here are some pants, a shirt, and sandals for you to wear today," she said, handing him the package she had gotten from the *tienda.* "I thought we might walk to the river and have our supper in the cool of the evening."

"I thought I smelled food," said Matt. He took her in his arms and kissed her, a long lingering kiss. She returned it with passion, clutching him to her bosom with a ferocity that surprised him. Then, abruptly, she pulled away and smoothed her dress.

"It is a long walk," she said. "Will your leg hold up?"

"I feel a tightness there, but yes, I feel like walking. With you."

"It is a beautiful afternoon. It will be cool by the river."

Matt began to dress. He enjoyed flexing his legs. Elena watched him with frank admiration. She laid out his other clothing neatly on a table, stacked the shirts and trousers together. She hung the coats on large dowels held fast in the adobe wall. Matt tried on the sandals. They fit, as did the light shirt and trousers. She furtively concealed the pipe and tobacco she had bought him in one of the empty sacks, stuffed into the wicker basket.

"You need a sash," she said. "And boots."

He twirled in a circle, and she laughed at his posing.

"Come," she said. "Can you carry the basket?"

"May I look inside?"

"No, Mateo. It is to be a *sorpresa*."

"It is already a surprise."

He lifted the basket. She took his arm and led him outside, then released him.

"Can we not hold hands?" he asked.

"Not in the pueblo," she said. "When we are beyond the prying eyes that even now watch us through the shutters."

Matt looked up and down the *calle*. Amazingly, there were sombreroed men standing outside the faceless adobes, women tending to flowers in clay pots or talking together quietly. He had not seen a soul when he'd taken his smoke, except for the trio of boys with their rolling hoops. Elena tossed her head proudly and began walking, and he followed her, caught up with her. He had to slow his stride to keep from leaving her behind him. It felt good to be walking. He felt giddy and his legs did not seem natural to him. They were rubbery and seemed about to collapse under him.

As they walked along the winding street, pigeons flapped in discordant formations, flew aimlessly from flat rooftops, bellies swollen as if they carried ballast and must struggle to stay airborne. Some swirled and wheeled in the air like debris in a whirlwind before they fanned out and landed again.

After a mile, as they left the main boundary of the

pueblo, his legs felt stronger. The slight tug in his hip did not bother him and he felt no pain.

They left behind the cluster of adobes that composed the village, large clay blocks with streamers of piñon smoke hanging like vaporous pennants above them. There were a few scattered adobes here and there, little farms and ranchos that seemed like afterthoughts, or the dwellings of outcasts and hermits. A roadrunner dashed from cover and bobbed down the wagon path toward the river until it left the road and disappeared. Yucca sprouted everywhere, and they heard quail calling in the distance. The land was dotted with sagebrush, rabbit brush, and juniper. The air was sweet in Matt's lungs, and when they dropped below a rise, the village disappeared like the wild birds and Elena took his hand in hers.

A pair of mourning doves in whistling flight hurtled overhead, twisting and turning like winged gray darts arcing along secret transits that bore some arcane relationship to the sun's slow magnetic path across the endless blue of the sky.

Lieutenant Melgares set a bulging satchel beneath the table that served as his desk and listened in stony silence as the surgeon told him of his patient, one Matthew Caine, a businessman from St. Louis, robbed and shot and left for dead on his way to collect a legal debt in Santa Fe.

"Why did you not tell me of this man before?" He fixed Larrañaga with a gaze hard and dark as a Spanish dagger. Although the soldier was seated at his desk in his headquarters, he appeared ready to leap across it and throttle the doctor.

"I did not think the man would live, at first, and then he was unconscious for a very long time. His brain was addled from the beating he suffered, and I was not able to determine who he was."

"He is a Yanqui?"

"Here on legitimate business, as I told you."

"Who were these *bandidos,* these *ladrones*?"

"I do not know. He does not know." The surgeon appeared very calm and poised, almost maddeningly so to Melgares, who was seething in a volcanic fury.

"Is he a big man?"

"He is a large man. He appears to be a gentleman."

"We have been looking for just such a man."

"Oh," the surgeon said airily, "I doubt you would have trouble finding this one had you searched for him."

"Perhaps he is El Gigante. If so, he is a spy. He must be taken into custody."

"No, I do not think Senor Caine is El Gigante. He had no weapons and he appears to have breeding. He is not at all wild."

"I want to see this man," said Melgares.

"Tomorrow," said the surgeon. "He should be fit enough to travel."

"How do you know he will not run away now that he is well?"

"He is not that well yet. His wounds were very serious. He is, ah, a cripple for the time being. He will not run away."

"Still, I think I should post a guard on this man."

"I will guarantee his appearance tomorrow."

Melgares snorted, turned away. When he turned back, he lay his hands flat on his desk. He booted the satchel beneath his desk out of the way.

"I want to question this Caine. Do you have any objection?"

"No. I want him to rest tonight, so that he may travel when we leave Taos. He really needs another week of rest."

"I do not like this," said Melgares. "I do not like secrets."

"A doctor's discretion," said the surgeon. "I beg the lieutenant's pardon if I caused you alarm. As I said, the man was in danger of losing his life. He had lost a considerable amount of blood and had severe contusions."

"He could have gained these in a fight with New Mexican soldiers."

"Oh, come now, Don Facundo. Had soldiers shot him, they would have either killed him or brought him to Santa Fe for questioning. Is this not so?"

"Perhaps." Melgares regarded a large fly that buzzed past his face. He seemed about to reach out and snatch it from the air. Instead he stood up, leaned over the table. He looked down at the surgeon as if he were, like the fly, a type of bug. "Doctor, I must make a full report of this incident upon my return to Santa Fe. If you are wrong about this man, then you will be punished."

The surgeon stood up, unruffled. He stared, eye to eye, at Melgares.

"I could have said nothing, Lieutenant. I could have left the American gentleman here in Taos, and none would be the wiser. I am sure he could have made it back to his own country, in time."

Melgares drew a deep breath through his nostrils. His lips were clamped down tight and he blew the air back out his nose before he spoke.

"I hope I am not making a mistake in trusting you, Doctor. I want that man brought before me in the morning at six hours of the clock."

"So early?"

"If you are not here, I will shoot you both."

"Good afternoon, Lieutenant," said the surgeon crisply.

"Until tomorrow, Doctor."

"Claro que sí, Teniente."

Lieutenant Don Facundo Melgares stared at the door a long time after the surgeon left his office. Then he reached down and picked up the satchel beneath his desk. He opened it, pulled out a sheet of foolscap, a container of ink, and a quill pen sheathed in a small wooden box. He began to write furiously in flowing script, blowing on the ink as he hunched over the report that he would send to the *comandante* in Santa Fe before the sun set.

When he had finished, he fanned the air with the paper, then folded it in thirds. He placed the dispatch in an envelope. He took a magnifying glass from the satchel, a stick of beeswax. He walked to the window with the letter, the wax, and the burning glass. He caught the sunbeam in the glass, aimed it at the wax until it began to melt. He held the envelope beneath it until a thick blob of wax formed at the apex of the flap. When it was of sufficient dimensions, he removed his signet ring and pushed it into the hot wax, sealing the envelope. He walked back to the table, put everything back in the satchel except the envelope, and called loudly for his aide. He sat there, waiting, with both of his fists clenched, until the bones showed luminous and white beneath the taut skin of his knuckles.

Elena and Matt sat on the sloping, rocky bank of the Rio Grande, staring into its swirling muddy depths as if seeking omens and portents. Shadows stretched toward them from the yucca plants a few yards away, their yellow flowers dried to shriveled cups, their stalks brittle and seared from the ardent sun of summer.

Matt had not surveyed the Rio Grande this far south; it was already running very low this far from its source. It was not the same river, but somehow it was.

"The river is thin here," he said.

"This time of year it will be dry farther south. Until the spring."

"Hard to imagine such a great river becoming so tame."

"You have seen it running full, then?" Elena asked.

"Yes," he said.

Bats streaked low over the river, scouring the air for insects, and they watched a snake inch along the opposite shore, flowing over the rocks like an elongated shadow until it disappeared in a cluster of rocks.

"Do you have hunger?" she asked. "The food may be cold by now."

"I have hunger," he admitted.

She spread the food out on the cloths.

"Squabs," he said, thinking it had been a long time since he had eaten young pigeon.

"Will you open the wine?"

The cork jutted from the bottle. He pulled it with his teeth.

"I forgot cups," she said.

They ate with their fingers, the fried potatoes, the squabs, the *pan dulce*. There were pastries dipped in sugar, and they ate, these two, sitting there in the gloaming as silent smelters razed the western sky.

"You looked funny wearing the sheet," she said when they were finished eating. There was still a third of a bottle of wine left, and a full bottle of brandy.

He looked down at the trousers she had bought him, his sandaled feet. "I look funny now," he said. "But decent."

"I wanted to have this evening with you. Alone. Away from the pueblo."

"Yes. I am very happy."

"I too am very happy," she said.

"You have not always been so," he told her.

"No."

"Tell me about yourself. Where you were born. What your parents were like. Where you studied."

Elena laughed. "You want to know so much," she said. "The truth is that my parents sent me to a convent. I ran away and went to work for Dr. Larrañaga. My father was Spanish, from Andalusia, and my mother was mestiza. I do not know much about them. They died while I was in the convent. I was their only child."

"Why did you run away."

"I did not like the life. I wanted freedom."

"And Dr. Larrañaga just took you in."

"I cared for the sick at Our Lady of the Sorrows convent. I wanted to be a nurse."

"But not for the good sisters."

"No." Elena looked away, off into the gathering coral twilight. Her eyes looked wistful. A church bell tolled in the village of Taos as if echoing the sadness. It sounded faraway.

Matt looked at the brooding Sangre de Cristo range, the tallest peaks mantled in snow, backlit by a pageantry of cold fire emblazoned on the sky's distant backdrop.

"Who are you, Mateo?" she asked when she turned back to him, her face darkened like the dusky sage that rimmed the ridge of the riverbank. "Where did you come from?"

"I am just a wanderer, Elena. An American."

"You do not want to tell me."

"My father was Scots-Irish. My mother was English, I suppose. We do not take much stock in where we came from. We are just glad we're Americans."

"I think there is more to you than just that, Mateo. I see a man here with me. A strong man. A man of adventure perhaps. A man with a mission."

Her hand found his and they were silent for several moments as the sky turned iodine, the shadows deepening in the flowing river.

"You are very perceptive, Elena," he said. "You look at me and see only one man. But I'm really two. There is a hidden person inside of me, making me move and talk and keep secrets. Secrets I don't want to keep, but must."

"You are a man of mystery, then."

"And so are we all."

"Who is hidden inside you, Mateo? A monster?"

"Maybe. Sometimes he seems like a monster."

"I cannot see this other man. I see only a gentle one."

Matt sighed, as if releasing something pent up inside of him, something he had held deep inside him for a long time. When he spoke, he had to struggle for the exact Spanish words to express himself. His speech was halting at first, then flowed from him as if the tongue were his native language.

"Sometimes I feel ... empires moving through me," he said, "... the surge of civilization itself ... flowing westward like a great river, knocking down everything in its path, sweeping me and millions of souls along with it. At other times, I feel utterly alone and lost, like the last man on earth—or the first—and I wonder if this isn't all a dream."

"Do you have fear, Mateo?"

"I am confused. But then, I look at the river, this grand thing, this mighty outpouring of nature's lifeblood, and I feel part of it all—part of the sky, the earth, part of all mankind from the moment of creation until now and even beyond—into the future."

"You are a puzzling man, Mateo. You sound almost like a priest. Or a poet."

"I am a soldier," he said, "and that means I am all three."

"Truly?"

"Truly."

"Then it is very dangerous for you here."

"Yes. But I knew that when I came to the mountains."

"You seem to know many things," she said.

"What things?"

"There are things you do to me that make me think you know how to make a woman happy."

"I want to make you happy, Elena."

"You do. Very happy. You must have known many women."

"Not many."

"You are unlike any man I have known."

Matt said nothing.

"You are tender, Mateo. You seem to know a woman's heart."

"I do not understand what you are saying, Elena. I am just a man. You are a woman. We come together and we make love."

"Your Spanish is strange when you speak on this subject. Love."

"It is a difficult subject," he said.

"The way you touch me. The way you kiss me. That is very pleasing to me. You know so many ways to give pleasure to a woman."

"Perhaps you show me the ways I might give pleasure to you. You are like a flower, and I am a bee at your mouth, taking honey."

She wriggled against him, shivering with desire. Her voice dropped to a husky whisper when next she spoke.

"I will not ask you anything more," she said. "You must forget all this when you meet Melgares."

"Yes," he said. "I will remember who I am supposed to be."

"That will not be difficult for you, Mateo?"

"No. I have been someone else for a long time."

He kissed her then, and they made love there as the

nighthawks whispered overhead, coyotes called across the darkened land, and the fallen sun painted a last flaming memorial of the day beyond the towering peaks of the Sangre de Cristos, rising like distant white monuments above the ghostly plain.

Chapter

Nineteen

D awn was a raging inferno in the eastern sky, silent as a painting, eloquent as a lion's roar. Matt watched the flames spread across the horizon and knew that there would be rain before the day was done. He looked westward toward the mountains and saw the sullen clouds banked behind the ragged towers of the Sangre de Cristos, scrawls of mare's tails straying aimlessly, lost to the north, beyond Raton Pass. The mountains themselves were bathed in the soft blood of dawn.

Dr. Larrañaga emerged from his quarters, followed by a young man carrying his luggage. The surgeon carried his surgical bag, however.

"Are you ready, Señor Caine?"

Matt picked up the two bundles of clothes. Elena had put them in large flour sacks, tied them with twine. He placed them on his shoulders like a stevedore.

"Ready, Doctor."

"It is too early. Even thieves sleep at this hour."

Matt laughed. "Then we are lucky."

"Perhaps. I don't trust Melgares. Take care you do not say too much to him."

"He wants blood, does he?"

"He is a most dedicated soldier."

"The best kind," said Matt. The surgeon gave him a sharp look but said nothing. He started out, followed by the youth carrying his baggage. Matt followed. A lone church bell pealed a solemn invitation to morning mass, its echoes hollow among the silent adobe buildings.

"I wished to have dinner with you last night, but I could not find you."

"I walked to the river," said Matt.

"With Elena?"

"Yes. She brought us food and wine."

"She is a fine young woman. Like a daughter to me."

Matt wondered if the surgeon was warning him off. "She spoke of you," he said. "With affection."

"She is very young. With little experience."

"She seems to know her own mind."

"Perhaps."

The men spoke no more as they walked down the deserted street amid the raucous cockcrows of morning, the distant bark of dogs aprowl. Matt, wearing one of his new suits and shoes, dwarfed the surgeon, and when they entered the plaza, Matt had to duck under the arch. Across the way he saw Elena and Federico standing by a carriage in front of Melgares's headquarters. She wore a simple dark dress, black shoes. She looked elegant, Matt thought.

"Ah, there they are," said the surgeon.

"We are riding in a coach?" asked Matt.

"Yes. It will be quite comfortable. Come. I want to introduce you to Lieutenant Melgares. Be careful what you say."

The Mexican troops stood by their horses, lined up in twos. All of their horses were white. At the head of the column an orderly held on to the reins of a coal-black horse bearing a silver-studded Mexican saddle, finely tooled. All of the horses were magnificent, their coats curried and clean, their tack polished, gleaming even in the muted light of the *madrugada*.

"Good morning, Mateo," said Elena. "Good morning, Doctor."

"Good morning," chorused both men.

"Good morning," said Federico.

"We'll be a moment," said the surgeon.

"The lieutenant is waiting for you in his office," said Federico.

The surgeon told the boy to put his baggage aboard the coach. He held on to his medical satchel. Federico and Elena divested Matt of his bundles. Federico climbed atop the carriage and placed the bundles there, strapped them down.

"Come with me, Señor Caine," said Larrañaga when their luggage was loaded. "This should not take long."

Matt followed obediently, ducking through the doorway as they entered the outer office of the temporary headquarters. The room was bare, stripped of its army identity a few moments before. A single orderly stood at attention before the lieutenant's door. He rapped twice on the door.

"*Entran,*" said Melgares. The orderly opened the door for Matt and the surgeon, closed it behind them.

Melgares stood next to a window, peering out at the sky. His eyes tracked a flock of pigeons wheeling overhead in tight formation only to disintegrate like a scattering of confetti as they lit in the branches of a dead tree standing before a vacant clerestory just beyond the courtyard. The lieutenant turned when the two men entered his office. His desk was completely bare, the room bereft of any sign that he had ever used it for an office. A granddaddy longlegs inched across the ceiling like some arcane measuring instrument defying the laws of gravity.

"Lieutenant Melgares, may I present to you Matthew Caine."

Matt towered above the lieutenant. He did not offer
his hand, nor did Melgares offer his. Instead the two men
looked at each other. Matt stood with shoulders squared,
his back straight, his shoes close together. He might have
been a larger version of the Mexican officer except for his
lack of uniform.

"Do you care to sit, Señor Caine?"

"No."

"You are an American?"

"I am."

"Will you state your business in the state of New
Mexico?"

"I came here to beseech your governor to assist me in
the collection of a legal debt."

"You speak our language very well," said Melgares.
"Where did you learn it?"

"I learned some in school. Some in New Orleans."

"Do you have proof of your citizenship? Papers de-
tailing this debt of which you speak?"

"No, Lieutenant. I was set upon by bandits and
robbed of all my possessions."

"Where did this event occur?" The lieutenant's eyes
never left Caine's, and Caine's did not avert nor flicker.

"Somewhere near the Cimarron cutoff," Cain lied.

"How did you get to the pueblos de Taos?"

"I do not know. The surgeon told me that I was
brought in by Indians."

"I see. Well, we will proceed to Santa Fe at once.
There, you will be granted an audience with Governor
Alencaster. In the meantime, you will consider yourself
my prisoner."

"Lieutenant Melgares," sputtered the surgeon. "I
must protest."

"You will not be shackled or bound, Señor Caine, but
you will be guarded by my troops. Should you try to run
away, you will be shot."

"Lieutenant ..." The surgeon stepped forward, was halted in his tracks by the flat of Melgares's hand.

"Those are my orders," said Melgares. "Do you understand?"

"I understand," said Caine. "I assure you that I am unable to run even if I wanted to."

"He is still a patient of mine," said the surgeon. "I must protest this insulting treatment of an American citizen seeking sanctuary in our country."

"We will see what sanctuary awaits the American in Santa Fe," said Melgares coldly. "Now, let us depart."

Melgares ushered the surgeon and Caine through the door, closing it behind him. When they left the room, two soldiers with rifles fell in beside Caine.

Outside, the lieutenant rattled a series of orders to his men. The two guards opened the doors of the coach, stood there while Elena, Federico, and Larrañaga climbed inside. Then they nodded to Matt. He climbed into the coach, sat next to Elena. They faced Federico and the surgeon in the opposite seat.

The guards climbed up on the rear boot and sat there, rifles across their laps. A driver and a rifleman climbed up on the front seat high above the horses. The driver took up the reins, held on to the brake. The horses snorted and shook, rattling the harness and jingling the buckles.

"I brought refreshments," said Elena, pointing to the carpetbag at her feet.

"So did I," said Larrañaga, jutting a thumb toward the medical bag at his feet.

"Melgares will ride all night. He will not stop except to allow us to relieve ourselves. Even that will not be often."

"I have a slop jar," said Federico. They all laughed.

"When will we be in Santa Fe?"

"Tomorrow night," said the surgeon. "Perhaps sooner. The road should be good. It has been dry."

"There will be rain tomorrow," said Caine. The others looked at him as if he had just made an oracular pronouncement. But none questioned his prediction.

The coach began to move, its wheels grating on the cobblestones. They moved from the pueblo slowly, picked up speed as they cleared the village. Matt looked out when they made the turn south, saw the troops riding two by two on their white horses. Melgares stood out on his black horse. They looked like a military detachment in a parade, with their banners flapping in the breeze, their lances glistening in the rising sun.

The talk inside died away. At noon the column halted and they ate outside in the shade of the coach. Cold tortillas and *bistec, frijoles refritos,* lemony tea. The soldiers sat in the shade of their mounts, eating the same fare. Matt noticed that the food came from a wagon that had been following them, was passed out by a man he took to be a civilian cook. He wore a leather apron, a straw sombrero, and the white garb of a peon. The meals were served in small *canastas* covered with moist cornhusks. When the meal was over, the *cocinero* collected all the baskets and carried them to the wagon. Matt's two guards sat nearby, their rifles never far from hand.

Several of the soldiers relieved themselves. Matt, Federico, and Larrañaga did the same. Caine wondered about Elena, then saw her returning from behind a small hillock where she had gone to urinate.

When the order was given, the foursome got back in the coach, the troops formed up, and the procession moved out again.

Dust spooled past them as they rode, and even with the leather curtains pulled down, grit filtered inside the coach. It became unbearably hot, and Federico slid the coverings up so that they could have a little breeze with the choking dust.

The surgeon and Federico both slept, leaning against opposite sides of the couch. Elena held Matt's hand.

"You look very beautiful today," she whispered. "Very handsome."

"Thank you."

"The suit fits you well?"

"Perfectly, Elena."

The surgeon began to snore. Elena giggled, squeezed Matt's hand.

"You look beautiful today yourself, señorita."

"A million of thanks, Mateo."

They rocked from side to side in the coach as it rumbled over the rough road. Soldiers passed them every now and then and looked inside the coach. Elena and Matt ignored them.

"Tell me, Mateo," she said, "tell me more about these *juptis* you talk about. You spoke of them when you were dreaming. When I asked you about them before, you would not tell me. I am dying of curiosity."

"Hoopties? *Arquitos. Chiquitos cercos.* They're just the peculiar way I see life, Elena. As a little hoop each man carries. No beginning, no end, but rolling on through time and space until he and his little hoop of life disappear."

"This is a very difficult thought, no? Deep?"

"Maybe. Seeing life as a hoop makes it easier to understand. And if you make the hoops small, hoopties, then life does not seem so formidable."

"It is hard for me to see life as a hoop. Even as a little hoop."

"The Indians believe that the heavens, the earth, all life, is round. A circle. And the circle is sacred. Holy."

"Where did you learn that?"

"I lived with the Shoshones," he said.

"Heathens."

"They are not Catholic, but they believe in a great

god, a great spirit that is in all things—rocks, trees, grass, people, animals."

"Those are pagan beliefs, Mateo," she chided.

"They are beliefs, nonetheless, and who is to say that they are not true?"

"The priests. They would say that these things are not so."

"Perhaps the priests do not know everything there is to know about life."

"Mateo, shh. You must not talk this way. You sound like a heretic."

"Perhaps the world needs a few more heretics," he said, his whisper growing louder.

"I love to hear you talk," she said, her voice almost a sigh.

"Is your curiosity satisfied?"

"About the hoopties, yes."

"Well, do not get too curious about other things."

She put an arm around his waist and snuggled into him. The land blurred by, and the soldiers stopped checking on them. Soon they slept, and when they awoke, the surgeon and Federico were awake. Elena pulled away from Matt and straightened her dress, patted her hair.

"Did you sleep well?" asked Larrañaga, looking at Matt.

"Very well, Doctor."

"Call me Jorge, *por favor*."

"Jorge."

"Governor Alencaster will probably detain you. He might put you under bond."

"I would not be able to post a bond."

"It is a technicality. I will help all I can."

"Thank you, Jorge. I am grateful to you."

"It is nothing."

They spoke no more for a long time. The afternoon seemed endless. The heat inside the coach was oppressive, ιike being inside a furnace. Later the breeze began to cool. The horses slowed as the coach pulled a grade, and then they were going downhill. Matt looked out and saw nothing but barren desert, rocks, junipers, sage, an occasional jackrabbit, and the Sangre de Cristos looming above a murky haze, their edges softened, the snows on their peaks like dirty rags. The heat shimmered off the land in the foreground like a surrealistic painting reflected in a smoky mirror.

Elena slipped a rosary from her pocket, crossed herself and began saying her beads. She had given her confession that morning, was now completing the penance given her by the priest. Matt dozed again. Federico was sound asleep. The surgeon fanned his face with a handkerchief, dabbed the sweat dry on his forehead.

They passed an occasional adobe dwelling, drenched bloodred in the waning afternoon sun. Matt awakened when the column stopped at a well, and they spent thirty minutes watering the horses at the stone trough. The passengers drank from canteens, constantly refilling them. The mountains began to fill with shadows when Melgares gave the order to continue their journey.

"It's going to be a long night," said Larrañaga as he held on to a strap to keep from sliding back and forth across the seat. The coach rocked and swayed, its wheels clattering on rough stone. The sun sank behind the mountains, leaving behind a massive blaze across the firmament like the mute core of a banked blast furnace.

Melgares halted the column and they ate a cold supper with the sunset still hanging in the sky like a reflected prairie fire from some distant unknown plain. The land seemed like a landscape on another planet as the shadows stretched long and thin from bush and tree, thickened beneath the brooding fortress walls of the mountains. The canyons harbored the darkest shadows, and these began to spread upward and outward as the golden sky faded to dust and smoke.

Later, when the column was moving again, the coach rocking its passengers to sleep, the clouds moved in from the north and rain began to patter against the sides of the coach. Matt and Larrañaga awoke and closed the windows, plunging the interior into darkness, like pulling the lid down on a coffin.

The wind stiffened and hurled the rain against the coach like scattershot. The driver and his companion huddled in slickers as the mounted soldiers rode on, their white horses ghostly in the dark, Melgares seated on his invisible black steed so that he appeared to be riding on the night itself.

Chapter

Twenty

The coach, its black lacquered hide layered in dust, its wheels spinning off mud from the storm of the night before, escorted by Melgares and his men, pulled into Santa Fe late the next afternoon under clear cobalt skies. The column proceeded down Calle San Francisco, slowly, the tired troopers still proud and stiff in their saddles, pennants flapping in the light breeze. The street was filled with people, burros, dogs, cats, children, chickens. Beggars squatting against adobe walls, both men and women, held out empty palms or blindly clawed at hair lice scrambling on their skulls, sent scurrying through follicle forests by the beat of the sun. Many of the drab adobe buildings were one-storied, but some were two stories, with balconies, which did little to break up the monotony created by flat planes of the stacked mud bricks in an endless row of hovels. Soldiers, off duty, waved to the procession as it passed, saluted Melgares.

Burros, loaded with wood, clogged the street, and the soldiers drove them and their drovers to the sidelines. Small boys jumped onto the chuckwagon and tried to break the lock and get at the food, but they gave up and leaped off, landing on the run, laughing at their own daring. The coach filled with the smells of juniper smoke and corn tortillas steaming on the domes of *hornos,* animal dung and urine, lye soap and the fresh scents of laundered clothing flapping disconsolately in the breeze. A thousand smells and a thousand sounds displaced the high desert air inside the coach, jarring the passengers out of the wild empty spaces and back into the turmoil of civilization.

The coach stopped just outside the guarded gates of the presidio. A few moments later the gates opened and the coach started up again. Once all the troops were inside the compound, an officer ordered the column to halt.

"We are here," said Elena, patting her hair.

Several soldiers appeared at the coach door. One of them opened it, while another held his rifle at the ready.

"Outside," barked the soldier, pointing his rifle at Caine.

"What is the meaning of this?" asked Larrañaga.

"We have orders to take this man into custody, Doctor," replied the trooper.

"Whose orders?"

"The *comandante* of the presidio."

Matt stepped outside. He was immediately surrounded by a half-dozen armed foot soldiers.

"I don't understand," Elena said to the surgeon.

"I'll see what I can find out," replied Larrañaga.

"A coach will take you to your homes, Doctor," said the soldier. "It should arrive very soon. The governor extends you a most cordial welcome. He requests that you call on him once you are refreshed and rested."

"Thank you, Corporal," said the surgeon, somewhat mollified.

Matt stood there in his rumpled suit, a Gulliver among Lilliputians, hatless, his jaw shadowed by beard stubble. His new shoes pinched his feet some, but they felt better than they had when they started out from Taos. He flexed his calf muscles and feeling returned to his legs. He carried only his pipe and some tobacco. The soldiers flanked him, dropped into formation, marched him away. He turned to look at Elena. He saw that she was struggling not to weep. She looked small and stricken.

No sign of Melgares. The parade ground was empty except for clots of soldiers staring at the guard detail and the tall American walking toward the headquarters building, with its flags flying above the skyline, its cannons pointing toward the front gate. Matt saw the castlelike churches rising above the adobe city like medieval fortresses, bricked and formidable.

The soldiers halted outside the headquarters building, between two cannons. After the detail was announced, they entered into a cold, dark passageway and marched down a corridor. Matt was ushered into a large room. Behind a large cherrywood desk sat an imposing man in khaki uniform, his chest bedecked with ribbons and medals.

Matt looked sharply at the large map on the wall behind the desk. It showed the territory north of the Rio Grande claimed by Mexico. He wished he could study it more carefully, check it against his own notes on the grand river's source in the Rocky Mountains. He quickly averted his gaze, scanned the room.

Melgares stood at rigid attention next to the desk. On the right, in a large leather chair, a well-dressed man sat, his legs crossed, one arm draped over the back of the chair. He looked important, with his embroidered shirt, his polished kidskin boots, his sharply pressed trousers. He smoked a small cigar, blowing long thin plumes of blue smoke into the air after each puff.

The man at the desk, who resembled a human gargoyle, with his round face, bulging eyes, deeply-furrowed forehead, tousled curly hair, handlebar moustache, broad sideburns, leaned forward, spoke to Caine.

"I am acting *comandante* of the presidio of Santa Fe," he said in Spanish. "I am called General Carlos Tomás Cardoza de Molina." The *comandante* stood up, gestured to the distinguished-looking man in the chair to his left. "And this is the most esteemed Joaquin Reál Alencaster, governor of Santa Fe. You already know Lieutenant Don Facundo Melgares."

Matt nodded to each man, but his gaze lingered on the governor's. Their eyes met and there was a flash of recognition between them, as if they were gladiators in the emperor's arena, facing each other for the first time, neither armed, but knowing they would soon be engaged in mortal combat.

"I will be as brief as possible," said Cardoza.

Matt turned to look at the *comandante*, but his glance swept the room, with its walls of armored breastplates and conquistador helmets; crossed swords with their gleaming Toledo blades; a pair of Spanish dueling pistols; a matchlock rifle and an old blunderbuss; a fowling piece, hand-tooled; a globe on a small table; books; a bar, with a model of a Spanish galleon atop it. On the *comandante*'s desk stood a replica of an artillery piece, a four-pounder cannon on wheels, sitting next to an inkwell, a feathered stylus jutting from its stygian maw.

Cardoza glanced at the stack of reports on his desk, most of them written on foolscap. He riffled through them as a fortune-teller would shuffle the tarot deck and extracted one sheet that made the muscles on his neck swell like a bulldog's in the rut.

"I will speak in English, so that you understand me perfectly. Everyone in the room here speaks your tongue. You will please respond in that language."

"Why, shore," Matt drawled. Out of the corner of his eye he saw the governor twitch visibly.

"What are you doing on Spanish soil?" The *coman-*

dante's speech was heavily accented. Clearly, English was a painful second language to him.

"Hell, I'm just a trader, lookin' to collect an honest debt, Comandante. I'm half wild, brother to the grizzly b'ar, dumber'n a stump about territories. I heard this feller what owes me money come to Santa Fee, and I come a-lookin' fer him."

"What is this man's name?"

"Paul Gallard," Matt said easily. It was the name of a river rat in New Orleans.

"There is no such man in Santa Fe," said Cardoza.

"Well, somebody said he come here."

The *comandante* held up the paper he had extracted from the pile, shook it at Matt.

"Do you know who El Gigante is?" he asked.

"Nope," said Matt easily. He looked at the others in the room and grinned idiotically.

"I think you are this El Gigante. If so, you face serious charges. The murder of many of my soldiers. Trespassing on foreign soil. Spying. Are you a spy, Mr. Caine?"

"Hell no."

"But you have no papers."

"I was robbed."

"That is what you say."

Matt pulled out the pockets of his trousers, showing that they were empty.

"Have you been living on the Rio Grande del Norte for the past year?"

"Hell, I don't know one river from the next. But no, I ain't been nowheres. I got jumped up on the Cimarron cutoff and some Injuns brought me to Taos."

"We will see," said Cardoza. He turned to the governor, nodded to him.

Alencaster rose from his chair. He walked over to Caine, circled him as if he was admiring a suit on a mannequin, stopped in front of the tall man. He looked up into Caine's eyes.

"You speak as one who is unschooled," said Alencaster, "but you have the bearing of a military man." His speech was precise, his English impeccable. The accent was slight.

"Yes sir. I mean, no sir. I ain't no military man."

"Hmm." Alencaster folded his hands behind his back. He continued to stare up at Caine. "What should we do with you?"

"Sir, I think he should be incarcerated," said Cardoza in Spanish.

"Perhaps," said Alencaster. "But if this man was set upon by thieves and robbed, and if he was coming to Santa Fe on a legitimate mission, then he deserves our hospitality. I am told you speak Spanish, Mr. Caine."

"Some," Matt said.

Alencaster spoke to him in Spanish then.

"For the time being you will not be imprisoned. Instead, I will provide a house for you. But you will not be allowed to leave Santa Fe. You will not be allowed to possess a firearm. You will be guarded and watched. Is that clear?"

"Claro."

"I have already sent a message to Chihuahua. They will find out who you are. If we find that you are El Gigante, then you will be put in front of a firing squad and shot. Is this agreeable to you?"

"It is most agreeable, Your Excellency," Matt said in perfect Spanish. "I will honor your conditions and hope that my name is cleared so that I can return to my home in St. Louis and take up my trade again."

"You speak better Spanish than you do English. Why is that?"

Matt shrugged. He did not know how to sound like a lout in the Spanish tongue.

"I think you are a young man of presence," said the governor. "But you act like a lowborn peasant."

"Yes, sir, I reckon."

"Confine him to the Palace Hotel," said the governor to Cardoza. "We should have some information on this man within two months."

"Yes, Your Excellency," said Cardoza.

"We will meet again, Mr. Caine," Alencaster said in English. "You intrigue me."

"Anytime, Governor."

"You will be allowed to walk around our beautiful city, but if you try to run, you will be shot."

Matt nodded.

Alencaster left the room then. Cardoza spoke to Lieutenant Melgares in rapid Spanish.

"I will assign men to take this man to the hotel, along with his belongings," replied Melgares.

"Then get some sleep. You look tired Don Facundo."

"Yes, sir."

Melgares saluted. He took Matt's arm and they marched from the room.

"You do not fool anyone," he said to Matt in Spanish when they were outside.

"I was not trying to fool anyone," Matt replied, but he knew he was playing a dangerous game. He wondered how good his cover was. If the Mexican government started checking on him in Washington, or St. Louis, they might well find out that he was a major in the United States Army and that he had been sent illegally onto Spanish soil for the purpose of surveying the upper Rio Grande. His sweating was not entirely from the heat as he and the lieutenant walked across the parade ground, the four soldiers falling in step as an escort to the barracks where he would await transportation to the Palace Hotel.

*   *   *

Matt lay on the bed in his room at the hotel, puffing on the pipe Elena had given him.

One of the soldiers had kindly given him a tinderbox, with flint and charred cloth. At least he could smoke his pipe until someone brought him some food. The room was homely, but clean. A bed, little more than a cot, actually, a dresser, a table, two chairs, a pitcher of water, a jar for drinking, a chamber pot, a pair of towels hanging from dowels stuck into the wall. There was a view only of the street outside. Two windows, a soldier outside at each one.

Matt's room was on the ground floor. There was only one door, and two windows. He was hemmed in by other apartments. Not a jail cell, exactly, but the room served its purpose. He was a prisoner, and while it was permissible to go outside, to walk around, he would always have two shadows with him, armed soldiers who would think nothing of shooting him dead if he even looked as though he might escape.

One of the first duties of a captured soldier was to escape. Matt knew that, but he also knew he was in a peculiar position, charged with a peculiar task. Yes, he knew it was his duty to formulate an escape plan. But it was also imperative that he gather as much intelligence as he could. He was in the enemy camp. This afforded a rare opportunity to collect information on the New Mexican forces, population in Santa Fe, troop morale, anything he could pick up that might prove useful to his government.

He began to make mental notes of tasks he might carry out, objectives he might attain, even while a prisoner. If he was allowed to work, making cabinets and furniture, he might earn money with which to buy weapons: a knife, a rifle, lead, powder, flints. He would eventually need a horse, food to pack on the trail when he made his escape, a compass. Perhaps he could even manage a brace of pistols.

He would need to make friends. Friends he could

trust. He had one or two already, he felt. Elena. How much
could he trust her? The surgeon? They might feel differently now that they were back at their homes. Were they
disloyal enough to risk their lives? Matt doubted it. But he
might use them to widen his circle of acquaintances in
Santa Fe. If there was discontent among the villagers, the
Pueblo Indians, as he suspected, then he might find men
who would help him, men who would store the things he
needed until he was ready to make his escape.

Matt paced the room, his mind teeming with plans.
He looked through the barred windows. The bars were
wrought iron. He could probably bend them wide enough
to slip through, but he doubted if it would come to that.
The place and time to escape would present itself, he
knew, and he must be patient. There were flowers growing
in a box on the outside sill, geraniums, he thought, their
sturdy petals rimed with a clotting patina of dust. The
guards were relaxed, stood at ease, smoking and talking.
From their speech, he knew that they were Mexicans, not
Spaniards, and they were bored. A good sign.

Shadows began to form on the street outside as the
sun fell away in the afternoon sky. The room took on a
chill. There were no drapes, so he knew the soldiers would
be able to see him at all times. There was a single lamp
in the room, inset into the wall. The cubicle was blackened
by smoke. No tapers with which to light it.

People streamed past the window, unaware of his
presence inside the room. A few peered toward him but
quickly turned away. The soldiers were an indication that
the room was occupied, but none was so curious as to stop
and risk a harsh word from one of the guards.

The bells of the angelus tolled and the street outside
grew quiet, with only a few passersby to break the monotony.

Later one of the guards entered the room. Matt heard

the key in the lock and then the door opened. One of the soldiers came inside, a taper burning in his hand.

"Stand back," said the soldier. "I will light the lamp."

"I have hunger," said Matt.

"Someone will bring you food. Later."

The soldier lit the lamp, as another guard stood in the doorway, his rifle pointed at Matt, his thumb on the cock. After adjusting the flame, the soldier left. Matt heard the key turn in the lock.

A feeling of loneliness assailed Matt as he lay down on the bed, suddenly weary. Yes, he thought, he must make plans to escape. He felt like a wild thing in a cage. He thought of the mountains and the big river where he had made his home for the past year, and the Shoshone, free under the big sky and the stars. Here, in this room, this bleak cell, he was suffocating, drowning in the darkness that seeped through the windows. The smell of the burning oil from the lamp choked him, strangled him. He wondered how long he could stand to be cooped up in this small cave, this shadowy sepulchre, like a mole, shut off from the sun, the sky, the pure sweet air of freedom.

Never before had Matt felt such despair, been so lonesome for human company. Never before had he felt so alone.

Chapter
Twenty-One

Jorge Larrañaga scowled at Governor Alencaster over the snifter of brandy he held to his lips. All through supper, the governor had avoided talking about Matthew Caine. Instead he had asked innumerable questions about the vaccinations, the various populaces along the Rio Grande del Norte, the weather, the temper of the townsfolk, housing accommodations, table fare, game sighted, and travel conditions.

They dined in the patio behind the governor's house, a place of flowers and flagstone, a trellis overhung with wisteria and honeysuckle vines, under a New Mexican sky littered with diamond stars and a full moon spilling soft pewter on the big wrought-iron table. Candles flickered in silver holders; cats prowled the high wall beyond the flower garden, with its tall yucca and cactus mounds, its statues and fountains.

"Governor, I think we ought to talk about the Yanqui, Matthew Caine."

"Yes, of course. That is one reason I wanted to have this private dinner, Jorge. Do you think Caine is a spy?"

"Of course not, Your Excellency. He is a victim of

214

circumstances. I do hope that you will not keep him cooped up in that hotel like a prisoner."

"What would you have me do with him?"

"He is a tradesman; he should be allowed to work."

"And what is his trade?"

"He is a maker of cabinetry, an artisan of fine wood. He should have a home and a shop until the matter of his citizenship and, ah, affiliations are cleared up to your satisfaction."

"But," said the governor, "he has no money, no tools."

"I will provide what he needs," said the surgeon.

"You put a lot of trust in a man you hardly know. One might suspect that you might harbor treasonous thoughts of your own."

"I hope you do not give me reason to resent that speculation, Your Excellency."

"Of course, I am only joking, Jorge. But you do seem most interested in a man with a suspicious background, a man who has no papers, no identification, an American, a stranger."

"I believe what Caine has told me about himself. We might offer him some hospitality, some chance for him to regain his dignity. After all, the man was set upon by thieves and nearly murdered."

"So he says." A *mozo* appeared out of the darkness, refilled the snifter of brandy, cleared off more of the dinner plates. Alencaster produced a pair of cigars, offered one to the surgeon. Larrañaga shook his head. The governor lit his cigar on one of the candles, blew a plume of smoke into the air. It fanned out like a silver mist in the moonlight.

"When Caine returns to his own country, what he says about Santa Fe and our hospitality may one day be important."

"What you say is true, Jorge. We will have to deal

with the Americans one day. Already, they are eager to trade with us, and someday I envision our two countries will be engaged in heavy commerce. They have goods that we need, and we have goods that they desire. Which reminds me. Have you need of any more horses?"

"Always," said Larrañaga. "Why?"

"An emissary from a tribe of Shoshone Indians arrived yesterday to tell me that we can expect some two thousand head of wild horses they wish to sell. Even now this herd is being driven down the Rio Grande, and should arrive in Santa Fe within the week."

"That is good news."

"The timing is especially favorable, since this is the time when we make preparations to attend the fair in Chihuahua. Do you plan to go there?"

"I have had my fill of travel, Your Excellency. While that is a journey I usually look forward to, I wish to rest my bones."

"I understand. We will have a large contingent this year, and we must leave within the month."

"Will you, then, put Caine in my charge before you leave?"

"I will allow a certain amount of freedom, providing you post bond."

Larrañaga reared back in his chair. Alencaster laughed harshly, drew on his cigar.

"Your word will be your bond. Understand that he will still be under guard at all times, free to travel within the city, but not beyond its boundaries."

"Understood, Your Excellency." The surgeon finished his brandy, anxious to leave before the governor changed his mind.

"And the government will not provide the American any subsistence if he begins to earn money for his labors."

"That is most generous of you, Governor."

"Very well, then. I will give the order tomorrow. Where do you plan to quarter the American?"

"I will find a family with room, perhaps in the home of the French family from St. Louis."

"Ah, yes, the family of Don Pierre Chatelaine. Very good. They are honorable people."

"Caine is not fully recovered from his wounds, and I will want to see that he is in no danger of infection."

"Will you have more brandy?"

"No, Your Excellency. The hour grows late and I will stop by the home of Don Pierre and seek his cooperation. I am most grateful to you for your generosity in this matter."

"I trust I will not have reason to regret my decision."

"Good night, Governor," said Larrañaga as he rose from his chair. Alencaster nodded and blew a series of smoke rings, as if the surgeon's leaving was of no consequence.

Antelope stood his horse on a hill and watched the slow-moving column of wild ponies stream by, two thousand head driven by Shoshone braves down from the mountain meadow where the tribe had summered. The horses walked in bunches, held to the trail by young braves flanking them on both sides, turning back those animals wanting to bolt away. Well behind the herd, the women and children rode horses pulling travois poles carrying their lodges, food, and clothing. A pack of dogs plodded at their heels, some braced with small travois poles and bundles, some carrying little packs. These were driven by fleet-footed boys carrying stones and sticks to keep the dogs on the trail.

Dust rose in the air like spirit smoke, hung over the river bottom in the still afternoon air. In just a few suns they would be in Santa Fe. The runner had come back that

morning with news that the governor would buy every
head. This was good news for the Wind River Shoshone.
They would set up their lodges outside the pueblo and buy
goods for the winter before they journeyed to the High
Plains for the winter buffalo hunt.

Later the scouts would ride in and tell them they had
found graze for the night. Antelope looked at the horses
and knew that they were fat and strong, that they would
bring much wealth to his brothers. He waved to Gray Deer
as he passed by, then rode down to take up his place on
the east flank.

Among the women, Morning Lark rode a pinto of
liver spots and black shields, a gift from Big Man. The
pony's mane was braided every eight or ten inches, and at
the tips of the braids fluttered bright yellow and red ribbons. She carried a pack with Big Man's papers. On the
travois, carefully bundled and tied, Matt's surveying kit
rode safely. Inside were his bulbs full of quicksilver, his
sextant, compass, various thermometers, a measuring
wheel, a box that created an artificial horizon, his round
watch, no longer ticking, parallel glasses, his books, including nautical charts and tables, an almanac, and a folding measuring stick.

She looked back at the travois often, as if to reassure
herself that it was still there. And she looked beyond the
travois to the empty plain that bristled with the brown
plants of late summer. She looked into the emptiness long
and hard, as if seeking someone following in their wake.
She looked to the horizon for puffs of dust, and her heart
pounded until she saw that there was no one there. Her
eyes burned with the looking. But she saw no one. She did
not see Big Man, and her heart fell to the ground.

Antelope had told her to bury Big Man's things in the
high meadow.

"Leave this cache here. If Big Man returns, he will
find it."

"He said he would come back. Perhaps he has already gone to the Mexican village."

"You will not find Big Man in Santa Fe," he told her.

"He said he would go with us to the Mexican pueblo," she had argued stubbornly.

"He is dead," said Antelope.

"No, Big Man is not dead. I would know if his spirit had flown."

"How would you know that?"

"I am his woman," she said. Antelope had gone away, shaking his head. But she knew in her heart that Big Man was not dead, that one day he would return. Until that day, she would carry his medicine things with her. She would guard them with her life.

Broken String rode up alongside Morning Lark, her shawl wrapped around the lower part of her face, covering her nose. Her pole travois scarred the ground, adding small spools of dust to the cloud overhead. The sun falling away to the west was shrouded in dust, so that it shimmered in the haze like a quivering disk burnished to a burnt-sienna glow.

There was no sound but the creak of rawhide and the scratch of poles gouging the earth. Even the dogs were silent, their tongues lolling from mouths bristling with teeth, their ribs showing through their thin summer coats.

"You still look for Big Man," said Broken String, making the sign with her hand.

"He will come," said Morning Lark.

"Black Quill and Basket Woman say that Big Man is dead, that his spirit has gone to the sky."

"They do not know this."

"They say he would have come if he was alive."

"Big Man will return," Morning Lark said stubbornly. "Talk does not make him dead."

"You do not see him. I do not see him."

"I see him," said Morning Lark.

"Where is he?"

"I do not know. Go away. I do not like this talk, Broken String."

"You must find another man."

"I do not look for another man. I do not turn my face away from Big Man."

Broken String snorted loudly, touched a hand to her head, made the sign that said Morning Lark had lost her senses.

"There are many good men for Morning Lark. Many men who want to take you to the willows."

Morning Lark spurred her pony, slapped its rump. She rode away from Broken String, her face impassive, her eyes bright as polished obsidian beads. She slowed her pony when her side began to ache. She looked back at her travois to see if the bundle was still there.

But she did not look beyond to the empty plain. She would not give Broken String the meat that she wanted to chew on. Let them think she was crazy. In her heart, she knew that Big Man was alive. She knew that he would return.

Chapter ──────── Twenty-Two

E lena Cuevas looked darkly at the soldiers who stood under the shade of the drooping willow tree, her face shadowed by the shawl she wore. The two men smoked cigarillos, their rifles slung over their shoulders. When they looked at her, she turned her back on them.

"What is wrong, Elena?" asked Matt.

"Those soldiers," she whispered. "They make me nervous."

Matt laughed. "You get used to them."

"They never talk. They just look."

"They send two different ones each shift to guard me. My guardians. They discourage my attempts at friendship."

"They are pigs," she said under her breath. "I wish they would go away."

"I was getting used to them."

They sat on separate benches, facing each other in the Chatelaine garden at the side of the house. It was cool there in the late afternoon, a place of flowers and shadows, of graceful willow trees and roses, pansies and morning glories, all in carefully tended beds. There was a fountain and a small pond filled with goldfish. Beyond the house,

in a fenced field, horses grazed alongside the two milk
cows. The Chatelaine property might have been in another
country, but it was in the middle of Santa Fe, not far from
the plaza, on a quiet alameda. The house was two-storied,
large. Matt had a workshop under a shed, all the tools he
needed. Larrañaga had seen to that. The best part of it was
that Elena lived in an apartment a few streets away.

"I wish we could be alone," she said softly.

"I'm sorry. At least it's better than that cold room at
the hotel. But I will see if the soldiers will leave us alone."

Matt stood up, walked over to the soldiers. They appeared startled as he stood hunched over under the tree.

"Have the goodness to leave us alone. Stay outside
the fence." His voice was low, steady.

One of the soldiers started to jerk his rifle from his
shoulder.

"If you take up your rifles against me, I'll bend them
around your necks like bracelets," Matt said evenly.

The soldiers looked him up and down, decided
against making a show of force.

"We wish to have privacy," Matt said. "I am not going to run away from this beautiful woman. You will be
able to watch us through the fence. But if you stare too
much, I will come over there and talk to you again."

The soldiers nodded, and Matt knew they understood
him. They put out their cigarettes and walked out the gate.
They stood against the fence but did not stare unduly. Matt
walked back and sat on the bench facing Elena.

"Are you comfortable?" she asked, a smile flickering
on her lips.

"Very. Don Pierre and Tomasina are very nice people."

"What about their daughter, Perla?"

"I have seen her only once, when the surgeon brought
me here yesterday. Are you jealous?"

"A little," she admitted. "Perla is very beautiful. She is very young."

"So are you, Elena."

She blushed. She could feel the soldiers staring at her back through the fence. She pulled the shawl farther over her face, as if to hide her discoloration.

"You give compliments," she said. "*Tan pequeños piropos.* I want to hold you in my arms. I want you to kiss me."

"I think that is a fine thought."

"But the soldiers—"

"Pay no attention to them." He rose from the bench, squatted in front of her. He took her head in his hands, pulled her face to his. He kissed her. She clasped his arms with her hands. The fingernails dug into his flesh as she held on, held the kiss. In the dappled sunlight they created a small, intimate arbor of coolness and shadow. They made the kiss last a long time, and Matt could feel the energy flowing between them like electricity from cloud to earth and back again, soft, silent lightning. When they broke the kiss, they stared at each other for a long time, as if reading each other's thoughts, as if wishing they could mate right then and there, like animals without shame.

"My," she said, sighing. "You have gotten your strength back."

Matt laughed. "I want you," he said. "Now. Here."

He stayed close to her, so the soldiers could not hear them talking even if they raised their voices. She wore a brightly colored skirt with a red sash, a white blouse with puffed sleeves that came to her elbows. In her hair she had a red ribbon that complemented her sash and the red border on her green and yellow skirt.

"Oh, Mateo. Not here. Not now."

"You could come to my room tonight," he said. "It has a separate entrance." The Chatelaines had given him a

furnished room out back, connected to the stables. In the
spring it served as quarters for the gardener/handyman.

"The soldiers will be there. They would know."

"Yes, that is true. I think they take turns sneaking into
the cantinas at night, though."

"I will come anyway," she said.

"Good. Very good. I will leave the door open so that
you do not have to knock. Just come right in."

She had seen his room, briefly. He had shown it to her
when she'd come to see him, after lunch. She had seen his
workshop too. He was making some cabinets for the Chatelaines, his first job. It had been three days since she had
seen him, and she missed him. But she knew that the surgeon was arranging for Matt to live in this place. He was
still a prisoner, but he had some freedom. He could walk
through the city. He could visit her. But the guards would
be there, always. Always close by.

"Let's walk around," said Matt. He stood up, took her
hand. "There are some things I want to talk to you about."

Matt spoke to the soldiers.

"We are going to walk around the garden. No need
for you to worry."

The soldiers scowled at him, but remained beyond
the fence. They unslung their rifles, leaned them against the
wrought-iron struts, sat down so that they could still see the
garden.

"What is it?" Elena asked as they strolled away from
the benches.

"I need some favors, but I do not like to ask you."

"Why?"

They walked over to the fountain, where the flow of
the water kept their voices from carrying. Small brown
birds flapped in a nearby bath bowl that stood on a
wooden pedestal. They sprayed water in all directions and
the droplets glistened with miniature rainbows. Pigeons
cooed on the roof of the Chatelaine house, their claws

clicking on the tiles like abacus beads in a Chinese counting house.

"It could be dangerous for you."

"And for you?"

"Yes. Most dangerous. But I can't just stay here and be a prisoner. The Chatelaines have given me permission to wall up the open three sides of the shed, so that I can work this winter. But I must get back to my own country. It is most urgent."

"I understand," she said, her gaze scanning his face. "But I hate to see you leave. I may never see you again."

Matt did not want to get into that. He knew that if he left Santa Fe, in all likelihood he would never return again. But as a soldier he was bound to try and escape his captors. And he considered himself still on a mission under the orders of General Wilkinson.

"I will do all I can to return under more auspicious conditions. In fact, I learned from Don Pierre last night why he is allowed to stay here when he is an American citizen."

"I know," she said, still gripping Matt's hand. "He is a trader from St. Louis. He foresees trade between our two countries, and the governor favors him."

"I think he is right," said Matt. "We have goods that New Mexicans want, and surely they have fineries that our country would welcome."

"What is it that you want me to do, Mateo?"

"I would like you to see if there is a gunsmith in town, find out what a good rifle would cost. I cannot buy it now, but I want to save money for one. You would have to keep it for me until I needed it."

"Oh, Mateo, that would be forbidden."

"I will need protection when I make my escape. Will you do this for me? I will need powder and ball, some other things."

"I will try," she said. "You could stay here in Santa Fe. You will not always be a prisoner."

"I have to return," he said, and looked away. He wished he could tell her more, but he did not dare.

"I will not be here next month," she said suddenly. "I am going away."

"Where?"

"To Chihuahua, to the fair. And I have something to tell you. Something I found out from Dr. Larrañaga."

"Oh?"

"He told me that the Shoshones would be here in a few days with two thousand head of horses for the governor."

Matt's blood quickened. "When will they arrive?"

"In a few days. That is all I know. I remember you told me that you had lived with some Shoshones. Are these of the same tribe?"

A vision of Morning Lark arose in his mind. He saw again the warriors, Antelope and Gray Deer, men he had hunted with, fought with. He had known they would come to Santa Fe, of course, but had not thought of them in a long time.

"Yes, I think these are the Wind River Shoshones. Will you let me know the minute they arrive?" he asked her.

"I will," she said, but her eyes darkened with suspicion. "But it would be very dangerous of you to see them. The soldiers, your guards, will report it to the *comandante*."

"I know. But I must see my friends."

"I am very afraid," she said, slipping his arm around her waist. "I am afraid the soldiers will kill you."

"Why should they?"

"Dr. Larrañaga said that Melgares, the lieutenant who escorted us from Taos, believes you are El Gigante. He has spoken to the *comandante*."

"And what did the *comandante* say?"

"He told Melgares that he must have proof."

"And how will he get this proof?"

"I do not trust him," she said.

"Nor I," said Matt. "But we will not worry about things that have not happened. I will see my friends when they come. And I hope you will find out about the rifles, and I will need two good horses."

"You ask a lot for a man who is a prisoner, who is under the deepest suspicion of the government."

"I know."

"I must get back to the clinic," she said. A cloud passed over the sun and she shivered. Matt kissed her briefly. "Adios," she said.

"*Vaya con Díos,* Elena."

He watched as she walked to the gate, passed through it. The soldiers watched her too, and Matt could see them talking about her.

As he started to walk back to the shop on the other side of the house, his eye caught something moving in an upstairs window. He thought he saw someone step back from the window, but he could not be sure. He had the strangest feeling that he was being watched.

Perla Chatelaine stepped away from the window where she had been watching Matthew and Elena. Just in time. She saw Caine look up at her.

"Did he see you?" whispered the man standing behind her in the dark bedroom.

"I—I don't think so."

"That is El Gigante. I know it. Damn him. The bastard."

"Don Facundo," she said, turning to Lieutenant Melgares, "don't be angry."

"He will trip over his big feet one of these days."

"Yes, yes." She burrowed into him, and he put his arms around her. But he was still smoldering with anger. "Do not worry about him now. I want you."

"Keep your eyes on him, Perla," said Don Facundo. "Tell me everything he does, everyone he sees."

"You want me to be your spy?"

"Yes, if that is what it takes to get this man hanged."

"I will do anything for you, Don Facundo. You know that."

She began unbuttoning his tunic. She purred like a cat as he slipped her dress up over her head.

Downstairs they could hear Caine hammering, and then it was quiet as they tumbled down onto the bed, both naked, their arms locked around each other like twining serpents, and she cried out when he entered her and thought of the big man staying at their home and wondered how he would be in this very bed, how it would feel to make love to a man who would one day hang from the gallows in the plaza of Santa Fe.

Chapter
Twenty-Three

Two days before the Shoshones drove the two thousand head of horses into Santa Fe, the whole city knew they were coming. Riders from Taos, twenty leagues to the north, rode ahead and proclaimed the coming of the Indians and horses. All day and all night, new riders, for the sheer joy of it, brought further news of the Shoshones' imminent arrival. By the time the first Shoshone scouts approached the outskirts of Santa Fe, the road was lined with curiosity-seekers all the way to Ocate Crossing.

Matt stood on the low, flat hill above Santa Fe with hundreds of onlookers, flanked by his soldier escorts, watching as the cloud of coral dust in the sky drew closer and thicker. He felt his blood racing as the vanguard of the herd came into view. Trailed by half-naked Shoshone braves, the first bunch of horses galloped the last few yards into a rope and log corral hastily erected by workers on orders of the governor.

Caine recognized the horses, not as individuals, but as part of the herd he helped the Shoshone capture, and his blood raced hot as he saw them streak by, a sea of them like chunks of colored glass in a kaleidoscope, waved into

the corral by young braves with flashing blankets. The
crowd cheered as the first animals galloped to the end of
the corral, turned and began to mill as the Indians held
them at bay.

Matt saw Lieutenant Melgares and his mounted honor
guard ride up and form a line at the entrance of the corral.
Pennants flapped in the breeze. The troops, all on white
horses, were dressed in parade uniforms. Melgares sat a
jet-black horse, its coat rubbed to a brilliant, glistening
sheen. Melgares did not look at Matt, who stood a head
taller than the tallest man in the crowd.

Late in the day a troop of soldiers marched up to the
corral and formed a picket line to hold the horses in, a
man every fifty paces around the makeshift fence. The
Shoshones put out their own pickets too, to guard their
valuable property; boys armed with short-hair ropes and
sticks, eagle feathers in their hair, some with breastplates,
all moccasined and breechclouted—to the delight of the
young Mexican maidens who stared at them with the lights
of lust in their dark flashing eyes.

All day long the horses and Shoshones came and into
the night. Lanterns and candles twinkled on the mesa like
clusters of stars. People brought food and tobacco to the
Indians, and the New Mexicans ate supper and drank wine
under the fluttering stars. They sang songs to the sorrowful
twanging of guitars, the plaintive keen of mouth harps, and
the beat of small tambours.

The people of Santa Fe watched as tepees blossomed
on the mesa and a city grew before their eyes. Smoke
poured from the smoke holes and fires gleamed through
the open flaps as the Shoshone women cooked food for the
evening meal. Shadows moved among the lodges like
ghostly warriors in the dusk; children played hard after
long days on the trail, their laughter floating into the night
like melodic fragments from ancient songs.

Melgares and his men wheeled their horses and rode

off in a column of twos as the night came on, disappearing over the edge of the mesa until it seemed that they had been dreamed in the minds of dreamers and had never existed on an earthly plane.

Other guards came and relieved those with Matt. They brought food with them in cloth sacks, and he ate cold chicken and warm tortillas with his captors.

"When will the governor come?" Matt asked one of the soldiers.

"Tomorrow, when all the horses have arrived. He and the *comandante* will bargain with the Indians."

"Have you ever seen anything like it?" asked the other. "So many horses."

"It is a sight," said the first soldier.

"I would like to be there for the bargaining."

"Yes. They will talk and talk for days."

"Haggle over the price."

The soldiers both laughed.

Later they told Matt that they had to return him to his quarters. It was just as well. The Shoshones were busy with the horses and setting up their lodges. It had been a wondrous day, though, like a huge picnic or a fair, with so many people coming and going, all in a festive mood. The reek of cigarillo smoke primed the still evening air, and little golden lights winked in the darkness like summer lightning bugs. As they walked down from the mesa, Santa Fe glittered with pinpoints of yellow light, and it seemed like some great city basking in the darkness. The stars seemed big and close in the clear air, and the Sangre de Cristos loomed above the winding snake of the Rio Grande del Norte, their snowy peaks shining mute in the night like distant beacons. And the river ran careless and creeklike in the August heat, dreaming of winter snows in the mountains and the sweet rains of spring.

Santa Fe teemed with night people, the air lushly rank with the heady aromas of tequila and mescal, sharp in the nostrils like wet wormwood and sour oaken wine casks. Music and laughter poured from the cantinas, and girls in gaily colored skirts flirted with the soldiers and with Matt. They reached the Chatelaine house, entered through the gate. Dogs barked down the street, and somewhere a desert owl hooted and the little dogs of coyotes yapped in the hills, chasing shadows sculpted by the moon among the blackened phalanxes of junipers.

Matt wished *buenas noches* to the soldiers and went into his quarters at the stables. He lit a candle lamp so that he could get his bearings. He would not be there long. He had already figured out how he could climb through a window and escape his guards through the back pasture. From there he would climb up to the mesa by the back way, not go through the city. He had to slip into the Shoshone camp and talk to his friends without being under the watchful eyes of the soldiers.

After a time, Matt blew out the candle, loudly making sounds of a man lying down in his bed, as if to go directly to sleep. The corn husks rattled as he pressed down on the blankets with his hands. Then he lifted off carefully, soundlessly, and stood there in the dark, listening.

"El Gigante has gone to bed," said one of the soldiers.

"Fool."

So, thought Matt, they believed him to be the man the soldiers had hunted for so long, soldiers now dead and part of the earth along the Rio Grande.

"All Yanquis are fools."

They laughed softly, and then Matt heard them strike a flint on iron to light their cigarillos.

After a few minutes Matt crawled through the open window. It was a tight fit and he had to move slow so that he wouldn't scrape his clothes against the adobe sill. He dropped to the ground silently, like a panther, and listened intently for a few moments. The soldiers were talking quietly, arguing about who was to slip into town first, whether or not to bring girls back to the hacienda.

Then Matt hunched over and crept toward the pasture. He kept the stables between him and the soldiers so that he could not be seen. When he reached the log fence, he dropped to his belly and crawled under the lower pole. He kept going until he reached the back fence, and crawled under it too. When he was well away from the Chatelaine hacienda, he stood up straight. Keeping to the shadows, he walked upright toward the mesa by a circuitous route, passing dark adobe huts in the darkness, walking softly so as not to startle the dogs that roamed the outskirts of the village.

Matt climbed up the slope and slipped through the musky junipers, marking his path by the stars. He stole slowly through the trees like some giant predator, prowling soft among the dark pools of shadows. He came up on the other side of the Shoshone camp, realizing that this was the most dangerous part of his journey. He tried to remember the circles, how the tribe laid out its lodges. As he stepped away from the scrub trees and walked across the plain, he hunched low again, knowing the Mexican pickets were all around the corral.

He went to the farthest tepee, stopped to get his bearings. In the shadows of night it was difficult to assess the layout of the camp. Matt stood just outside the perimeter of the Shoshone camp, listening for familiar voices.

In one of the lodges he heard a deep booming male voice, then another, higher-pitched. There was a strange quality to the voices. They seemed almost unreal, as counterfeit as an echo of an echo. They seemed the voices of braggarts who were trying to overcome the fear inside them. He did not recognize them, but he had heard the tone before, from the throats of both white men and red.

"Damned shame," he muttered under his breath.

From the slurred speech of the men inside the lodge,

he knew that the New Mexicans must have provided the Shoshones with whiskey or brandy. Perhaps as a friendly gift, but more likely to befuddle their brains for the trading that would begin tomorrow. Any white trader knew that whiskey had an immediate effect on an Indian. Whiskey usually made them either belligerent or docile, but it also was immediately addictive. Once a brave had drunk from the burning cup, he always wanted more, and would trade everything he owned—furs, horses, weapons, even his woman—for a bottle of whiskey.

Matt walked between the lodges until he saw some boys playing among the lodges.

"Boys! You there!" he called. "I am Big Man. I am looking for the lodge of Antelope."

"Aaiiee, Big Man!" yelled one of the boys. "You look strange. What has happened to the hair on your face?"

"Little Lance? Is that you? Come here."

Little Lance was the son of Two Lances. He had nearly sixteen summers, but he was small-statured and looked just like boys much younger than he.

The three boys came over to Big Man, stood respectfully before him.

"I am lost among these lodges and I look for my brother, Antelope," said Matt.

"I do not know where his lodge is," said Little Lance. One of the other boys pointed toward the road from Taos.

"He is somewhere in the first circle of lodges," said the boy. Matt did not know his name.

"I will go there," said Matt.

"Let us take him there," said Little Lance. The boys dashed off through the labyrinth of lodges, and Matt followed. He heard low voices from some of the lodges, but many were silent and dark, and he heard snoring in others as he passed by. Horses whickered in the corral beyond the Shoshone village and he caught glimpses of them, restless and milling, the smoke from their breath silver in the moonlight, their backs flashing like fish spawning in shallows.

They wound through the maze of tepees, Matt loping several yards behind the boys until they rounded a bunch of lodges and disappeared. When he turned the corner, he saw the boys pulled up short, caught by warriors with lances. They squirmed in the hands of their captors like rabbits caught in snares.

"Big Man, help us, help us," cried the boys.

Matt stalked to the warriors. Gray Deer was one of them.

"So, it is you, Big Man. You have returned as Morning Lark has said."

"These boys were taking me to the lodge of Antelope. I wish to make talk with him."

"We thought they had whiskey," said Gray Deer, his face shadowed so that is appeared to have been carved out of the darkness itself. Standing with him were three other braves Matt knew, Lazy Beaver, Jumping Puma, and Whistling Elk. Lazy Beaver and Whistling Elk held the boys between them with spears and shields that fenced them in.

"We have no whiskey," said the oldest boy.

"Let them loose," said Gray Deer. "You boys go to your lodges. Be quiet."

The boys ran off like scattering birds released from a cage.

"The soldiers asked about you, Big Man," said Gray Deer. "They wanted to know if we knew El Gigante. We told them we knew no such man. They made much talk. We took their gifts and gave them tongues that were forked like the snake that crawls in the grass."

"Good. I am prisoner of the Mexicans."

"Come. Antelope will make talk with you."

Matt followed the soldiers to Antelope's lodge. Gray Deer scratched lightly on the flap. It opened and Antelope's woman, Night Loon, showed her face briefly, then disappeared inside.

Matt heard Antelope speak from inside the lodge. "Enter," he said, and Matt ducked down, humped through the flap. Night Loon closed it behind him, locking the others out. Matt heard the Shoshone warriors move away, their moccasins whispering in the sand, crunching the small stones.

Antelope sat at the center of the back flap of the lodge, his pipe and medicine pouch close at hand. The small fire, surrounded by blackened stones, flickered. A tendril of smoke strung skyward in lazy serpentine scrawls. He beckoned to Matt, patted a place beside him on his right. Matt moved left, as was the custom, and sat next to his friend. Antelope spoke to his woman.

"Go to the lodge of Morning Lark. Tell her that Big Man is here."

The woman left without a sound.

"We will smoke," said Antelope. "We will make talk."

"Yes," said Matt.

Antelope offered tobacco to the four directions and to the sky. The men smoked, passing the feathered and quilled pipe between them. The tobacco was harsh and hot at first, biting Matt's tongue, scorching his throat, but once he was accustomed to it, it grew cool and soothed him.

"Morning Lark said that you were alive."

"How did she know?"

"Who can tell what is in a woman's heart, what she sees without eyes?"

Matt told him all that had happened.

"The soldiers wanted to know if the Shoshone knew you."

"I know."

"Sometimes the Shoshone are very good liars."

Matt laughed.

"Will you come with us to hunt the buffalo?"

"No. I will go back to the lodge that the Mexican soldiers guard. I must go to the big white man's fort on the Great River."

Antelope pondered this for some time. Then the flap opened and Night Loon crawled through it, her face like the dark scowl of a raccoon, her eyes glittering like beads, struck by the firelight.

"Morning Lark is not in her lodge," she said. "They say she took the talking leaves of Big Man with her when she went to look for him. One of the people of the Pueblo tribe told her that Big Man was living in a white man's house."

"She has gone?" Antelope asked.

"She is looking for Big Man."

The hackles on the back of Matt's neck tingled and stiffened, as if teased by the furtive apicals of bats. Something leaden and cold sank through his stomach with a dead weight that froze his senses for an eternity of seconds.

Antelope rose from his robe, his shadow daubing the lodge behind him with a giant sprawl of lampblack. When Matt started to rise, he felt a strong firm hand on his shoulder forcing him back down.

"You stay, Big Man," said the Shoshone. "We will find Morning Lark and bring her to you."

When Matt started to rise again, Antelope's fingers dug into his shoulder, shooting knives of pain through his flesh until his arm went numb and he felt paralyzed on one side.

"Stop," said Matt.

Matt looked up and Antelope shook his head, then released his grip on Matt's shoulder.

"Stay," the Shoshone said again, and then he was gone, leaving Matt there, rubbing his clavicle as the pain receded and feeling returned to his arm.

Matt looked at Antelope's wife, who had fallen to her
side when Antelope had burst through the tepee flap. Her
face, struck strangely blue–green and splotched with ver-
milion in the fractured glare of the fire, was impassive as
bloodstone.

Chapter
Twenty-Four

M att listened to every sound. He tried to remain calm, but his brain was screaming with loud cries of alarm. Yet he knew that Antelope had been right. If the Mexicans saw him with Morning Lark and found his satchel full of surveying data on the Rio Grande River, they would promptly execute him without blinking a single eye. He shuddered to think of what they might do to Morning Lark if Antelope didn't find her before someone saw her wandering around Santa Fe.

And how did she get his papers? He had hidden them in the cleft of a tree when the soldiers had been chasing him. He was puzzled and confused.

"Night Loon," he said, "how did Morning Lark find the talking leaves?"

"A scouting party found them," she said. "They knew you had been in a fight with the Mexican soldiers. Morning Lark keeps your medicine. She prays to the Great Spirit for you."

Well, thought Matt, that explained some of it.

"I should be looking for Morning Lark," he said.

"Antelope says that you stay here."

"Yes."

Matt heard voices in the distance, but he could not make out the words. He heard the horses in the corral, muffled whinnies and snorts, the stamp of hooves on hard ground. Coyotes let forth ribbony hunting phrases, all across the dark prairie, as they chased after shadows and rabbits and mice.

Night Loon, croned by the dimness inside the lodge to appear older than her seasons, put more sticks on the fire, but the flames did not take away the darkness in Matt's mind. He felt locked in a cave, not knowing where Morning Lark had gone, or if Antelope could find her before she fell into the hands of inquisitive soldiers patrolling Santa Fe's streets.

"Many said that you had given up your spirit," the woman said as she rocked back from the fire and squatted like a grasshopper with her arms folded across her knees. "Others said you had gone to the white man's town and would not return."

"We all ride in circles," Matt said.

"Ah, that is so," said Night Loon. "Our paths have met again as Morning Lark said they would do. Will you stay with the Shoshone? Will you take Morning Lark to your blankets?"

"I am a prisoner of the Mexicans," said Matt.

"But you are free. You can ride away."

"I have no weapons. I have no horse."

"You have many horses here."

"That is true. I do not know where my path will take me."

"You should stay with the Shoshone. You should stay with Morning Lark."

Matt considered this. If Morning Lark had his satchel, then he could still complete his mission. He would be many months late in getting to St. Louis. Perhaps all his contacts would be gone by the time he arrived. He thought they might send someone else to take his place. And what about Elena? If he left now, he would be putting the Shoshone in jeopardy, and Elena would never know what had happened to him. Perhaps the surgeon and she would be punished by the governor. Once again he was torn between duty and a strange sense that he belonged here, in this wild country; perhaps not in Santa Fe, but with the Shoshone. The land did something to a man if he stayed long enough in it, and Matt had already stayed too long. Was he still a soldier in the United States Army, or a wild man of the mountains? Or was he a prisoner still in service to his country? He did not know the answers. Night Loon made it all so simple. He had walked away from his prison, and so far the soldiers had not missed him. Why could he not just ride out in the night and meet up with the Shoshone in the next moon somewhere along the Rio Grande del Norte?

"You have many questions," he said finally. "And I have no answers."

"You have the answers," said Night Loon. "You just do not listen to them."

He grunted, knowing that she was right. "I will talk to Morning Lark," he said. "Then I will know what is in my heart."

"That is good," said Night Loon, and she rocked on her haunches and stared at the big man across from the fire. They both listened to the little wolves singing on the prairie and the ebb and flow of voices outside and far away. Finally they heard the pounding of footsteps, and then there was a scratching on the tent flap. A man ducked his head inside.

"What do you say, Two Lances?" asked Night Loon.

"Greetings, Big Man. Antelope tells me to take you to your lodge, where Morning Lark waits for you. She was in the lodge of Basket Weaver. It is good. She did not go to the Mexican village. She has the talking leaves in her lodge."

"Go," said Night Loon, a faint smile bending on her face in the darkness.

Matt rose and hunched through the opening in the lodge. Two Lances motioned for Matt to follow him. He stalked off down a row of lodges and followed its circle until he came to the lodge that Matt knew well. Antelope stood before it, like a sentry.

"Morning Lark is inside. She waits for you," he said.

Matt nodded, clapped a hand on his friend's back. The flap was open. He bent down and slipped inside. The two braves stood outside. Matt turned around, looked at them.

"We will watch for soldiers," said Antelope.

Matt closed the flap.

Morning Lark was trembling when he crawled to her side. He took her into his arms. He clenched her tightly to him, and her soft breasts pressed against his chest.

"My heart soars like the hawk," she said.

The lodge was dark as the inside of a dead stove. But he could see Morning Lark even so. Light filtered down like dust from the smokehole, and touching her was seeing her too. She grazed his face with her lips, and he felt the storm of desire rise up in his loins and there was the first whisper of breath blowing on coals in his belly. He kissed her and ignited the fire between them as if it had been waiting there all along, waiting to be fanned by their touching, their collision like planets skidding off course in a wild and unsettled heaven.

There were no words in Shoshone to express the way Matt felt. He had not realized, until that moment, how much he had missed Morning Lark. Nor had he known the depth of her feelings about him. Now it was certain that she believed that she was his woman and that he, lost, had come home.

They found each other in the darkness, on the buffalo robes, amongst the blankets. They tossed their clothing into the void and came together like creatures in the rut, mating once, then again, and still again, until the camp was quiet and even the horses no longer nickered and the coyotes were silent.

They did not sleep, but sat and talked long after Morning Lark had sent Antelope and Two Lances back to their lodges. She built a small fire as the nightchill crept into the lodge.

"I must go before the soldiers come looking for me," Matt told her.

"My heart is falling to the ground."

"I will return. When the next sun has gone to sleep."

"Morning Lark will wait for Big Man."

He dressed and kissed her one last time before he opened the lodge flap and crawled outside. Distant lost cities sparkled in the sable sky, more than a man could count. Matt closed the flap, walked to the far edge of the last circle and retraced his steps back across the plateau, then down into the basin where Santa Fe dozed in mud and darkness. He crawled through the fence, stole across the pasture. He listened long and hard before he tried to climb back through his window. The guards were apparently asleep. He heard no sound from them. After he crawled inside, he heard another's breathing, and his own breath stopped short in his throat as his blood coursed hot in his veins, his senses pricked to an alertness that brought him to a crouch, his muscles coiling for action, the cords in his arms and shoulders tautening to face the danger.

"Who is in here?" he husked.

A small laugh whispered from her throat. "You are a naughty boy," Perla said.

Matt's eyes strained to see through the darkness. "Christ, you scared hell out of me," he whispered as he saw the barest outline of her shape on his cot. "Perla?"

"Yes. Whom did you expect?"

"What are you doing here?"

"Waiting for you."

"Why?"

"Come here," she said. He heard her pat the blanket.

He groped his way to the bed, touched her shoulder. She grabbed his hand, pulled him down next to her.

He sat on the bed and she came into his arms.

"Where are the soldiers?" he asked.

She laughed again. "I paid them a few pesos to go away."

"You are crazy, Perla."

That laugh. More like a bird's warble. Throaty, sensuous, like the soft growl in a cat's throat. It made Matt feel like prey.

Over the past week, Matt had gotten to know Perla better. She had come to his workshop and watched him build the cabinets. They had just made small talk. She was pretty, with her black hair cut short, her brown pixie eyes, and her petite, yet somehow full, figure. She seemed spoiled, though, and somewhat brazen. She was not afraid of men, Matt knew that. She seemed to genuinely like him and was not shy.

But he had no idea what Perla was doing in his room. He certainly had given her no reason to suspect that he wanted her to share his bed, although she had dropped enough hints to him that she wouldn't mind him sharing hers.

"Have you been with her?" she asked in her faintly accented Spanish. He had not told her he spoke French. She would probably be more at home in her parents' native tongue, he thought. Her Spanish was not the best.

"Who?"

"That nurse. Elena. I do not like her."

"I have just been out walking," he lied. "And now I am very tired."

"Walking? I have been waiting hours for you, Mateo. Hours and hours."

"I did not ask you to come here, senorita."

"Do not be mean to me," she pouted. He could see more of her now that his eyes had adjusted to the pale moonlight that bathed the room in a kind of soft mist. She smelled of perfume, a smoky scent that he couldn't identify; violets perhaps, or lilacs, but subtle, not overpowering.

Perla began to stroke Matt's hair.

He drew away from her, caught her hands as if she were a child exploring the cookie jar. He held them for a moment, then dropped them when he knew she would not resist.

"Mateo," she said chidingly, drawing the syllables out into a chromatic ribbon studded with vowels that wrapped around his neck like a scarf.

"You should be in bed, young lady."

"I am in bed, Mateo. Besides, it is almost morning."

"Your own bed." His voice was firm.

"Oh, Mateo. Do you not want to play?"

She came at him again, slinking toward him until her arms draped over his shoulders. She clasped her hands behind his neck and scooted so close he could feel her minted breath on his face.

He broke the hold and stood up.

"Mateo. You run away."

"Perla, I do not want to be rude to you."

"Then do not be rude."

He walked to the highboy dresser, found his tinderbox. He opened it, found flint and steel by touch, struck sparks into the scorched cloth until it glowed. He blew on it while he added wood shavings he had brought from his workshop, until the blaze was high enough to light the candlewick he touched to it.

He took the candle to the wall lamp, lit the candle there, then walked back to the bureau, closed the lid of the tinderbox to snuff out the fire. He blew out the first candle. He looked at Perla on his bed. She looked like a startled nocturnal elf, bright-eyed and small in her black dress and open-necked blouse with the puffed sleeves.

"I am tired and sleepy," he said. "I want you to go home."

"But this is part of my home, Mateo. Maybe you would like to sleep with me. I can sing you a song, rub the tiredness away."

"No, Perla."

Her eyes blazed for a second. Matt thought that Perla could be a very dangerous woman. He certainly did not trust her. He hardly knew her. He did not know her well enough to sleep with her, even if that was all that they did. He had the distinct feeling that he might have to search her for a concealed dagger first.

"You are not very polite."

"I am a prisoner. You should not even be here. I am sure the *comandante* would frown upon it."

"Don Facundo would not." Even as she said it, Matt knew that she had made a mistake.

"Melgares? So, that is why you came. Is he a friend of yours?"

She rose from the bed. Matt could see that she was angry.

"That is none of your business, Señor Caine. I am going, but I have a good mind to tell Don Facundo that you were not in your room tonight. He might throw you in jail."

Matt thought for a moment before he spoke. His eyes narrowed. No, Perla was not to be trusted. He was pretty sure now that Melgares had sent her to check up on him. He did not believe that she had to pay the soldiers to leave their posts. They had gone away under official orders. It made his skin crawl. Perla could upset all his plans.

"I did not mean to hurt your feelings, Perla. I did leave here, but only because I was choking on my confinement. I wanted to breathe the air, look at the stars. I sat alone in the hills and felt free for a little while."

Somewhat mollified, Perla sniffed. She straightened her skirt and patted her hair, which was drawn up in a bun behind her left ear. She was a very beautiful young woman, he thought, but treacherous as a viper.

"Well, I hope the next time I come to your room, you will be more polite."

"I will. I promise."

"Are you sure you do not want me to stay?"

"No. I am very tired. Truly."

"Good night, then."

"Good night, Perla."

He opened the door for her. She lingered in the doorway. Matt knew she wanted him to kiss her, but he looked past her just to confirm that his guards were not outside.

"I hope you enjoy your damned sleep," she said as she sauntered away through the darkness. With her black dress and hair, she disappeared into the shadows but a few yards away. Matt closed the door, dropped the bar to lock himself in.

He would have to be very careful from now on. Perhaps, he thought, he could not wait long enough to acquire horses, a rifle, knife, powder, ball, food, and the things he would need to journey to St. Louis. Perhaps he would have to ask the Shoshone for help and ride away while he still could.

He lay on his bed, his head near the open window. The sky was washed with moonlight, seemed to be floating beyond a gossamer mist.

He fell asleep under the glow of that pale light, felt the moon's naked alabaster glow on his face until it seeped into his mind, his dream, and became harsh and glaring, seemed to sink into his soul like a bright shooting star fallen from the far black sky.

In the dream, he was running for his life. And behind him, on a black horse, was Don Facundo Melgares, trailing white horses in his wake like giant silver fishes that were endless in their coming, ghosts rampant and ravenous upon the fear-fraught nightscape.

Chapter
Twenty-Five

Matt awakened to a soft tapping on his door. He climbed out of the dream like a swimmer surfacing from the bottom of a dark lake, shook his head and blinked his eyes to clear his head.

"Who is it?"

"Larrañaga."

"A moment."

Matt rubbed his eyes, lumbered to the door. He shot up the bar, lifted the latch.

Larrañaga stood there in his white suit and polished boots. He was not carrying his surgeon's bag. Several soldiers stood guard with their rifles, eyeing the surgeon suspiciously. Matt counted at least a dozen scattered among the trees. None of their faces looked familiar. And none of them appeared friendly.

Beyond the trees, the city of Santa Fe, the majestic Sangre de Cristos seeming to rise out of the dawn, glowed sanguine under the onslaught of sun, the silk-white clouds aurous and gelid as glaciers over the high, snowcapped peaks.

"May I enter?"

"Enter," Matt replied in Spanish.

"Close the door," said the surgeon once he was inside. Matt could barely hear him, Larrañaga spoke so low.
Matt dropped the bar.

The surgeon looked around the room, saw the rumpled bed, the candle lamps on the wall, the wooden
dresser, a table and two chairs, a slop jar, a water pitcher,
Matt's clothes hanging on pegs, his shoes under the bed.

"A soldier in Sparta lived better," he said.

"Seat yourself, Doctor."

"Good. Good. After we talk, we are invited to break
our fasts with Don Pierre Chatelaine and his family."

"All those soldiers out there," Matt said, taking the
other chair. He ran fingers through his tousled hair, felt the
bristles of the beard on his cheek and chin. "Are they with
you? Or did I inherit them during the night?"

"They're here to watch you, prevent your escape,"
said the surgeon, leaning forward to speak in a confiden-
tial tone. "You were seen going to the Shoshone camp last
night. Lieutenant Melgares is having fits. He went to the
comandante and asked if he could bring you inside the
presidio. He wants to stand you against a wall, have you
face a firing squad."

"For going to see the Shoshones?"

Larrañaga nodded. "He is convinced that you are El
Gigante and that you are responsible for the deaths of
many soldiers."

Matt said nothing as the surgeon scanned his face.
The room was so quiet they could hear their own heart-
beats.

"The *comandante* said he would talk to the governor.
By luck, I was dining with Alencaster last evening when
the *comandante* arrived. I made some strong talk in your
favor."

"Thank you," said Matt.

Larrañaga shook his head impatiently. He swatted at

a fly that had risen early. It orbited the surgeon's head like a diminutive vulture.

"The *comandante* wanted to arrest you immediately, I fear. There was a discussion earlier, between the governor and myself, concerning the latest dispatch from Chihuahua. It appears that a United States general, Wilkinson, might be planning to march to Natchitoches to establish headquarters in territory claimed by Mexico. Perhaps early next year."

Matt's pulse raced, but he kept his face placid. "And?"

"And Mexico believes that your country is planning to invade the northern territories almost at any moment."

"I think the Mexican government is misinformed. Jumping to conclusions."

"Perhaps. Your name was sent to General Wilkinson in Washington. So, your government knows that you are under house arrest in Santa Fe. The only reason you're not under full arrest now is that the *comandante* and Governor Alencaster are both afraid of you."

"Afraid of me?"

"In more ways than one. You could become an international embarrassment to Mexico. That's the long-range view of Alencaster."

"What's the short-range view?"

"Matthew, I believe that Melgares will arrest you as soon as the horse trading with the Shoshones is completed. The minute the tribe leaves Santa Fe, you will be put in irons. Or you will be killed."

Matt still wondered how much he could trust Larrañaga. While the surgeon had saved his life, helped him, he might have done all that in order to gain information that might be useful to the Mexican government.

"I doubt if this, ah, General Wilkinson would bat an eye."

"Matthew, I am your friend. Elena told me that you

had asked her to help you escape, at some time when you
could afford to buy a horse, a rifle, and other things."

"Oh?" Matt said.

The surgeon waved a hand in the air as if to clear it,
as if to show Matt that it didn't matter what Elena had told
him.

"That was as far as it went. But I believe it is very
dangerous for you in Santa Fe right now. Lieutenant
Melgares has given orders to his troops to shoot you if you
act suspicious or try to sneak out from your quarters again.
I believe that he wants very much to kill you at this very
instant. He believes you are El Gigante and seeks revenge
for the loss of an expedition that searched for him to the
north. Many of the soldiers were Melgares's friends. He
hates Indians and he hates Yanquis."

"Maybe now is the time for me to leave Santa Fe."

"I believe that is so," said the surgeon. He sighed
deeply and leaned even closer to Matt. "Listen with care,
Matthew. I have procured you a fine rifle, with plenty of
powder and ball. I have also gathered a knife, small
hatchet, food, a compass, things you will need when you
return to your country. I have one horse for you. I think I
can help you escape, but you must be very careful. And
you must do exactly what I say."

"That is very generous of you. How can I get away
from all those soldiers out there, however?" Matt waved a
hand toward the door.

"Tomorrow is Sunday. You will ask if you can go to
church and hear mass. Ask them to take you to the San
Francisco Cathedral. It is at the end of Calle San
Francisco."

"I have seen it," said Matt.

"Once there, you will go to the last confessional on
the left section of pews. A panel has been loosened in the
confessional. When you tell the priest who you are, he will
summon someone to remove the panel, and you will go

behind the drapes along the wall, which conceal a narrow passageway. This will lead you to the sacristy. There, you will don a priest's cassock. You will then leave by the back entrance with another priest and make your way to a secret location where you will find a horse and the things I have gathered for you. You must wait for dark, then ride away to the north."

"The soldiers will search the city. Even if I wear the robe of a priest, I will stand out like a fly in a bowl of cornmeal."

Larrañaga laughed softly. "Yes, the soldiers will search for you, and yes, you will be difficult to conceal even in a priest's robe, but no, they will not find you."

Matt's eyebrows arched.

"There is an old stable right next to the presidio. It was once used by the military, but was abandoned when they built the new fortifications. It is full of old livery, carriages, tack. There is room for you and your horse, but the soldiers will not think to look for you there. It is considered, at night, to be a haunted place."

Matt laughed. "There is a problem with your plan," he said.

"Oh?"

"I must leave here tonight."

"Why?" asked Larrañaga.

"A promise I gave."

The surgeon thought for a moment. "That can be arranged," he said. "Confessions will be heard this evening. Tell the soldiers you want to confess your sins. It will impress them. I am sure some of them will want to take advantage of the opportunity to whiten their own black souls. I will make the necessary arrangements."

"Good," said Matt.

"One other thing."

"I am listening."

"Elena wants to see you today. Can you stop by the clinic?"

Matt shrugged. He felt uneasy thinking about Elena. He would have to tell her farewell. During the past weeks, he had grown very fond of her. He knew that she had grown more affectionate toward him. She had said that she would miss him when she went to Chihuahua for the fair. That had been the time when he planned to make his escape. While Elena was gone. That way, he hoped, the parting would be without sorrow.

"Does she know that I am leaving?"

"Yes. She was helpful in making the preparations for your escape."

"Doctor, why are you doing all this for me? You are a loyal Mexican, are you not? And the priests. Why would they be a part of such a scheme?"

Larrañaga took his pipe from his coat pocket, offered Matt some tobacco. Matt shook his head. The surgeon filled the bowl. Matt went to the dresser, brought back his tinderbox. He had a flame going by the time the doctor's pipe was ready. The tobacco caught fire and the room quickly filled with a pall of blue smoke.

"Those are good questions," said Larrañaga. "I will try to answer them. Yes, I am a loyal citizen of Mexico. And so too are the priests, and all those who helped us. But we believe that your country, the United States, is prepared to conquer all the country held by Mexico from Louisiana to the Rio Grande border."

Matt's eyes narrowed. The surgeon had a good mind. While he had never heard such a plan mentioned, officially, that was his belief as well.

"It is inevitable," said Larrañaga. "When Spain ceded Louisiana to that Corsican, Napoleon Bonaparte, some of us could see the proverbial handwriting on the wall. After Napoleon lost the armies in San Domingo that were to occupy the newly regained territory, three of your country's commissioners stepped in and asked to purchase a small parcel of those lands. Napoleon sold them a vast empire. When your government sent Lewis and Clark on that expedition, many of us knew that more would come, and Santa Fe would eventually come under American rule."

"That's quite an assumption," said Matt.

"Is it? This territory is ripe for conquest. Taos is a powder keg, swarming with a dozen different races all ready to take up arms in revolt. Alencaster sits in the *palacio* looking down on the plaza, knowing that he is but one of many governors who have tried and failed to unite the people along El Rio Grande del Norte. The soldiers hunt down the Navajo and the Apache, but come back to the presidio under drooping flags. Iron sells here for a dollar a pound, tobacco at four dollars a pound, and none but the very rich can afford it. Only a blind man can fail to see that Mexico's hold on its northern territory is slipping. Every wagon that rolls into Santa Fe from the east is another nail in New Mexico's coffin. We all know that our days are numbered, but none will voice it aloud. Not the governor, not the *comandante,* not the priests, not the *alcalde.*"

"What about Don Pierre Chatelaine?" asked Matt.

"Ah, he knows. He is one who will breach the wall that opens the way for America's invasion of New Mexico."

"I am surprised at all this, Doctor."

"Come, let us break our fast with Don Pierre."

"Does he know that I plan to escape?"

"I am sure he does, but he would not tell his wife and daughter. Don Pierre is a wise and careful man."

"So, apparently, are you and many others here in Santa Fe," said Matt.

The surgeon smiled, covering the bowl of his pipe with his thumb as he rose from the chair.

Matt began to dress while the surgeon stared out the window across the empty field. A half-dozen crows marched up and down the fencerow, feathered sentries guarding the border.

Matt enjoyed a long and leisurely breakfast with Don Pierre, his Mexican wife, Tomasina, and Perla, who avoided any mention of her visit to Matt's quarters during the night. There was no talk of politics or Matt's situation. He had an eerie feeling of being a condemned man at his last meal. The conversation was pallid and forced.

Don Pierre was a forceful presence, self-assured, well-groomed. Tomasina was a heavyset, square-framed woman who wore her corpulence well. She was round-faced and jolly, proud of her finely appointed home. Matt was impressed with the simple opulence, the high-beamed ceilings, the whitewashed walls, the tapestries and floor rugs, the polished furniture, the gleaming silver everywhere one looked. He demolished his breakfast of delicately poached eggs; cheeses; tortillas; *frijoles refritos* liberally doused with *salsa picante;* sliced apples and peaches floating in cream; *jamón;* thin, almost translucent crepes packed with goat's cheese. Don Pierre drank a mild white wine he told Matt he had made himself. Perla pecked at her food. She seemed still half asleep, and Matt was grateful that she was silent for most of the meal. Larrañaga and Don Pierre did most of the talking. Tomasina spoke mostly to the maid, ordering her in and out of the kitchen.

"I must get to the clinic," said Larrañaga as the men stood on one of the balconies overlooking the backyard. "It was a fine meal, Don Pierre."

"You must visit us more often, Doctor."

"I must leave too," said Matt. "Thank you for breakfast, Don Pierre."

Don Pierre walked them to the front door. There, Larrañaga and Matt said good-bye again, asking Don

Pierre to thank his lovely wife for serving such a fine breakfast. After Don Pierre opened the heavy door, they shook hands on the tiled front steps.

As Matt stepped down, movement caught the corner of his eye. The door closed behind them.

"Ah," said Larrañaga.

Lieutenant Don Facundo Melgares strode across the lawn, intercepting the two departing men at an oblique angle. Matt thought of rolling hoopties, circles that kept forming so fast he could not keep up with them.

"One moment, Caine," said the officer.

Matt stood there, regarding Melgares as he approached.

"Caine, I have just one thing to say to you," said Melgares. He spoke so low that Matt could barely hear him. "I know you are El Gigante and I intend to prove it. You are to consider yourself my prisoner. You are not to visit the Shoshone camp. You will be watched very closely."

"I know that," Matt replied.

"If you do not respect my orders, my men will shoot you dead."

"Is that all you have to say?" asked Matt.

"Good day, Doctor," said Melgares, glaring, with a look of pure hatred, one last time at Matt. The lieutenant clicked his heels and marched away. Beyond the gate his aide stood holding the reins of a black horse.

"I am surprised he didn't draw his pistol and hold it to your head," said Larrañaga as they watched the officer walk to the gate.

"I don't think Melgares would shoot me," said Matt.

"You do not?"

"No. I was looking at that sword he wears. I think the lieutenant would like nothing better than to draw it and run me through a dozen times. He would make me die slow, and he would be laughing at each thrust."

Larrañaga shuddered.

He did not think Melgares would be able to stick Caine more than once with his sword. He was quite sure that Matthew would make the arrogant lieutenant eat that Toledo steel blade, a centimeter at a time.

Chapter
Twenty-Six

Elena and Matt sat at a table outside a small café a few doors from the clinic. Overhead, vines scrambled along a large latticework trellis, providing shade. They were surrounded by soldiers standing under the acacia trees, across the street, down the block. The sun stood straight up overhead at high noon, and the sky was beginning to cloud over from a light wind blowing from the north. All morning long cobwebs of high cirrus clouds had whitewashed the blue, until now it appeared only in patches. A pair of white-throated nuns in black habits strolled by, saying their beads in silence, their white-winged cowls giving them the look of strange flightless birds.

Elena's face glowed with radiance, a pale blush like a misty morning on her cheeks, the faint pastel of a rose petal on her lips. She wore a white blouse and blue skirt, a velvet blue ribbon in her hair. Matt thought she had never looked more beautiful, and he wondered if it was because he was going away, might never see her again.

"Are you hungry?" she asked.

Matt shook his head.

"My stomach is full of butterflies, Mateo. I could not eat. I ordered *tepache* for us. To calm ourselves."

"I brought you something, Elena."

He handed her a small package. She hadn't noticed it before in her eagerness to see him. She took it, undid the twine, unwrapped the brown paper. It was a small box, highly sanded and stained, with little brass hinges and latch. She opened it up. It was lined with plush velvet. The tacks didn't show.

"Did you make this, Mateo?"

He nodded. "It's a jewel box, or for small trinkets. Something to remember me by," he said. "Tomasina gave me the velvet for the lining."

Elena clutched the jewel box to her breast. She drew in a breath, trying her best not to cry. "You are a very dear man, Mateo. I hate to see you go."

"I will miss you, Elena."

She reached out a hand, touched him. He took her hand in his, held it warmly, gently.

A small herd of Shoshone horses raced up the street, driven by caballeros. Matt and Elena watched them pass in a dusty haze, like imaginary beings emerging from a sunlit dream. The soldiers watched them as they ran down the wide street toward the presidio.

"Look at them, Mateo. They are so beautiful, so powerful. And wild."

"And once they ran free," he said. "Free as the wind."

"Yes. Like you. It is very sad."

"No," Matt said ruefully. "I have never been free like that." He watched the horses pass by, and his jaw hardened as he thought about the high mountain meadow where the Shoshone had kept the herd before driving them to Santa Fe.

After the hoofbeats subsided, Elena leaned over the table. Then the waiter came with a couple of glasses of *te-*

pache and she drew back. She paid for the drinks, and when the waiter left, leaned over the table again.

"You must not go to the church tonight," she whispered.

"Why?"

"It is dangerous. I think Melgares knows all about the plan."

"How?"

"I do not know."

"Larrañaga?"

She shook her head. "I think one of the soldiers was listening outside your window this morning when the surgeon told you of the plan."

"That is possible," said Matt. He should have looked outside before he and the surgeon talked.

"You must find another way."

"I do not have much time. You can see that there are many soldiers guarding me."

"Perhaps this is not a good time to leave."

"You do not want me to go."

Elena shook her head. "That's not why I am telling you this, Mateo. Look at them. They know that you are planning to escape. They cannot wait to shoot you."

Matt gazed at the soldiers. They seemed to be very alert and watchful. All the more strange, since it was very near siesta time. Each of them turned away when he looked at them.

"I will think of something," he said.

"Maybe that will not be enough."

"What do you mean?"

"In a few days, when the trading with the Shoshones is over, Lieutenant Melgares, the governor, and many people will journey to Chihuahua for the fair. I think Melgares wants to kill you before he goes."

"What about the rifle and the horse?"

"I do not know. The priests have them, I think."

"Perhaps the priests have changed their minds."

Elena shrugged. "Perhaps," she said. "I do not trust Melgares. He has eyes everywhere."

They drank the *tepache* in silence. Matt felt something squeeze his heart as he looked at the fine strands of hair that blew over her cheeks and forehead. He felt empty inside, a longing for something he could not explain. It was not the parting he had imagined.

"Thank you for warning me," he said. "I had better get back to work. I have one more cabinet to finish up for Don Pierre before I leave."

"Then you are going to try and escape?"

"I am going to think about it," he said. "Can you spare a few pesos?"

"What for?"

"I need to buy a few items."

"How much do you need?"

"Five pesos."

Elena opened her purse, took out a bill. "Is that enough?"

"I think so. Thanks."

He did not want to tell Elena too much. She might have to face serious consequences if she knew his plans, although at the moment he didn't have any. But he knew he could not risk staying in Santa Fe another night. If Melgares knew he was trying to escape, he might force the issue.

"Mateo. I am worried about you. You must not go to the church tonight."

"Do not worry, Elena. I do not want to be shot down."

"Even if Melgares does not shoot you, he will most surely arrest you and put you in jail. He would not leave Santa Fe without knowing you were under lock and key."

"Where is the surgeon? I would like to talk to him."

"I think he is at the Shoshone camp with the governor. Melgares and the acting *comandante* are there buying horses."

"Does Larrañaga know that his plan has gone bad?"

"Yes. He said he would try and find another way. He will come to your room tonight. If he can."

"If he can?"

"He says that you should be careful. Melgares is very persistent in getting what he wants."

Matt was beginning to get a pretty good picture of his situation. Larrañaga had done as much as he could. Now he was on his own. He could not count on anyone's help in Santa Fe. Somehow, he would have to give his guards the slip and make his way to the Shoshone camp. If he stayed in his room, however, he would be trapped. And even if he got away from the Chatelaines' place, he would have a hard time fleeing the city. Melgares would have the full garrison out searching for him.

Another fifteen or twenty horses pounded up the street toward them. People lined the alameda, watching as they passed. Matt looked longingly at the horses, thought of his friends, the Shoshones. He wished he could be there while they bargained with the Mexicans. A thought struck him.

"Where do they drive the horses before they turn on this street?" he asked Elena.

"They come up Calle San Francisco, turn at the cathedral."

"That's what I thought," said Matt.

"Why?"

"No reason. I was just curious."

"The horses have been galloping past all day. They are so beautiful."

"Good-bye, Elena," Matt said. He rose from the table, walked around it and lifted her from the wooden chair. He kissed her. She hugged him tightly. She did not cry.

"Will I ever see you again?"

"Perhaps. Someday."

"I truly hope we will meet again, Mateo."

"I have the feeling that we will."

Elena bit her lip as if afraid to say more. She opened her mouth, but no words came out. She hesitated, and the moment passed, flown and gone into some eternal place where gather all such crucial events in the lives of all beings in the universe.

"Adios, Elena."

"*Vaya con Diós,* Mateo."

He looked back at her as he walked away, his military escort flanking him, catching up his rear. She stood there in the patio, holding the jewel box he had made for her. She waved and he waved back. He felt again something squeezing his heart, and then it filled up with a loneliness that constricted his throat, brought sudden tears to his eyes.

Matt stopped at a small *tienda* with an *abarrotes* sign. A soldier stood in the doorway while he made a purchase from the lady inside. He bought a packet of black dye and a package of cigarillos and tobacco, which the lady had hidden underneath the counter. She eyed the soldier nervously.

"Do not worry," Matt told her. "The cigarillos are for him." He concealed the dye inside the package of pipe tobacco.

The lady did not smile as he paid her.

After he got his change, Matt walked to the door. The soldier stopped him.

"What did you buy?" he asked.

"Tobacco." Matt held up the package. The soldier looked inside but did not disturb the contents.

Matt gave the soldier the pack of cigarillos, put his tobacco and the dye in his pocket.

"For me?"

"For you," said Matt.

"Many thanks."

"It is nothing."

Another herd of horses passed them on the walk to the Chatelaine estate. Matt and the soldiers watched them fly by, all white-eyed and nervous, dust, like the flotsam blown by a sudden storm, billowing in their wake.

The sky darkened on the way back to the Chatelaine hacienda and the breeze stiffened almost imperceptibly. The soldiers chatted about the weather as they passed through the gate. Matt went to his room, gathered up his other white suit. He put it inside the slop jar, filled the jar with water from the pitcher on his dresser. He poured dye into the water, made sure the suit was soaked through. Satisfied, he went back outside, walked to the shed on the other side of the house. Some of the soldiers lay under trees and took their siestas, while others sat in the shade and smoked as Matt worked. He took a gourd from the wall and ladled water from a drinking trough. He drank and thought about the plan forming in his mind. It might work, if he was lucky.

None of the soldiers seemed interested in what he was doing. Those who were awake looked bored and sleepy. By the time the sun disappeared behind black clouds, most of the men were dozing in the shade of the big willow trees.

He shaved several boards with a hand plane, set them aside. During the afternoon, he surreptitiously picked up the dry shavings and filled his pocket. He walked back to his room, accompanied by four soldiers, and once inside, emptied his pockets of shavings. He pulled the suit from the slop jar, wrung it out with powerful twists from his hands. He hung it over the windowsill in the sun, hoping the wind would dry it before it began to rain.

Matt walked back to the shed, continued to plane

boards so that he could collect the shavings. He heard footsteps on the back stairs. A moment later Perla rounded the corner of the house, treading regally as she smiled at the peasant soldiers. She came into the shed, watched as Matt finished off a whipsawed pine board and stacked it with the others.

"*Buenas tardes,* Mateo."

"Good afternoon, Perla."

She wore a black skirt with a wide red band above its hem, a bright yellow sash around her vespinous waist. She wore sandals, and Matt saw that each nail was painted bright red to match her fingernails. Her white blouse, with crocheted trim, billowed from her breasts in front and at her elbows. She wore a crimson carnation in her shiny black hair, and her eyes were lined with kohl, giving her face the look of an Arabian princess.

Matt picked up another board, spanned it across the two sawhorses. He picked up the plane.

"So, you were planning to run away," she said.

"What makes you say that?"

"Oh, I heard you and the surgeon talking."

"And you told Melgares."

"Yes."

"Why?"

"He is my lover."

Matt set down the plane, looked at the young woman. Her painted lips were bent in a mocking smile.

"How many bruises does he have on his body, Perla? How many teethmarks on his neck? How much of his blood have you drunk?"

"*Tu cabrón.*"

"I know the kind of woman you are, Perla."

"What kind is that?" she spat.

"You want to cut off a man's eggs, make him beg for mercy on his knees."

"How stupid you are."

"I have met your kind before. If you kiss a man who likes you, you bite his lips so you can taste his blood. You have to leave your mark on every man you take to your bed."

"That is ridiculous," she seethed.

"Is it? You claim men like a hunter takes trophies. You scar them once and think they are yours forever."

"You are nothing but a savage."

Matt smiled. "Then we are alike."

She struck at him, not with her fist, but her long fingernails distended like claws. Matt grabbed her arm, twisted it until she felt the pain.

"Bastard," she said again. "I hope they shoot you down like the dog you are."

"Such a pretty face. Such a black heart."

She cursed him so loudly, the soldiers looked at them. When she saw their faces, she whirled and walked away. Matt watched her go, then picked up his plane again and went back to work. He heard her ascend the stairs and then the back door slammed. It sounded like a rifle shot.

Matt finished the cabinet, stained it, set it out in the sun to dry. He looked at the sky, and filled his pipe. He struck flint to iron, blew on the charred cloth until the small shavings ignited. He put a coal in his pipe, drew on the stem until smoke filled his lungs.

In the distance he heard another herd of horses turn at the cathedral and gallop toward the presidio. He thought about his chances of getting away from here without being shot. In his mind, the rest of his plan began to form. It would take perfect timing, and he might have to knock a soldier or two down. He might even have to kill one or two. But it might work.

He wandered to the cabinet, touched it. Almost dry. He sat down in the shade of the hacienda, going over the plan in his mind until every detail stood out in stark relief. Larrañaga had said that General Wilkinson was planning

to set up headquarters in Natchitoches. That was still disputed territory, the present boundary between Louisiana
and Texas on the Red River. However, Matt knew that the
United States considered the Rio Grande to be the actual
boundary. But he had heard Wilkinson declare, when the
general sent him to map the Rio Grande, that he would
"soon plant our standards on the left bank of the Grand
River."

If Wilkinson did go to Natchitoches, the Mexican
government would view that as an act of war. Matt knew
if he were still in Santa Fe by then, he would surely be
taken to Mexico and thrown in a dungeon. So it was imperative that he somehow make his escape from Santa Fe
as soon as possible.

He did not know if he could trust Larrañaga. Now,
too many people knew about the escape plan, if Elena was
to be believed. And he was sure that she could. She was
probably in love with him, but he didn't want to think
about that.

Even if he did manage to escape from Santa Fe, he
had some tough decisions to make after that. He felt so isolated and alone. He looked again at the sky and felt the
warm south breeze shift to the north. There would be rain
sometime after the sun set, he was sure. He had a lot to do
before then, if his plan was to work.

Matt got up, checked the cabinet. It was dry. He
picked it up, walked around to the front entrance. The soldiers watched him like vultures sniffing blood spoor. He
knocked on the door. Conchita, the Chatelaines' *criada,*
opened the door.

"I have the cabinet for the señora," Matt said.

The maid called to Tomasina, who appeared at the
door a few moments later.

"Yes, bring it in," she said, regarding the soldiers
with malevolence. She pushed the maid aside as Matt entered, then slammed the door herself.

They went to the kitchen, where Matt fitted the cabinet next to the others he had made. He was proud of his work.

"You have done a good job, Mateo," said Tomasina. "When Don Pierre returns, I will tell him to pay you for your work."

"That is not necessary," said Matt. "I owe the nurse, Elena, some money. He can give it to her."

"I will tell him this. Conchita will bring you supper."

"A million of thanks."

Matt wondered if she too knew about the escape plan. She didn't say anything, so he left the house and walked back to the shed, his military remoras in tow, like shadows. He made a big show of working until the soldiers relaxed once more and ignored what he was doing. He filled his pockets with more shavings as the sky darkened and the day wore on.

Finally, as the north wind began to rattle the leaves on the trees, Matt put away his tools, stacked up the planed lumber and walked back to his room under a sky turned to iron. He relieved himself before going inside. A few moments later the church bells pealed and the guard changed. The new men wore black rain ponchos, serapes that dripped from their shoulders like huge shawls. Matt's suit was half dry. He turned it so the wet parts were outside the window. There were windows on either side of the room, large ones, and two small ones in the front. The room gradually darkened, but Matt did not light a candle.

Soldiers passed by the windows, looked in at him. None of them acknowledged his presence, nor did Matt nod to them, but only watched them pass, faceless and nameless as mendicants.

He hated to do what he had to do, but maybe the money he had earned would pay for some of the damage.

Matt emptied his pockets of the shavings, placed

them at the bottom of the front door. He gathered up all
the other curls of wood and added them to the pile.

Matt sat at the table, lit his pipe. He got up, checked
his dyed clothing. It was dry. He changed into the now-
black suit and continued to smoke. He looked around the
homely, spartan room. Tomasina had given him a bottle of
wine to sip in the evenings, but he did not want to cloud
his thoughts.

When the rain began to fall, gently at first, the small
room seemed to fill Matt with an odd feeling of sadness.
Rain always brought a homesickness to him, a nostalgia
for his childhood back home on the farm. In the tattoo of
the rain it seemed he could hear the mill wheel grinding,
that he could see again the groomed fields of grain, hear
the lyrical call of a mockingbird, smell the aroma of fresh
bread baking in the cast-iron oven, hear the rattle of the
copper kettle on the hearth.

Soldiers came to the side window near the Chatelaine
house and stopped, peering inside the room. In the darkness, Matt was invisible.

"Why do you not light a candle?" asked one.

"I like it dark," Matt replied.

"Stupido," said the other.

When the rains grew hard, the soldiers left him alone
and Matt rose from his chair and went to the door. He
puffed on his pipe until the bowl grew hot, then shook
the hot ashes onto the shavings crammed around the door.
He looked out through the window, saw the soldiers huddled together under the trees.

He smiled and knelt down. He began to blow on the
hot ashes until they glowed. The sparks ignited the shavings, and flames licked at the fresh, thin wood. Matt stood
up and lifted the latch. The flames grew higher. It would
not be long now. He went over by the far window and
stood there, ready to make his move.

The wind rasped sporadically beneath the eaves in

gusty whispers. It fed the flames, and soon the door was engulfed. Smoke filled the room and sought the open windows.

He heard the soldiers yell as flames ate through the door. Matt screamed.

And waited for the soldiers to come.

Chapter

Twenty-Seven

Matt leaped through the window as the soldiers rushed his room. The soldiers made such a racket, he knew they did not hear him. He hit the ground running as the soldiers beat on the front door with their gun butts. He knew the door would burst open and one or two would brave the flames and rush inside. This gave him precious moments.

Matt made a wide circle to the left, heading toward the church. He could not see the cathedral through the wind-staggered rain, but he knew where it was. In moments he had blended into the vespertine darkness and the rain. He ran until his lungs burned, then slowed as he reached an alleyway. He slipped down it quietly.

In a few moments he was on Calle San Francisco, standing in front of the church. A few people came and went, holding small swatches of cloth over their heads as Matt waited in the shadows, hoping more horses would come into the city and turn toward the presidio.

The rain beat down hard, rattled against the tiled roof of the cathedral, ran down the gutters and flooded onto the dirt street, turning it to mud. Lightning gashed the sky, pouring forth webs and lattices of quicksilver, and thunder rolled across the heavens like thousands of heavy barrels loose in a caravel's hold.

No one noticed the giant man in the shadows, but penitents paused in front of the church and looked down the street. That's when Matt heard the hoofbeats, muffled in the rain-sheeted distance. His heart tugged at its moorings as he peered down Calle San Francisco. The thunder grew louder, and he saw a dark mass moving toward him. He poised himself and waited.

On they came, the dark, rain-slick horses. As they approached the cathedral, Matt saw three jinetes driving them, one on either flank, another bringing up the rear. They were not moving fast through the downpour, but they were proceeding steadily.

Matt removed his pipe, tobacco, and tinderbox from his coat, shoved them into his trouser pockets. He took off his wet coat, started moving away from the shelter of the church onto Calle Presidio. As the horses turned the corner, he ran into the center of the herd, waving his coat overhead and shouting at the top of his voice.

"Heeya! Hooooweeeaaaahhh!"

The horses skidded in panic, turned inward on themselves. Matt ignored them, raced toward the nearest jinete on his flank. He flapped his coat at the horses as he passed them, and they collapsed on one another and those caught in the whirlpool, milling in confusion. He lost sight of the two other *cabarillizos* as he neared the horseman managing the herd's right flank.

"*Que haces?*" yelled the jinete.

Matt slung his coat back on as he raced toward the young boy. The horseman pulled back hard on the reins, tried to turn. But he was too late. Matt grabbed the reins, pulled them out of the boy's grasp. Then he reached for his shirt, grabbed a handful of cloth. He pulled the hapless rider from the saddle and flung him aside like a sack of meal. The horse backed away from Matt, but its hooves slipped on the mud. Matt rammed his shoe into the stirrup, grabbed the saddle horn and pulled himself aboard.

When his weight settled in the saddle, Matt wheeled the horse away from the pack and rammed both heels into the animal's flanks. He and the horse raced past the tangle of horses, just barely missing the downed *jinete,* whose arms stretched out as if to retrieve his horse. Matt saw the startled look on his wet face and hurtled past, bent over the horse's withers like a coal-black panther mounted for the kill.

Matt rode through dizzy streets, past bewildered soldiers searching for a large man on foot, and thought he heard commands hurled his way through silver sheets of rain. He zigzagged toward the hills, and then he was beyond the boundaries of the city, swallowed up by the rain and the night. He eased the horse to a walk, heard its breath whistle through rubbery nostrils, felt its sides heaving against his legs.

He looked back over his shoulder, saw nothing but the dim and ragged silhouette of the city, its edges softened by the blur of rain. He rode into the hills, and no one followed him and he heard no sound of pursuit.

He patted the horse's neck, calmed him down from the wild ride. Matt dismounted and walked the horse through the trees along the ridge. Gradually the animal's breathing returned to normal. Climbing back into the saddle, he saw something out of the corner of his eye.

And then he saw them.

Soldiers. They were riding in columns of two, all carrying torches that flickered in the rain. They rode toward him, a pair of scouts in the vanguard, following his tracks.

Matt stared in disbelief.

He wiped his eyes, rode to the edge of the trees. He saw one man riding at the side of the column, on a black horse. The other troopers sat white horses, their hides winking in the darkness like dozens of eyes.

Matt sucked in a breath and cursed softly.

"Melgares," he whispered. "You son of a bitch."

Elena saw three soldiers run past the window of the clinic, their rifles held at the ready, their dark serapes slick with rain. She went to the door just as the open buggy pulled up. Larrañaga set the brake, wrapped the reins around the handle. He stood down to the street, dashed to the doorway. Elena opened the door for him, let him inside.

"You are soaked to your skin, Doctor," she said.

"I know," he panted. "Did you hear what happened?"

"No. Those soldiers—"

"They are looking everywhere for Caine. He has escaped."

Elena choked back a soft sob as the doctor removed his coat. She took it from him, her heart thrumming like a trapped bird in her chest, her pulse racing. She hung the coat on a rack.

"Let us go into my office," said the surgeon.

"Did he get away?"

"I do not know. I think they are still looking for him."

They passed through the narrow waiting room, past two examining rooms, the linen closet, and back to the surgeon's office. He closed and locked the door. The room was filled with medical books; a small skeleton on a rod; several cabinets; shelves crammed with nostrums, unguents, powders, pickled human organs in glass containers, ancient surgical tools, couch, chairs, a desk and several lamps.

One lamp was burning. The back window looked out over a tree-filled sward, with a high back wall overgrown with ivy. Larrañaga closed the shutters and they listened to the clatter of rain on the roof, the gusts of wind blowing against the adobe, the far-off boom of thunder.

"Sit down," said the surgeon.

"I am too nervous to sit down, Doctor. Please, tell me what you know."

"Did you see Caine?"

"Yes. We—We said good-bye."

"Was he disturbed that our plan had been found out?"

"He seemed very calm."

"Hmm." The surgeon patted his pockets, then opened a drawer of the desk. He pulled out a spare pipe, a pouch of tobacco. "I wonder," he said as he filled the bowl and lit it, "how Melgares found out about our plan."

"That man has eyes everywhere."

The surgeon blew a plume of smoke out of the side of his mouth.

"Well, we cannot help Caine now. It is in God's hands. Did you tell him?"

"What?"

"About being *encinta*."

Elena shook her head. She struggled to keep from weeping but could not hold back the tears. The surgeon rose from his chair, went to her. He put a hand on her shoulder.

"Why did you not tell him you were pregnant, Elena?"

"I did not want his pity."

Larrañaga sighed and went back to his chair. "Is there anything I can do?"

"What do you mean?"

"I can force labor."

"No. I want to give light to Mateo's child."

The surgeon clucked, sucked on his pipe. A gust of wind shook the shutters, blew spray through the cracks. A flash of mercurial light bled into the room, then vanished. The thundercrack made them both jump in their seats.

"Do you want to raise a bastard?" the surgeon asked quietly.

She rubbed the tears from her cheeks, looked at Larrañaga. "Maybe Mateo will return some day," she said.

"Perhaps," the doctor mused. He wanted to say that she should have been more careful, but there was no reason to make Elena feel any worse than she did. "Perhaps he will return one day."

"There is going to be war, is there not?"

"I do not know, Elena."

But he knew there would be war. If not between New Mexico and the United States, then between the government and the Pueblo Indians. The river kingdom was even now seething with discontent, and he believed that it was only a matter of time before the Americans took advantage of the situation.

"He will come back to Santa Fe," said Elena. "He told me he would."

"Then I am sure he will do what he says."

The surgeon almost asked the question uppermost in his mind. *Will he marry you?* But he kept silent. This night would be long enough for both of them without bringing up unpleasant matters.

Larrañaga wondered where Caine was at that moment, and as if in reply to his unspoken question, the thunder crashed louder than before and the room shook with the force of its energy. The surgeon shuddered inwardly.

The thunder sounded like heavy cannon fire, and it

echoed through the city as though it were a solemn pronouncement of doom.

Matt rode a zigzag course through the junipers and the stunted pines. Later, when he was far out on the plain, he saw the torches among the trees and knew what he had to do. He dismounted, pointed the horse toward Santa Fe and slapped it hard on the rump. The animal galloped away in the darkness and disappeared.

It took him two hours to walk to the Shoshone camp. He tried to leave no tracks. The rain was hard enough to wash them away, but he could not be sure. Soldiers on horseback surrounded the camp, riding short distances, overlapping each other's posts, so that it would be difficult to slip through the pickets.

Matt hugged the ground, crawled parallel to the roving horsemen. He thought about what he had to do. The Shoshone had taught him so many things during the year he lived with them. He had learned how to stalk, how to remain motionless so that he could not be seen by game. This was how he moved now. Slowly, carefully. When the soldiers looked out upon the plain, they did not see him. Only shadows and rain.

Matt crawled to the northwestern corner of the Shoshone camp, and found a weakness in the Mexican defenses. There was a juncture where one guard sat his horse and did not move. The closest any of the riders approached him was a distance of thirty or forty yards. It might be possible to slip through that gap and into the camp, Matt thought. He would have to crawl all the way. He would have to make no sound.

The rain helped. The wind and thunder helped muffle his progress. His suit shredded on the rocks and grew heavier as it collected mud and water. The dye seeped

from the fabric, but the dirt concealed the natural white-
ness of its original state.

Matt slid along, three inches, four inches, six inches
at a time. Waited and listened after each move. Froze
when lightning streaked from burly black clouds and
flooded the land with ignited phosphor. He got so close to
the lone horseman, he saw his dark face when the lightning exploded and made the lodges dance, splashed mer-
cury on every shadow, turned every object into alabaster
stone as white as milk.

Closer and closer he came to the circle of lodges, circles within circles, and each time he heard the voices of
the soldiers in the darkness, his blood turned gelid in his
veins.

"La lluvia chingada."

"El viento debe que mamarme la verga."

"Chingate Pedro."

"En su boca."

The filthy words of imbeciles, the infernal and eternal
complaints of soldiers since time began, the curses of the
damned as they rode like blind men back and forth in a
godforsaken cacophony, wet and miserable, unable to
smoke, without drink, and their asses soaked and saddle-
sore, their legs numb as sticks, their toes cold, their hands
a pudding of flesh, useless and wrinkled as sodden prunes.

Matt bumped up against a tent stake before he knew
he had made it through the pickets. He lay there, eyes
closed to the spattering rain, listening to it rattle against
the hide of the tepee with every savage gust of wind, and
then he crawled around the lodge and got to his knees. He
floated through the camp, the fires inside the lodges flickering through their skins, and came, like some swamp-
freed hulk, upon his own lodge, the fire inside small and
barely visible.

Matt opened the flap, crawled inside.

"Morning Lark," he whispered. She sat in the darkness, a buckskin garment across her lap, awl and sinew in her hand. Orange light played upon the delicate features of her face.

"Big Man comes back."

"There are many soldiers looking for me."

"I know. They want to search the camp. Our leaders will not let them."

"Good."

She looked at his sodden clothes, shook her head. "I have dry buckskins for Big Man," she said. "And moccasins."

She brought him the clothes she had made for him over these past moons. They smelled of piñon smoke and sage, supple in his hands, sure to fit him as perfectly as a pair of fine gloves.

"I would speak with Antelope and Gray Deer," he told her, and hated himself for sending her into the night when he wanted to take her into his arms and lay her on the blankets and hide inside her, bury himself in the fragrant night of her while the world blew itself to cinders in the thunder of the night outside.

She slipped away as silent as a whisper, and when next he saw her, Antelope and Gray Deer were with her. They listened to Big Man as he told them of Melgares and the hunters with torches riding somewhere out there in the hills like a pack of hungry wolves.

"I need horses, a rifle, powder and ball, food for the journey."

"Where will Big Man go?" asked Antelope.

"To the place where the Rio Grande del Norte comes out of the mountains. There, Morning Lark and I will wait for the Shoshone and journey with them to the hunting grounds."

"We will go to the Moonshell," said Gray Deer. "Will Big Man go to the white man's fort on the Father of Rivers?"

"No, I will live with the People."

Morning Lark made a little sound in her throat.

"How will you escape this place?"

Matt told them. In the dark, crawling through the mud, he had figured it out, knew how he and Morning Lark could elude the soldiers and leave the Shoshone camp.

"That is a good plan," said Gray Deer.

"It makes me laugh it is so good," said Antelope.

"We have many good weapons from the trading of the horses," said Gray Deer. "We have much powder and ball, good knives, parfleches of food for your journey."

"Come, we will find others to help us," said Antelope, and they took Big Man with them, hid him in the lodge of Two Lances, next to his own. Morning Lark began to set their belongings outside, covering them with a buffalo robe to keep them dry.

When Matt next saw his lodge, it was collapsed and horses stood there with travois poles hooked to their saddles, with men he hardly knew holding the reins of horses.

They packed Big Man and Morning Lark onto the travois and covered them with a buffalo robe and bulky objects so that their shape could not be seen in their concealment.

Morning Lark and Big Man clutched each other as the horse began to move and bounced on the slender travois poles. Hoofbeats pounding on the plain and through the robe, they could see the wavering flames from the torches, hear them hissing in the rain. They heard angry Mexican voices, and Matt recognized the voice of Melgares as he asked to search the camp for El Gigante and the Shoshones replied that their people were tired and sleepy and would not allow him to disturb them, and the interpreter's voice shrill and high-pitched and finally silent.

Through the night they journeyed, not knowing where they were, but only feeling the shape of the earth as they moved over it under the smothering sepulchre of the heavy robe.

And somehow Matt slept, with Morning Lark in his arms, and he dreamed on that jouncing bed as if the dream would free him from the nightmare only if he saw it once again in the shadows of his mind.

The universe seemed to break inside him. Images tumbled from parapets, toppled into seas of swirling dark thoughts, fractured into a horror of the mind, where sudden hammers shattered icons, blurred everything together into a boiling caldron that exploded and erupted into shattered fragments of disconnected shards, turbulent with dark and arcane meaning: mucus and punctured eyes, scabs and vomitus, suppurating boils and torn-open chests, mangled bones and the fluttering blood of wild bulls, gaudy smoke racing ghostlike over ruptured landscapes where mountains grazed the sky like gigantic arrowheads and scratched sparks from black skies. And out of the chaos rolled a hoop of finest gold, all shining and perfect in its magical symmetry, a perfect circle rolling smooth over the ashes of a razed and desolate land.

When the dream broke, Matt felt as if shackles had been sundered from his wrists and ankles and that he was finally free.

Finally the horse stopped and Antelope jerked the blanket away and they emerged from their cocoon like creatures released from Hades, half blind and lost in the cold wind and the needling rain.

Antelope, Gray Deer, and Two Lances rode back to Santa Fe, promising to join them in a few suns. Matt and Morning Lark rode off through the rain, pulling the travois behind a third horse, until they found a place to stop and build a shelter. There they made love until, like children, they fell asleep, and this time Matt did not dream, but floated somewhere outside of time and space, free as the high-soaring hawk between all heaven and all earth.

Matt and Morning Lark rode along the Rio Grande del Norte, heading north by its twisting course, the sun's warmth seeping through them, the wind fallen to a light whisper, the earth smelling new and fresh.

Caine looked at Morning Lark on her pony, and his heart filled with that same glow from the sun that warmed his skin. For the first time in his life Matt knew what he wanted. He looked up at the mountains and felt at peace with the world. This was a time of armistice, a time to shake off the trappings of civilization and live with the People.

"Hoopties," Matt murmured, thinking of the dream. He smiled. "Worldwide hoopties."

"What does Big Man think?" Morning Lark asked when they lay in their shelter in the foothills that night staring up at the stars.

"Big Man is happy."

"You will not go to the white man's fort?"

"No, I will stay with Morning Lark, with the People."

"What will you do with the talking leaves?"

"I will keep them. When the other white men come, I will give them the talking leaves."

He could not tell her that he would be considered a deserter, that he might be arrested, brought up on charges and perhaps put in prison. He hoped that whoever came after him would understand that he no longer lived in their world, but had chosen another.

He had found something with the Shoshone, had seen it more clearly when he was a prisoner in Santa Fe. He had found a river and a life, and a woman deeper than either of them. There, under the great vast sky that watched over mountain and plain, he had found that which every man sought and often never discovered. He had come westward with the sun, like all men had done since ancient times, and had found what each had dreamed of finding.

Home. He had found a home.

Epilogue

The year after Matt Caine escaped from Santa Fe, in September of 1806, Lieutenant Zebulon Pike and his expedition encountered a band of Pawnees who gave him some fascinating information.

Pike was under orders from General Wilkinson to make binding treaties with all horse Indians and to record the natural history, map the terrain, and describe the people he encountered. He was further instructed to keep an accurate log of mileages, make astronomical observations, and collect botanical specimens, just as Lewis and Clark had done on their expedition.

Further orders were quite specific, though not written down in their entirety, and came directly from Secretary of War Dearborn. Pike was to infiltrate into New Mexico and make note of the New Mexican defenses along the Rio Grande del Norte and in their towns, and map or otherwise consider a way to open a trade route to Santa Fe. He was to avoid any direct confrontation with the New Mexicans. As Wilkinson noted in Pike's orders: "Your conduct must be marked by such circumspection and discretion as may prevent alarm or conflict, as you will be held responsible for consequences."

The Pawnees told Pike that a large troop of New Mexican soldiers riding white horses had been there in the previous moon. They were from Santa Fe, these horse soldiers, and they had been looking for the American soldier. They had also been looking for a man they called El Gigante.

Pike spent two weeks with the Pawnee, making friends, then pushed on to the mountains, where winter caught his party. When he reached the Rio Grande, he left behind five men with feet frozen so badly they could not depart the mountains. The remaining ten were demoralized and exhausted. On his map Lieutenant Pike wrote down "Red" as the name of the river, knowing full well that he had finally reached the Rio Grande. But if he ran into trouble, he intended to tell the New Mexican authorities that he must have gotten lost.

Pike continued his march until he came to the Conejos River, which flowed into the Rio Grande. He and his men hiked upstream for five miles and found a clearing where he could harvest firewood from the cottonwoods.

There, Pike and his men built a small stockade, thirty-six feet square and twelve feet high, as protection against, in his words, "the insolence, cupidity and barbarity of the savages." The fort was built of cottonwood logs and protected by sharp stakes slanted beyond the walls for two and a half feet. The bottom ends of the stakes were anchored in a ditch they dug all around the inside of the walls. The fortress had no gate and was accessible through a tunnel under the walls and a plank laid over the moat. They put gun ports in the walls, eight feet high, heavy planks below them for sentries and marksmen.

Unknown to Pike, Lieutenant Don Facundo Melgares had already returned to Santa Fe to report that he had failed to find either the American soldier, Pike, whose presence in the territory was reported to the Mexican government by spies in St. Louis, or Matthew Caine, whom he believed to be the legendary El Gigante.

Bull Heart, a chief of the Muache Ute, rode to Pike's fort one day, out of curiosity. With him were a number of his braves, including Deer Hoof and Broken Knife. Pike noticed the amulet that Bull Heart was wearing around his neck. It was a miniature American flag sewn from cloth.

"Where did you get this?" he asked.

"El Gigante gave me this," said the chief proudly.

"Where is El Gigante now?"

"He lives with the Wind River Shoshones," said Bull Heart.

Pike gave the Utes more presents and a larger version of the American flag.

After talking to Bull Heart, Pike was convinced that El Gigante was his friend and fellow officer, Major Matthew Caine. It would be over a year before Pike and Caine finally met. During that time, Pike was held prisoner in Santa Fe by Governor Alencaster, sent to Chihuahua, and later expelled from New Mexico. Pike returned to the Rio Grande in June of 1807. Pike had carried out his orders, however, while managing to keep details of his expedition secret.

At an overnight camp along the Rio Grande, Dr. John Hamilton Robinson, a member of Pike's expedition, saw them first. A line of riders approaching from upriver.

"Zeb, we got company."

"I see them," Pike said, and ordered his men to slowly ready their arms.

The column approached the campers from the north. The Indians were not painted for war; Pike noted that. At the head, though, was a huge bearded man in buckskins, who looked more savage than any of the half-naked warriors who followed after him on tough, fat ponies.

"Zeb, that you?"

"Major?"

Caine's grin shone through his thick beard. "You're a sight for sore eyes, Pike."

"Set down, Matt. We'll have a smoke."

Matt was riding with Antelope, Gray Deer, Two Lances, and four others. There was a bundle tied behind the cantle of Caine's saddle, wrapped in buckskins. After the introductions, the Americans and Shoshones sat around a circle and smoked. Later, Pike and Matt walked away and spoke for a long time.

"You played out the hand, Zeb," Matt told him. "But I got something for you to take back to General Wilkinson."

"You're not going with me?"

"It's a long story, Zeb."

Matt smiled wryly. He called to Antelope, made sign. A few moments later Antelope came up with the buckskin-bound packet he had retrieved from Matt's horse. Matt handed the bundle to Pike. Antelope returned to the circle where the men were still talking and smoking.

"What's this?"

"Maps of the whole Rio Grande from up yonder" —he pointed—"clear to Santa Fe."

"Are you saying you know where the river rises? I never could find its source."

"This river," Matt said, "what the Mexes call the Big River, has three tails up in them mountains. Only God has seen 'em all. I heard it from the Shoshone. It gets born up there where the Rockies is the highest, and it swoops right on down past Santa Fe and clear to the Gulf of Mexico."

"Makes a fine boundary."

"It's all one big river, Zeb. Since I left Santa Fe, I made notes of all I learned there."

"I met some friends of yours, Matt."

"Where?"

"In Santa Fe."

Matt's heart swelled in his chest, skipped a beat. "And who might that be?"

"A surgeon named Larrañaga and his nurse, a beautiful young woman named Elena Cuevas. Both told me you had been there, had escaped, and asked me if I had seen you. I was sorry to say I hadn't."

"And how were—how was Elena faring?"

"Just fine. You and she have a beautiful son."

Matt swallowed something that suddenly blocked his throat. "A son?"

"She calls him Manuelito. Looks just like you."

"Well, I'll be double damned."

Pike laughed. "You going back there, Matt?"

"I got me a woman, Zeb."

"Injun?"

"Rightly so. Her name is Morning Lark."

"Have you gone savage, then?"

"I reckon."

"What about your commission?"

"I don't give a damn about soldiering, Zeb. I found something here in these mountains, with these people."

"I think I understand. Well, I'd better get along. Thanks for these maps. I'll put in a good word for you with General Wilkinson."

"Wilkinson better give you a promotion, Zeb. Maybe somebody'll name a mountain after you some day."

"We got what we came for," said Pike. "I have been expelled from Mexico. My whole journey and my observations will bring the Spanish West to my country's notice for the first time. We have blown the mist away from the map, and before us are the shining mountains of New Mexico, and the Rio Grande, and beyond, the Pacific Ocean. A great land, and rightfully ours."

Matt and Pike said their farewells. Pike watched his friend ride away into the mountains and wondered what his life must be like, away from civilization and all its comforts.

Pike set out across Spanish Texas some days later, and in three weeks reached Louisiana, where on July 1, 1807, at four in the afternoon at Natchitoches, he felt his throat go dry, his heart pound, when he saw the American flag.

But his memories were of a great river and a great land full of decent and honorable people.

ABOUT THE AUTHOR

JORY SHERMAN is the Spur Award–winning author of *The Medicine Horn*, *Song of the Cheyenne*, *Horne's Law*, *Winter of the Wolf*, and *The Grass Kingdom*, as well as a previous novel in the Rivers West series, *The Arkansas River*. He is a former cowboy who lived in Texas for many years and worked the rodeo circuit. He now resides in Branson, Missouri.

If you enjoyed Jory Sherman's epic tale, *The Rio Grande,* be sure to look for the next installment of the Rivers West saga at your local bookstore. Each volume takes you on a voyage of exploration along one of the great rivers of North America with the courageous pioneers who challenged the unknown.

Turn the page for an exciting preview of the next book in Bantam's unique historical series.

Rivers West:

THE PECOS RIVER
by
Frederic Bean

On sale in summer 1995 wherever
Bantam Books are sold.

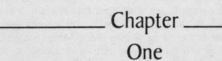

Chapter
One

Buck Wallace knew what it meant to be alone. Completely, totally alone. As far as he knew, the closest white man was better than three hundred miles to the east. And the closest red man was perhaps just beyond the next rise, or behind one of the shin oaks in his path with a fire-hardened arrow aimed at his chest. He was a lone white man in the land of the Comanche, the westernmost band of Comanches, the Kwahadie. In the universal sign language of the plains they were known by the sign for a snake crawling backward. When a Lipan or a Kiowa made the sign, it was accompanied by a show of fear. At Fort Mason, Buck had been warned about the dangers he would be facing. Few white men survived the journey through Kwahadie lands, he was told. He had been advised to take another route by the soldiers.

He halted the dun on a grassy knoll and squinted into the heat haze. In the distance, black volcanic mountains jutted into a clear blue sky. A westerly wind fluted through the shin oaks around him, the only sound in an otherwise ethereal silence. Broad grasslands stretched to the base of the mountain range, dotted with stands of scrub oak and mesquite. From a nearby tree limb a white-winged dove suddenly gave its soft, lyrical call to the wind and in some strange way the sound was a comfort, ending the eerie silence, the feeling of solitude. Farther away, a gentle cooing answered the dove's searching call. The dun gelding rattled the membranes in its muzzle, pricking its ears forward toward the sounds.

Buck patted the horse's neck. "Easy, boy," he whispered, with an eye to the horizon. "Only a bird. No need to worry."

Gusts of wind created waves across the tall prairie grasses, reminding Buck of the ocean. It had been months since he last saw the sea from the deck of a sailing ship, or tasted salt spray, heard the slap of waves against a wooden prow. Something deep within his soul had lured him away from life as a fisherman. He had always felt longings to see wide open spaces where a man could ride toward the sunset on the back of a smooth-gaited horse without ever encountering another living being. For years, fighting the pull of a fishnet, he had refused to harken to the voices that spoke to him about the mysteries of unexplored land, vast, empty prairies, the unknown places where white men seldom tread. He had dreamed of such lands, dreams fueled by the stories he heard from an old fur trapper he met down in New Orleans. Until last fall, all he had done was dream about those far-away places the old man described. That was before Clint Long offered to sell Buck his traps and the rest of his gear.

Like a grand awakening to a new existence, Buck saw himself free of the fishnets and rolling seas. He could make his dream a reality by the simple act of purchasing the old man's traps and then heading west. It had been an easy decision, really, after a summer of stormy seas and scant profits from his fishing enterprise. Thus he sold the boat and nets to equip himself for the westward journey into Texas. And beyond, perhaps even all the way to Santa Fe, if trapping was good along the Pecos.

He turned back in the saddle to inspect the bindings over the packs atop the mule. Everything he owned was encircled by ropes in a diamond hitch holding the packs in place. When he first mastered the art of tying the ropes, he wondered what a seafaring man would face, adrift on the western prairies without anyone to instruct him. He had listened to the old trapper's tales so many times he felt sure he knew what to do in most any circumstance, but when he found himself alone those first few weeks away from New Orleans, he discovered countless things he could not accomplish without difficulty. Even starting a campfire with flint had proven next to impossible. Yet he had cast away his anchor, so to speak, and there was no turning back. He could learn. When his mind was made up, it stayed that way even in the face of overwhelming odds. He had set out to reach the Pecos River, then the Guadalupe Mountains and even farther west, where he would run his traplines. Nothing short of death would turn him aside.

Death was, however, a distinct possibility in Comanche land. He had prepared for the redskinned fiends as best he could, with a Walker-model Colt .44 weighing almost five pounds and a Sharps .52-caliber carbine. Enough lead to make hundreds of bullets, bullet molds in both sizes, the percussion caps and patches, gunpowder, the gun-cleaning tools and oils. If it was a fight the Comanches wanted, he would oblige them, though he was at heart a peaceful man. He meant to live among the Comanches if they would allow it peacefully, or fight them off if the Indians chose otherwise. Though he felt he understood the danger, he never once considered that the risks might be too great. The old fur trapper had patiently explained that even the fierce Comanches were human beings who understood honesty and fair play. An honest man, regardless of the color of his skin, could live in peace among them if he treated them fairly and kept his word.

Still, there remained the chance that the Indians would kill him before he could demonstrate his honesty. He was an unwanted intruder into their tribal hunting grounds and unless he could convince them first that he meant them no harm, there was a strong likelihood of confrontation. It would be no small feat to convince the Comanches of his good intentions, since he neither spoke nor understood a word of their language. And he had been assured back at Fort Mason that no Comanche understood any English.

He had managed to learn a few hand signs from a sympathetic army scout who was half Indian himself . . . the sign for peace, another that meant "I speak true words," and a few more. The half-breed Choctaw had tried to convince Buck that riding through Kwahadie Comanche territory to set traps was downright foolish. He spoke of the terrible Kwahadies as though they were superior to other Plains Indians when it came to making war, and far worse, they were known to delight in torturing their enemies in the most cruel, inhuman ways. Yet none of this did anything to discourage Buck. He was a man following a dream and only death would keep him from his destination. He was forty-six years of age and nearing the end of his life, by his own estimate. Almost thirty years at sea had filled his lungs with a seaman's coughing sickness from which no one ever recovered. Of late, he sometimes spit up raw blood and tiny fragments of lung. So it was that he had no real fear of Indian arrows. He was dying slowly anyway. The years he had left would be spent trapping fur animals along the Pecos in peace and solitude, far from the cloying dampness of the ocean. Or dead at the end of a Comanche lance trying to reach the beautiful country Clint Long described so vividly.

He heeled the dun forward, feeling the pull of the mule's lead rope when the animal came reluctantly behind. Off to the west loomed the towering black peaks he had been seeking since he rode away from New Orleans. And unless a band of Comanches attacked him before he reached the mountains, he would make his destination and begin living his dream.

The creak of saddle leather was annoying then, robbing him of the peace and quiet his heart desired as he examined the craggy Guadalupes. On many a starlit night he had tried to imagine what the mountains would look like when he saw them for the first time. And now they lay before him, majestic, rugged, every bit as breathtaking as he guessed they would be. Only the damn saddle kept creaking, disturbing his quiet enjoyment of the sight.

The dun started down a gradual slope to the winding banks of the river at the bottom of a shallow valley. Scenting water, the horse lengthened its strides, forcing the mule to hurry, stretching the lead rope taut between the saddle horn and the mule's halter. Just across the narrow river, three white-rumped antelope lifted their heads, muzzles glistening wetly from drinking, to watch him approach the water. One at a time, their curious white tails flagged a silent signal, then they were off in a bounding, graceful run up the far embankment.

Buck halted the dun and the mule to watch them. He imagined he could hear their sharp hooves whispering through the grass, the soft thump of their feet, although the wind prevented him from hearing anything but the wind itself, flutelike whistles among the shin oak branches and the rustle of early spring leaves.

Suddenly a gray squirrel scolded him from a tree branch, rising on its haunches to chatter angrily over the intrusion, jerking its tail over its back to punctuate each sharp cry.

"Take it easy, little fellow," Buck said, grinning. "I'm not here to trap squirrels. That's a promise."

For a time he sat the dun quietly, overcome by the peace and beauty of the river, the grass-thick banks and bulrushes, the sight of distant mountains. He drew in a deep breath and let it out slowly, thankful to be away from muggy, salt-laden air. Some men found peace on the ocean, most often men who did not work it for their livelihood. Buck's inner peace had come from imagining scenes such as this . . . vast, open prairies and silent, rocky peaks touching the sky. There were no treacherous currents here, no undertow or fifteen-foot waves. Only Comanches, so the old fur trapper said, and they were men. Men could be reasoned with, unlike a boiling, storm-tossed sea. The only water Buck ever wanted to see again lay at the bottom of the slope, a crystal ribbon of sparkling river that would nourish him rather than trying to claim his life. Thinking this, he realized that he was thirsty and the wooden canteen hanging from his saddle was almost empty. A drink from a cool river was just what he needed to refresh himself before beginning the final miles to the base of the Guadalupes.

He opened the deerskin map the trapper gave him for the moment when he arrived at the mountains. Uncurling the soft deer hide, Buck glanced at the faint markings that told him where streams and game trails coursed through the peaks. An x marked the spot where he hoped to find the old prospector named Adams, near the highest peak, El Capitan. When Clint told Buck about the map, he showed him where he might find the only other white man ever to brave the Guadalupes and live to tell about it. Adams worked a silver claim high in the mountains, along a stream dubbed Silver Creek. The trail to Adams's diggings was plainly marked, though it had been almost a decade since the trapper had seen him. Clint Long left the mountains for good back in '41, due to failing eyesight and pain in his joints, so he insisted. When he sold his traps and equipment to Buck, he attached a certain amount of sorrow to parting with his belongings. Buck supposed that in the back of the old man's mind he planned to return to the mountains some day, perhaps for a final good-bye. Selling everything to Buck closed the door on the idea of making it back.

The gray squirrel chattered again, perhaps a bit more softly, as if its complaint were less over a human entering its domain. Buck chuckled at the squirrel's antics as he returned the deerskin to his saddlebags. When the map was restored to its proper place, he heeled the thirsty dun down the embankment to the water's edge, ending the horse's impatience over the delay. When they reached the river, the mule edged alongside the dun to drink. Upstream, a bluejay darted from a low cottonwood limb, fluttering to a higher branch farther from the disturbance made by a man and his animals.

Buck stepped from the saddle and tested his stiffened legs when both feet were firmly on the ground. His gaze fell to animal tracks in the soft mud beside the river. Deer and antelope tracks, the prints of coon and possum, coyote and wolf he easily recognized. A few widely scattered tracks made by huge buffalo. He had seen their droppings for several days, and the big wallows they made for themselves in the grass to rid their bodies of shedding winter hair.

"I'll make buffalo robes for the winter," he said quietly, so as not to disturb the peaceful scene with his voice. He had skinning knives in the packs, needles for sewing the hides to racks until they cured. It seemed impossible that he had all the things he needed aboard a single mule, but when he conducted an inventory, he couldn't find an item he was without. Two sharp axes had been added, to fell trees for the cabin he meant to erect when he found just the right spot. Clint had never fashioned a cabin for himself, preferring a tent made from animal skins like those of the Plains Indians. The difference was, in Buck's view, that he meant to stay here until he died. Of lung disease or an Indian arrow, whatever claimed him first. The cabin was to declare his permanence. It would be his home, and since he was a fair carpenter with some shipbuilding experience, he knew the cabin would be sturdy. It would serve as a monument to his conquest of the prairies, the mountains. Whoever found it in the years after his death would know that a man had come here with his mind made up to stay.

He stepped out on a flat rock and knelt to place his lips on the glassy surface of the river. He sucked water gently into his mouth and savored its sweet coolness, then he drank more deeply, filled with enjoyment. Lifting his face when his thirst was quenched, he smacked his lips as a starving man might over a bowl of delicious soup. "No salt," he said. It would have been a curious remark coming from a man who had never lived atop the deck of a fishing boat. He'd had enough of salty seas to last a lifetime. Water without a salty taste was a precious thing to a lifelong seaman.

Briefly, he examined his reflection in the river. A blond beard mottled with streaks of gray obscured most of his face. Clear blue eyes, the color of the sky overhead, stared back at him with a humorous twinkle. The eyes spoke of his exuberance over arriving at the mountains, ending four months of difficult travel across mostly empty, often harsh Texas land. With a seaman's skill for navigation, he had used the sun and the stars as guideposts to find his way, along with the maps the trapper gave him. And now, at last, he was at his destination, arriving without mishap for the most part, with all his gear and supplies intact despite dangerous river fordings and outbursts of inclement weather. At first, it had been a rough winter across parts of eastern Texas. But he'd made it into a warm spring with only minor difficulty, now to feast his eyes on the Guadalupes, where he would begin running traps, free at last of sailing storm-angered seas forever.

He stood up and looked around him, when he noticed that his mule and horse watched something along the western horizon, ears pricked forward attentively. Squinting, Buck looked in the same direction, puzzled by the animals' behavior. What had they seen?

Then quite suddenly he found it. Something was moving across the top of a distant rise. He saw a pair of short, curved horns and a furry brown head. "A buffalo," he whispered. But as his eyes took in more detail he quickly realized that he was not looking at a buffalo. What he saw had the head and horns of a buffalo, but the rest of it, this creature crossing the horizon, was something else. Underneath the buffalo's head was a horse, a brightly colored red and white spotted horse. It appeared that a man with the head of a buffalo was seated on the horse's withers—or was this some hitherto unknown creature, half man, half animal? At this distance he couldn't be sure.

His dun horse snorted, flaring its nostrils, trying to catch a scent.

"I don't know what it is," he said, as if to answer the horse's question, noting that the creature with the buffalo head appeared to be carrying a sharp-pointed lance. Or were his eyes playing tricks on him?

Buck's heart began to beat rapidly and he blinked in sudden, uncontrollable bursts. He was at once reminded of a story from Greek mythology, of terrible beasts called centaurs that were part horse, part man, with monstrous heads. Centaurs existed only in myths, didn't they?

The half-human beast halted on a hilltop above the river and then turned its massive, furry head toward Buck. Outlined against a blue sky the creature's horns were frightening things, curved up at the top of the buffalo's skull. For a time it sat watching Buck, as motionless as the black mountains behind it.

"It's a man on a pinto horse," he told himself moments later. "He's wearing a buffalo head to appear more threatening. I wonder if he is . . . a Kwahadie Comanche." He felt better when he concluded that he was not confronted with some awful, mythical beast, though his heart still labored inside his shirt and he noticed a tiny tremor in his hands. Very slowly, so his actions could not be mistaken for a threat, he reached for the heavy Walker Colt tied to his right leg, and when his fingers curled around the walnut grips he felt somewhat better, though not completely at ease.

Minutes passed as they stared at each other. The longer he looked at the thing, whatever it was, the more he began to doubt that what he saw was merely an Indian wearing a buffalo skull.

The dun gelding nickered at the creature and Buck wondered if his horse was also questioning the origin of it. But no answer came from the distant hilltop, nothing that would help identify it.

Then, very slowly, the beast turned away and went behind the hill. Or had it simply vanished, an apparition rather than a truly physical thing? He couldn't be sure, for it had been too far away.

His hand fell from the butt of the pistol. The brief appearance of the thing, whatever it might have been, left him seriously shaken. He left the flat rock and mounted the dun, still casting wary glances toward the hilltop. Some of the fearlessness that had always been a part of his nature was replaced by nagging doubts as he heeled the horse and led the mule across the shallow river.

Chapter
Two

A faint game trail winding along a rocky switchback took him from the prairie into the first of the ancient volcanic eruptions stretching westward as far as the eye could see. And with his rise from the prairie floor, thus did his spirits lift accordingly. He drank in every sight as one who thirsted for it, turning this way and that, entranced by breathtaking vistas on all sides. Breathing deeply, he caught the fragrance of wildflowers that were clinging to scant patches of topsoil between huge slabs of iron-colored stone. Once, at a bend in the trail, he swung down to examine a particularly pretty blue blossom of a kind he had never seen. And by happenstance he opened one of the odd, peashaped blooms to find a tiny cat's claw hidden inside. Cupping the flower in his big, callused hands, he held it close to his face and tried to inhale its scent. His dun seized the opportunity to graze on short, curled grasses beside the trail while its master was behaving so curiously. The mule stood hipshot, as though thankful for a moment of rest.

Buck came slowly to his feet with a broad smile across his face. For now, surrounded by so much beauty, the incident with the buffalo man was forgotten. He had reasoned with himself for more than an hour that what he had seen was nothing more than an Indian who wanted to present a fearsome appearance, thus to frighten away intruders. Centaurs were mythical beings. What he had seen on the hilltop was merely an illusion. If the Indian was a Kwahadie Comanche, he had failed to live up to his bad reputation as a wanton, bloodthirsty killer. He had ridden off as peacefully as a new spring lamb, allowing Buck to enter the mountains unmolested.

" 'Tis a beautiful sight, isn't it?" He asked the question of no one in particular, knowing full well that neither the horse nor the mule had any appreciation for grand scenery. He had developed the habit of talking to himself while moving about the slippery deck of his fishing boat. Alone at sea from dawn until dusk, he never worried that someone might think him daft for the one-sided conversations, for there was no one to hear him.

Looking higher up, he saw scattered half-sized pines of a type the trapper called piñon, which he claimed produced edible seeds that made excellent meal for crumbly cakes baked in the coals of a campfire. Right away, Buck wanted to taste one of the piñon nuts. His mouth watered at the thought, despite the fact that he had not yet sampled one.

According to the map, this trail would take him to high meadows where deer and antelope grazed in summer. There he could provide himself with fresh meat and perhaps rest a few days, enjoying the scenery while his animals filled their bellies on good grass. He climbed aboard the dun and pulled his flat-brimmed hat down on his forehead, then heeled the horse up the trail with the mule in tow.

"This is God's country," he said, swinging a look around at the mountains swaddled in spring greenery. "This is where I aim to spend the rest of my days . . . however many they may be." He listened to the ring of iron horseshoes moving across stretches of rock. On a ledge below the trail he found more wildflowers of a different variety, bright red and yellow petals around dark chocolate centers. Marveling at the show of brilliant colors, he almost missed a family of scrawny wild pigs trotting across the trail above him. He had learned from a Mexican teamster west of Fort Mason that the pigs were called javelinas, and in a moment of hunger he killed one at a river crossing, only to discover that the pig was mostly bristling hair and bones with huge razorlike tusks. When he cooked some of the hindquarter, the meat had a terrible smell and proved to be almost inedible.

The sow made a sharp barking noise, snapping her jaws at Buck as she led four baby pigs across the trail, then down a steep drop to a ravine thick with dagger-shaped plants that hid her from view. "I won't bother you if you won't bother me," he said, hearing the echo of his voice off the slopes on either side of him. Feeling no hurry, he allowed the dun to pick its own pace where the climb steepened, a slower gait more suitable to the mule and its heavy load. At every bend and turn, more vistas awaited him. Beds of cactus sporting pink blossoms seemed to cling to the smallest cracks in the rock where no root growth was possible. Sparrows and bluejays flitted about, always just ahead of the horse and mule, calling to each other with musical whistles and chirps, landing atop iron-gray stones to peck at colonies of lichen. Against the dark rock, the white and yellow lichen might have been the work of a careless paintbrush, an artist's whim, sometimes a vaguely familiar shape, more often simply irregular patches of color. Tiny white wildflowers with golden centers swayed in gusts of wind washing down from the slopes, making the flowers dance to a whispered melody Buck could not hear.

"Most beautiful place in the world," he announced, rocking against the cantle of his saddle. "Just like I knew it would be. I'm home. Wish I'd come a long time ago, when I was younger. If Callie could only have seen this . . ."

His beloved Callie had been dead for more than a dozen years, of galloping consumption, and he no longer thought about her. Her memory was too painful, especially those last few years after she had grown so sick he hardly recognized her. It had been a terrible death to witness, her rapid deterioration, the dreadful coughing so similar to his own, only far, far worse. For almost a year she had been totally bedridden, a mere skeleton with sad, sunken eyes, and when he did allow himself to remember the months before her death, he cried. But now, so many years afterward, as he viewed these wonderful sights he allowed himself to think of her again, the pretty girl she was before consumption took her from him. Her dazzling green eyes, the way they were before she got sick, would sparkle and fill him with great happiness. He knew her eyes would be sparkling now, were she alive and riding alongside him to see what lay before them.

As though Callie's memory reminded him of his own dying lungs, he leaned out of the saddle to cough. The wet, phlegmy sound that accompanied the coughing had worsened during the winter, and when he spat the fluid from his mouth it was always pinkish, colored by blood.

"Damn," he hissed, when the red ball of phlegm fell below his stirrup. He was dying faster than ever today, perhaps due to the excitement when he entered the mountains. A dollop of bloody spittle caught sunlight from above, and when he saw it he closed his eyes and turned his face away, seeking more promising sights. He wouldn't think about it, the dying. Not today. Nor would he think about dear, sweet Callie again.

A covey of quail darted from a pile of rocks and took off in low, soaring flight away from the horse. His mouth watered again, thinking of roasting quail dripping delicious juices into a firepit from sharpened sticks. He could almost taste the sweet meat of the breast, imagining it as he did now. He wondered if the cooler air in the mountains could be making him so hungry.

At a steep climb in the trail the dun was forced to scramble for footing. The surefooted mule had less difficulty in spite of its loaded packs. Near the top of the climb the trail bent to cross a grassy meadow, and around it grew the first piñon pines he could inspect closely. He rode to a nearby piñon and took a pine cone, feeling keen disappointment when he found no seeds. Swinging down, he picked up a fallen cone and crushed it in his hand, fingering one of the tiny seedlike flakes. He put one in his mouth and found it tasteless. Then his gaze fell to a spot of bare earth below the pine limbs where he found a faint impression that halted his chewing and quickened the beat of his heart.

Kneeling, he peered down at the hoofprint of an unshod horse. The track was recent, the edges still sharp when he traced a fingertip over it. "An Indian pony," he whispered, glancing around quickly, the hairs standing up on the back of his neck. Was this the track of the buffalo man? Was the thing shadowing him to see where he went?

The thought made Buck shiver. He stood up and took a careful look around the meadow, pausing when he came to a rocky outcrop or a shadow below a pine. "Don't see a thing," he said later. Then he looked down at the print once more, "But somebody was here not long ago, maybe a few hours," he added softly. Again he touched the butt of his pistol for reassurance. "He's just a man. That buffalo head is only meant to scare me off. It won't work. I'm stayin' here, no matter what."

He knew little about Indians in general, having no chance to meet one on the high seas. Clint told him many things about the plains tribes, those he came across at one time or another during his wanderings along the western frontier. Clint said that most all Plains Indians were warlike by nature, that warfare was a form of honorable conflict among many larger bands. Some were more inclined than others to fight, the Apaches to the west, who made formidable enemies, and the Comanches to the east. Comanches were considered to be so fierce and skillful in battle that other tribes gave them a wide berth. Most feared of the five Comanche bands were the Kwahadies, according to Clint, and for this reason white men and red men alike left them completely alone. The eastern edge of the Guadalupes marked the western boundary of Kwahadie territory, an explanation for the absence of civilization in or around them, since Apaches controlled the rest of the mountain range. But the isolation of the area was the very reason that a fur trapper could do so well here, for there was a plentiful supply of furbearing animals and no white men came with the courage to run traplines. Clint promised that if a man sought peace with the Kwahadies, bringing gifts of knives and glass beads, he would be left alone to make a living, so long as he kept his word. Clint had trapped here for five uninterrupted years by trading cheap trinkets for the right to trap coon and beaver, bringing gifts to the Kwahadie village every spring to renew the partnership, and to save his scalp. And as Clint had instructed, Buck carried a variety of trading items in the packs aboard the mule, to offer the Indians a similar exchange. But only if he got the chance to explain his proposal before the Kwahadies killed him.

He climbed back in the saddle and reined away from the piñon, burdened now by the sensation that he was being watched from somewhere up above. Swinging back on the game trail, he began to study the barren earth more closely for pony tracks.

Climbing again when he left the meadow, he rode past huge boulders fallen from steep slopes above the trail. Stands of shin oaks and piñon drew his attention, places where an Indian might hide. He practiced the hand sign for making exchange, a simple looping of one hand over the other, then an extended palm toward the man with whom you wished to make a trade. Would the Indian understand?

Again and again he practiced the sign language, including the sign for "I speak true words," and the sign for peace. He would have thought himself foolish, conducting sign talk with himself, were it not for finding the pony track and sighting the curious buffalo man earlier in the day. He understood that his life might depend on how well he used sign language, thus he continued his practice while the dun carried him deeper into the mountains.

As he made the signs, he whispered to himself, "I offer a trade. I speak true words. I come in peace."

AN ARMY SCOUT AND A COMANCHE WARRIOR...
BOUND BY A HATRED THAT WOULD NEVER DIE...

ENEMIES

Geo. W. Proctor

They had sworn to kill each other—an Army scout
haunted by the brutal slaughter of his wife and child
and a fierce Comanche warrior who'd suffered his
own tragic losses. And it's only a matter of time
before these two enemies meet, alone on the battle
field—warrior to warrior—in a bloody showdown
that can end only one way....

"An authentic, richly detailed novel set in a
neglected period of the American West—the
twilight of the frontier. Fascinating reading!"
—Chad Oliver, award-winning author of
The Cannibal Owl

- -

WINNER OF THE MEDICINE PIPE BEARER'S
AWARD FOR *BEST FIRST NOVEL*
FROM WESTERN WRITERS OF AMERICA

THE SIXTH RIDER

MAX McCOY

They were the hard-riding, hard-shooting Dalton boys
of Kansas, sired by a drunk, raised by a Bible-believing
mama, scratching to survive in a West being tamed by
the law. Samuel Coleman Dalton was the youngest
and at the age of thirteen he had dreams of an honest
life. But one day an older brother was gunned down
in cold blood, and Sam vowed to track down the
coward who'd pulled the trigger. The trail of vengeance
led straight into Indian Territory, and young Sam grew
up fast, gaining a reputation and a name: the Choctaw
Kid. When at last he rejoined his other brothers, the
legendary Dalton Gang was born, cutting a violent trail
in search of riches and renown that led to a last-stand
showdown in the Daltons' hometown, where the out-
law band—surrounded, outnumbered, outgunned—
faced death by hanging...or death from flying lead.

- - - - - - - - - - - - - - - - - - - -